# THE STARTER WIFE

ALSO BY NINA LAURIN

*Girl Last Seen*

*What My Sister Knew*

"There's no sophomore slump here; Laurin's riveting second novel is full of unexpected twists and dark turns.... [T]his is a read you won't want to put down."

—RTBookReviews.com

"One of the best things a novel can do is keep you guessing, and Nina Laurin's sophomore effort does exactly that. *What My Sister Knew* is a rich, complex story about the effects of secrets, the lingering consequences of abuse, the inner workings of deeply troubled households, filial love, and the way we are shaped by trauma. Fans of psychological thrillers would be remiss to skip this one."

—CriminalElement.com

"Nina Laurin delivers an action-packed, mind-bending ride. Just when you think you've discovered the truth, a new secret is revealed, making you question whether there really is a line between good and evil."

—Wendy Walker, bestselling author of
*All Is Not Forgotten*

"4 Stars! I am two for two when it comes to Nina Laurin's books! The book starts out with questions, suspense, and intrigue, and slowly builds to a bursting crescendo as we learn more about Andrea, Eli, and their family. If you had a chance to read the author's first novel and enjoyed it, I'm positive you'll gobble up *What My Sister Knew* as well. It was a fast read that had me flying through the pages and entertained me for hours on end."

—TheSuspenseIsThrillingMe.com

"A dramatic, suspenseful, incredibly thrilling novel that focuses on the sibling dynamic. It's a must-read for anyone who loves a good thriller."           —SarahScoop.com

# GIRL LAST SEEN

"Every good thriller has a shocking plot twist. *Girl Last Seen* has many. Author Nina Laurin's eerie novel will stay with you for days, months, even years to come."

—HelloGiggles.com

*Girl Last Seen* by Nina Laurin is a chilling suspense about two missing girls whose stories intertwine—perfect for Paula Hawkins fans."           —EliteDaily.com

"A well-written and compelling novel that offers more than suspense; it offers a deeper understanding of how sexual assault can leave its victims broken. Ms. Laurin is to be congratulated for her achievement."

—NYJournalofBooks.com

"4 Stars! This debut novel is a gritty thriller with dark twists you won't see coming. The heartbreaking, heart-racing journey...will keep you guessing to the nail-biting end."           —TheSuspenseIsThrillingMe.com

"Debut novelist Nina Laurin has created a memorable character in complicated, flawed and endearing Laine Moreno. From the very first page, *Girl Last Seen* jettisons the reader into the life of a crime victim trying to outrun her past. Fast-paced and hard-edged, it is a heart-stopping thriller that had me guessing to the very end."

—Heather Gudenkauf, *New York Times* bestselling author

"*Girl Last Seen* hooked me so quickly I might have whiplash. This is a sharp, twisting, intense thriller, the heartbreaking and fast-paced story of a woman who bears the scars of a trip to hell and back but who refuses to be defeated. Don't miss this smashing debut!"

—David Bell, bestselling author

"*Girl Last Seen* gripped me from start to finish. Lainey Moreno is a riveting heroine, a kidnapping survivor who will only escape her demons if she faces her greatest fears, and Nina Laurin brings her vividly to life. Psychological suspense doesn't come much grittier or more packed with satisfying twists and turns."

—Meg Gardiner, Edgar Award–winning author

"Laurin creates a compelling, vulnerable central character."

—*Publishers Weekly*

"Laurin's novel is nearly as compelling as it is depressing in detailing Lainey's story to a hair-raising, violent climax. A promising debut."          —BooklistOnline.com

"Disturbing and suspenseful...provides a great twisty ending that will satisfy."          —RTBookReviews.com

# THE
# STARTER
# WIFE

## NINA LAURIN

**GRAND CENTRAL**
PUBLISHING

NEW YORK   BOSTON

Copyright © 2019 by Ioulia Zaitchik
Excerpt from *What My Sister Knew* copyright © 2018 by Ioulia Zaitchik

Cover design by Lisa Amoroso
Cover copyright © 2019 by Hachette Book Group, Inc.

Grand Central Publishing
Hachette Book Group
1290 Avenue of the Americas, New York, NY 10104
grandcentralpublishing.com
twitter.com/grandcentralpub

First Edition: June 2019

Grand Central Publishing is a division of Hachette Book Group, Inc. The Grand Central Publishing name and logo is a trademark of Hachette Book Group, Inc.

The publisher is not responsible for websites (or their content) that are not owned by the publisher.

The Hachette Speakers Bureau provides a wide range of authors for speaking events. To find out more, go to www.hachettespeakersbureau.com or call (866) 376-6591.

[insert additional photo/art credits or statement "Additional copyright/ credits information is on page TK." or delete this line]
[insert credits and permission statements for text, e.g., lyrics, excerpts, or delete this line]

Library of Congress Cataloging-in-Publication Data

Names: Laurin, Nina, author.
Title: The starter wife / Nina Laurin.
Description: First edition. | New York, NY : Grand Central Publishing, 2019.
Identifiers: LCCN 2018052065| ISBN 9781538715710 (trade pbk.) | ISBN 9781549120589 (audio download) | ISBN 9781538715734 (ebook)
Subjects: LCSH: Psychological fiction. | GSAFD: Suspense fiction.
Classification: LCC PR9199.4.L38415 S73 2019 | DDC 813/.6—dc23
LC record available at https://lccn.loc.gov/2018052065

ISBN: 978-1-5387-1571-0 (trade paperback), 978-1-5387-1573-4 (ebook)

Printed in the United States of America

LSC-C

10  9  8  7  6  5  4  3

# PART ONE

# CLAIRE

# PROLOGUE

*Last night, I saw you, with the wifey. In the restaurant where I wait tables. You didn't see me, and neither did she, but that's normal because I wear a uniform that matches the walls, as if I'm meant by design to blend in, be furniture. That restaurant isn't fancy, hardly a place where you'd want to bring your date—not if you plan on getting laid afterwards. But for you two, it was a delicious joke you shared along with your popcorn shrimp appetizer. A little moment of kitsch, like going to ride the Ferris wheel at the town fair.*

*I thought it was an extraordinary coincidence. A sign from the stars. Surely you had no idea I'd be here—and I hadn't planned on seeing you. I panicked when I saw you two walk in, her first, because you held the door for her like a gentleman. My palms went clammy instantly, and I wiped them on the sides of my polyester shirt. In my cowardice, I even prayed that Lizzie the hostess wouldn't sit you in my section, but then again, I knew she would. The place was empty that night, and everyone there knew I needed the tips because I could only work weekends, no school nights. She was being nice to me because she, like everyone there, felt sorry for me, the youngest, least skilled waitress in the place.*

*But there you were, so I pulled myself together and went to give you menus, and even when I rattled off the specials (I didn't once screw up or give myself away in any way, of which I'm still proud), you didn't glance away from your wife's face and look at me. You both looked so flushed and happy, like you were popping in for a greasy snack after rolling in bed all afternoon. You only had eyes for each other.*

*It would have been just another ordinary night—you eat, you pay, you tip, and you leave, to go back to bed, maybe. But then a miracle happened, a miracle that sent my whole world spinning off its orbit. A true sign from above.*

*After I cleared away your plates and put in the order for your dessert (cherry pie with ice cream—two spoons, of course), I found myself overwhelmed, needing a moment alone. I raced to the bathroom and locked myself in a stall to catch my breath—okay, to slip my hand inside the elastic waist of my uniform pants and touch myself. But no matter how furiously I rubbed myself through my panties, it just wasn't happening—I hovered on the brink, frustration growing and threatening to crest into something uglier. That's when I heard the door open, and froze. If anyone*

*caught me hiding out in the bathroom, I might get in trou-*
*ble. I pulled my legs up onto the toilet seat so they couldn't*
*see me.*

*Your wifey's sneakered feet shuffled past. I couldn't have*
*missed these sneakers, hot pink edged in fluorescent yel-*
*low, the kind rich ladies wear to their workouts and to run*
*weekend errands. My own work sneakers were once plain*
*white but turned gray, a generic brand, bought on sale. I*
*stared at their toes the whole time she was there, in the stall*
*next to mine. She knelt on the floor, ignoring the scattered*
*bits of tissue, black yoga pants strained at her hips, and the*
*unmistakable sounds of retching followed almost immedi-*
*ately.*

*I'll never know whether she was making herself puke,*
*like those girls at school. It's not important. I remember*
*watching her get up, and then one foot came off the floor,*
*and the toilet flushed. The door of the stall clacked open;*
*the rush of tap water followed, and after it, the cacophony*
*of the hand dryer. At last, the door squeaked softly closed*
*behind her. I burst out of the stall, a mess of relief and gid-*
*diness, and then I saw it. The miracle.*

*Sitting there, on the edge of the sink, in a little puddle*
*of soapy water, was her engagement ring. Old looking, an*
*antique or heirloom—I imagined your mother giving it to*
*you, passed down from some great-great-grandmother, to*
*be given to the woman of your heart someday. A big emer-*
*ald glimmered darkly in a setting of tiny diamonds and*
*platinum leaves.*

*And she left it in the bathroom of a shitty chain restau-*
*rant, thoughtlessly slid it off her soapy finger and plunked*

*it down on the cracked porcelain like it was a cheap bit of costume jewelry. That's when I knew. I knew she didn't deserve you. And I knew I could—would—take you away from her, no matter what it took. A higher being was on my side, and he sent me the ring as an omen.*

*I snatched it off the sink and put it in a place where no one would find it, even if—when—she noticed and raised a stink, and in case the manager wanted to search all of us.*

*But I knew it wouldn't happen.*

*Fate was on my side.*

# CHAPTER ONE

Byron let me sleep in this morning.

There. That way, it sounds nicer than "my husband snuck out of the house while I was still asleep." Because that's exactly what happened and what's been happening every day of the week so far, and we're at Thursday.

This morning, the balmy September sun finally gave way to rain, and with the bedroom windows facing north, it's still kind of dark when I wake up. It could have been just dawn breaking, around seven a.m. Except Byron's side of the bed is empty and there are no footsteps downstairs in the kitchen, no water running in the bathroom.

I get up, grab the imitation ring from the nightstand, and put it on the ring finger of my left hand, where it settles into the groove it has made in the skin. He just presented me with it one day, and I didn't press the issue further. He never actually told me whether the stones were real. I decided to let it go and never asked.

It's ten thirty. I run my fingers through my hair, which is tangled and matted with sweat, and eye the digital clock in mild dismay. Yesterday it was ten ten. The day before, on Monday, it was nine fifty. Byron gets up at seven every morning like clockwork—to go running in good weather and to hit the gym at the college in bad. If he goes running, he comes back to take a shower before changing to go to work.

September has been beautiful this year, dry and sun filled. He hasn't gone running once, as far as I can tell.

At the start, I'd get up at six fifty and have breakfast ready for him: French toast and cheese omelet, with a glass of orange juice and coffee with cream. Now I'm wondering if he ate all that fatty food to be polite, because these days his breakfast is an energy bar. And I guess I can't complain—I see other men his age at university events when he takes me. By forty, they have paunches and double chins while Byron, at forty-seven, has the body of someone half his age. He's also one of the lucky ones who has his hair, all of it—except with age, the points of the M of his hairline have sharpened a little, and the blond color has grown bleak with gray hairs. When I met him, it was easier to forget the twenty-year age difference.

And that name. The name caught my attention even before he did, took me back to high school English lit where the teacher made us pick poems apart to the bare bones. I hated it—it ruined their beauty, made the magic evaporate.

Ironically, the original Byron never had a romance that wasn't thoroughly dysfunctional—ranging from mildly unhealthy to downright unhinged. Back when he was courting me, it didn't raise any red flags.

Then again, neither did the first wife.

I make my way downstairs and start the espresso machine. Byron is particular about his coffee beans while I could drink any swill from a filter—the way he puts it. The truth is I find the fancy espresso too bitter, too sour, like sandpaper on the palate. But today I'm feeling especially foggy so the caffeine buzz seems worth the tongue torture. And those exotic beans do deliver the buzz—can't complain about that.

While the machine hisses, I get my laptop from the little office Byron set up for me upstairs, the one I almost never use. Whenever I can, I sit outside or down in the living room in front of the giant bay window, basking in the natural light. That's what I do now, pulling up my pajama-clad legs and balancing the sleek Mac on my knee. I check both my email accounts, the personal one and the one I use for writing-related contacts, even though no one ever emails me on either. My friends, the few who still keep in touch, prefer to text, and the last batch of queries I sent dates back months. Some agents still have my manuscript but let's face it—it's not going to happen.

The cliché should make me sad. I admit I cringed a little all these months ago when I first wrote my bio for emailing literary agents. Back then, I was full of optimism and hope, with Byron leaning over my shoulder to peek at the screen and then kissing my temple and working his way down to my neck. Here's what it says, in clunky third person that's apparently industry standard: *Claire Westcott has a degree in English and creative writing from Ohio State University. Her work has appeared in the campus newspaper as well as several small literary publications. Presently, Claire writes full-time. She lives with her husband, a professor of literature at Mansfield Liberal Arts College in Ohio.*

This is a fancy way of saying I'm one of *those* women. Those girls my evolved, progressive classmates at Ohio State sneered at: the boring white women who married a man who can support them while they write their irrelevant little stories. I know I'm not exactly in the zeitgeist, but Byron loved to tease me about it, calling himself the Leonard to my future Virginia Woolf, a man destined to fade in his famous writer wife's shadow.

I didn't remind him how that story ended. I wasn't thinking about it at all in happier times.

Now, as I open the second inbox, it dings, a sound that now fills me with dread rather than anticipation. Looks like one of my queries has netted a response, months later. I scan the form letter shallowly when the ding repeats itself. Two in one day? But the ding is from my personal inbox this time.

There's no subject line, and the address is gibberish. I really shouldn't click on it—it's probably a virus—but my hands are faster than my mind today. As I rush to hit the Back button, the image downloads, and my hand freezes over the touch pad. It knocks the wind out of me. I stare at it, my eyes drinking in every pixel, but there is no explanation.

I'm looking at a close-up of the emerald in my ring. My replacement ring? The real thing? But it's . . . impossible.

Then I see the name of the sender, and it takes everything I have not to slam the laptop shut and hurl it away from me, as far as possible, like it's a venomous spider nestled in my lap.

COLLEEN.

# CHAPTER TWO

Colleen may have died but she never left.

The fact that we live in her house is hard to forget. Just like the fact that we live off her sizable savings, which went to her husband when she died since she had no other family. Byron never directly said so, but I know that's how he's able to support his future Virginia Woolf while maintaining our lifestyle, all on his generous but not exactly millionaire's salary at the college.

I haven't worked in two years but I get new clothes every season, and every eight weeks, I get my roots bleached and carefully toned to a perfect wheat blond and then streaked with corn-silk highlights. I drive an hour to the good salon in Columbus while everyone I know goes to the local place, run by a middle-aged woman with a bouffant hairdo who charges about a third of what the Columbus place does. Sadly, she's also a firm believer in wedge cuts for anyone over twenty-two.

So I drive and sit in that chair for hours, holding my head straight and smiling while my hair is pulled and tugged and slathered with chemicals, and then I hand over the family credit card. Another three hundred of Colleen's dollars, plus tip, changes hands invisibly. No crass cash.

I try to convince myself there's no reason to feel guilty. It's not like he left her for a younger woman or threw her out on the street or dumped her with three kids and no alimony, or any such sordid story, all too common in this town. She died. He grieved but then moved on. Selling that monolith of a house, in such a market, would have been insane. So would moving away from a perfectly good job with the prospect of tenure looming on the horizon. Byron repeated that to me hundreds of times. Everything makes sense.

Rationally, that is. What I feel is anything but.

Some days, after a not-so-great day in the Westcott household, I drive to the local mall and buy things I don't need, hideous clothes I'll never wear, tacky pink makeup. I tell myself it's my petty revenge against Byron, but really it's my revenge against Colleen, as if wasting some of her money can make up for the thousand little humiliations I suffer.

Eventually, I know the savings will run out, and I don't plan to make Byron support me forever. My novel is pretty much dead in the water. The next novel, the one I'm supposed to be writing while my husband is at work, is clearly never happening. So now I'm looking for work—

starting to. I've set up profiles on the big job-search sites and made a separate email address. I haven't sent out any CVs yet.

That's what I was going to do when I got the email from Colleen.

That, of course, is utterly insane. Every part of it: that Colleen is alive, that Colleen has my ring, and that Colleen just sent me an email from a dummy address. If that email wasn't sitting right there in my inbox, I'd think I was going out of my mind.

I put my laptop aside carefully and get up. There's no sun flooding in through the bay window today. The glass is speckled with rain, droplets and silvery streaks. I peer through them with mistrust, convinced—my skin crawling with the feeling—that someone on the other side is watching me, observing me like a fish in an aquarium.

Then I go back to the kitchen where the cup of coffee sits under the little tap of the machine, still steaming, but just barely. I've lost all taste for coffee. Adrenaline woke me up better than espresso could, and the thought of gulping down that gritty, bitter nonsense makes me shudder. I dump it in the sink and then go have a shower. I wash my hair, blow-dry it with the round brush, and put on makeup—the good stuff for special occasions, the expensive foundation and mascara, hoping that, if I look like me, I'll feel like me. Tough. I feel like the same jittery mess, but with makeup on.

From here, I decide to tackle it head-on. There are ways of figuring out where an email came from. IP address and such. I can google it. At least I could try. To get my real, rightful ring back, of course. Only to get my ring back from whoever stole it.

Not because I think it could actually be...her.

With a decisive intake of breath, I sit on the living room couch, back straight, knees together like I'm in elementary school, and open my laptop. I don't look at the email...yet. I google how to find out where an email comes from and spend another ten minutes blinking helplessly at walls of text studded with unfamiliar terms.

Okay, then. I'll just do it step by step, figuring it out as I go. I click on my inbox, realize it's the wrong one—still open on my form rejection. *I just didn't connect...*

With an impatient sigh, I click the red cross, and the writerly inbox disappears. I'm looking at my personal email now.

A message from Byron sits at the top, dated back three weeks. Below it, one from my sister, from three months ago. I'd promised myself I'd reply. I really did. But then I dreaded it, put it off, then forgot, and then gave up altogether because it would just be even more awkward after all this time. Below that, a couple of generic messages from those discount sites for Columbus that I keep track of, as if we really needed 48 percent off a meal at a restaurant chain or a knockoff Apple Watch for $199. Byron hates those sites, despises the very idea.

Frustrated, I scroll through the emails. They're going back six months now, seven, ten. Back to the top—nothing. I check the other folders. Nothing. Nothing in Trash or Spam.

It's gone like it was never there.

A little laugh bubbles out of me. Clearly, I'm going crazy. Ha ha. Imagining emails that never were.

My thoughts churn. I should have taken a screenshot, I should have saved the image—should have, should have, should have. How do I retrieve a lost email? Google has plenty of answers but they all apply only to emails that ostensibly existed.

Remembering that I have a phone, I run to get it from the charger in the bedroom. No new notifications. I write a quick text to Byron, who should be on his lunch hour by now: Bon appetit! Love, xoxoxoxo and a couple of emojis. It's cheesy but right now all I want is to hear from him, even if it's just a two-word text.

It's better than asking, Hey, by the way, are you absolutely sure your first wife is dead?

# CHAPTER THREE

*Are you absolutely sure your first wife is dead?*

Once you've been inside our house, the question doesn't sound as crazy.

Here's what I know about Colleen Westcott.

Her favorite color was lilac—because the entire first floor is painted pale lilac with gray accents. Why change it? Byron would say if I asked him. It's tasteful and makes the rooms look airier. As if the rooms, with their twelve-foot ceilings and lingering echoes in the corners, needed to feel any bigger.

She liked to cook—hence, the state-of-the-art equipped kitchen and a full set of Le Creuset cookware stashed away in its cream-colored cabinets. When I saw how much these things cost, on a trip to Williams Sonoma, I choked on my iced coffee. She was definitely the cook because I've yet to see Byron use the kitchen to make anything more complex than cereal or, on the odd occasion, pasta with canned sauce. The Le Creuset dishes gather sticky dust on their once-shiny enameled lids.

She was the coffee enthusiast too, because her books on coffee—heavy, glossy photo volumes—are stacked on a shelf in the dining room, right next to her cookbook collection. If the cookbooks are to be believed, she was fond of Mediterranean cuisine with an occasional foray into the Middle East. All the books are inscribed with her name on the flyleaf in silver, needle-thin Sharpie. She wrote in cursive. She must have had an elegant hand because...

...because the worst part. The paintings.

Colleen was a painter, an accomplished one as far as painters in the twenty-first century go. She taught at the same liberal arts college where Byron still teaches, something no one fails to remind me every time I go to a function with my husband. *Did you know Colleen used to teach in the Fine Arts Department? Students loved her. And what do you do?*

*Claire is a writer*, Byron would say, stepping in pointedly.

*Really, now? Makes sense—our Byron always goes for the artsy types, doesn't he?*

But back to the paintings.

Colleen's famous paintings—landscapes, faces, strange blurred figures, all big giant things in smeared colors—are everywhere. Yes, I guess I am an "artsy type" but I'm a writer, raised on printed words, and for the life of me, I just don't understand the appeal. I'm not going to say,

"A three-year-old could have painted that mess"—oh no, since my husband is a lecturer at a liberal arts college, I know better than that—but when it's not even a *beautiful* mess, what's the point?

Perhaps I'm just bitter. Perhaps in another context, I would have stood in front of one of those paintings in a trendy gallery in Cleveland or Columbus, tilted my head, and tried to see a deeper meaning. Noted how the colors seemed to flow together while at the same time were perfect in their integrity. Noticed the rich texture and thickness of the glossy paint.

But when I see them on the walls of my house, all I can see is Colleen.

Her paints, her easel, her kit of pricey, soft brushes made of real fur or hair or I don't know what—all has been moved to the storage room in the basement, reverently and with reluctance. The room she used as a studio is now my office.

But it's the paintings themselves. They're all over the house. Over the staircase, her sketches (études—I read in an art book once they're called études) hang behind glass, in tasteful, skinny frames of dark mahogany. Banal things in reddish-brown chalk that remind me of rust or dried blood. Some buckets piled up in the grass, next to a barely sketched-out shed. The faceless silhouette of a woman, naked and unselfconscious, her doughy thighs and rounded belly on proud display (not Colleen herself— she was wiry, thin not from workouts but thanks to a fast metabolism). A sketch of Byron's profile in the middle of an expanse of pristine untouched paper. I've inspected that sketch many times, noting all the little discrepancies between the drawing and real-life Byron yet never able to quite pinpoint why it looked so different from the face I see every day.

In the dining room: a quaint beach, almost mono-chrome in sienna and ochre. Someplace on Lake Erie? The hastily smeared copse of trees, the shabby little boat moored to a root, it doesn't look like something from the Caribbean—not that Colleen and Byron were the type to go sunning in an all-inclusive resort with the kinds of people Colleen would have probably found as bland and boring as my university classmates found me. They went to Peru for their honeymoon, which Byron reluctantly ad-mitted to me when I pressed him about the origins of a mask that hung in the hallway upstairs. But as far as I know, Colleen didn't paint Peru. Found the subject matter too predictable, maybe.

And then the living room. That giant sprawling canvas of the house itself. The house sits in the middle of a murky sfumato like an island lost at sea. The whole thing is in tones of burgundy, raw and rusty, and it makes the house appear sinister. Maybe she painted it that way to make a nice flashy contrast with the lilac walls and cream-colored couch. But Colleen was above painting decorative things. Colleen made true art, whatever that means.

All that without counting the other paintings, smaller ones, scattered throughout the hallways and in the kitchen and upstairs and in Byron's office. So far, in the two years we've been married, I have only succeeded in get-ting rid of the one in the bedroom. I was going to find something else to put up in its place but abandoned the idea—whatever I chose, it would inevitably fall short by comparison.

The paintings are worth something, which is unusual, I suppose, in an era when hardly anyone bothers to spend money on unique art—let alone serious money. I looked it up furtively, erasing my search history afterward; that hideous bedroom one could keep our bills paid for months. But my attempts to suggest we sell even one have hit a wall.

It all frustrates me to no end, and then I get angry at Byron, and then I feel guilty and down on myself for being angry, for being resentful and petty. What else is it but pettiness, to feel jealous of a dead woman?

When I met Byron, that undercurrent of tragedy drew me like a magnet; when I learned the truth, I was only more enthralled. Anyone else may have been apprehensive and chosen to fall back and keep her options open: surely a reasonably pretty girl in her early twenties can do better than a guy almost twice her age, with a dead wife you just know he will never truly get over. But instead, it made me love him even more.

Boys my age knew nothing of true loss and pain and grief—they smacked gum and swiped their phone screens, scrolling through profile after profile on the latest dating app, always in search of the next bigger, flashier thing. For them, everything and everyone was replaceable, and replaceable things have no value. Or maybe it was the writer in me who became drawn to so much raw feeling concentrated in one person. I still can't be sure.

Maybe if she'd had the courtesy to divorce him or to run off with some long-haired hipster from one of her college workshops, he'd at least be able to let go. But Colleen had to go and die. And who can blame Byron for going off the rails a little when his first wife committed suicide?

# CHAPTER FOUR

When Byron told me, I did the only thing anyone of my generation would do: I looked it up online. I found an obituary. Colleen, as it turned out, painted under her maiden name—truth be told, I don't know whether she ever legally changed it to Westcott.

> Colleen May, esteemed artist, passed away on April 11, 2010. She leaves behind grieving colleagues and friends as well as her husband, Byron Westcott.

There was no mention that she killed herself. But there was a photo of Byron and Colleen together, made grainy by the newsprint. Not a posed wedding photo like you'd expect—they didn't have posed wedding photos. In it, they were standing, him with his arm around her shoulders. Behind her, I could make out, even despite the bad quality of the image, the unmistakable wild streaks of paint on canvas. This was her gallery show. I didn't know which one.

I've reread this obituary more than a few times since, peering into the photo, trying to suss out any details lost between the lines, in the sparse words. To glimpse something of the life they had, the connection between them. As a result, I could recite it from memory by now.

But today, my fingertips are drumming on the touch pad of my laptop as if of their own free will, my nerves on edge. That simple text is no longer enough, and I know better than to casually bring up Colleen's death with my husband.

The ringing of my phone makes my head snap up. Disoriented, I race around the house in circles before remembering I left it on the kitchen counter, next to the emptied cup of coffee.

Luckily, I don't miss the call. When I see Byron's photo on the screen, my heart jumps. He never calls me during his lunch break anymore.

"Hey, babe."

I wince just a tiny bit. I can't ever picture him referring to Colleen, offhandedly, as "babe." Although of course they must have had the same silly little names all couples have for each other. Even though the thought poisons me, slowly, one cell at a time, hollowing out my bones like radium.

"Hi." I ask him how his day is going. The answer is the same as the one he gives me every day when he comes home.

Today, though, something is different.

"You know what? I was thinking. It's horrible outside. So do you want to come and meet me after I'm done? We can go catch a movie and then get dinner at some greasy spoon."

In my head, I'm making up excuses. But my mouth says, "Okay. Sure."

"It's been a while."

"Yeah." I'm not sure what he's referring to. A lot of things have been a while. A week since he last said bye to me before leaving for work. Two weeks, three days since we had sex. About a month since we did anything together outside the house.

"How's the book going?"

"It's going," I lie. "I wrote some pages."

"Good. Then we both earned it."

Did we? Really?

"I love you," he says out of nowhere. I'm so startled I let a couple of seconds tick by before I say it back.

He gives a soft chuckle. "I'll see you at six."

\*     \*     \*

I know it's just a movie and dinner but at least it gives me something to think about instead of obsessing over some email I may or may not have imagined.

I abandon my laptop and go upstairs where I pick out a dress, then layer on some more makeup to be sure to cover the subtle but creeping dark circles under my eyes. The circles appeared sometime last spring after a particularly nasty bout of insomnia. I got a prescription to treat the insomnia itself but the circles never quite faded. Instead, they've been getting just a little bit darker, a little bit hollower, every single morning.

It's one of those changes that creeps up on you until you wake up one morning, at thirty or thirty-five, and realize that a little bit of your beauty got away from you. But I see it. Is this when it starts? Twenty-seven? I read that your cells start dying faster than they renew at twenty-five. Is that all there is then—is it downhill from here?

It's laughable, the fact that my husband teaches droves of artsy nineteen-year-olds every day, and yet the person I feel most threatened by is his dead first wife.

Sort-of-dead first wife, who sends me emails from the other side.

My sharp, hollow laugh echoes through the bathroom, and I snap back to reality. And the reality is I smeared half a tube of high-end concealer under my eyes, like two giant half-moons. Reverse raccoon. I bought that tube during one of my rampages at the mall. It's soft as whipped cream, like rubbing pure silk into your skin, and it costs a fortune. I wipe off the excess with a cotton pad and stamp down the rest with a little makeup sponge.

Hours later, I'm finally made-up, my hair straightened, in my car, and driving to the college. The place where my husband works couldn't be any more different from the college I went to—not just the exorbitant tuition but the place itself. When you hear "elite university," the image that pops into your head is Gothic spires and mossy stone walls, arched windows, and, of course, ivy. Lots of ivy everywhere. At least that's what pops into *my* head.

The people who founded this institution had a starkly different idea. There are lots of geometric shapes, lots of tinted glass that gleams on sunny days like remnants of an alien spaceship. On a day like today, the buildings meld with the gray sky. In lieu of cozy winding paths, the entire territory is shot through with arrow-straight lanes, contemporary sculptures scattered on fluorescent-green buzz-cut lawns.

When Byron's colleagues were within earshot, I always expressed polite admiration of the things but Byron saw right through it and never stopped poking fun at me. *Oh look,* he'd taunt in my ear as we walked past one or another concrete masterpiece, *it's that wonderfully expressive cubist take on* Venus de Milo.

I could never conceal my loathing of contemporary sculpture. It's as if whoever conceived of all this was outright rejecting all things traditional, casting them aside with palpable disdain.

Rain has been dripping steadily all afternoon but a group of students still holds court on benches that surround yet another hideous lump of metal that passes for art. They follow me with curious looks as I hurry by. And I get it—I stick out, and not in a good way. With my dress and blond hair, I'm normal, hopelessly conventional, and to them, I must be the human equivalent of an impressionist landscape painting. Passé, pastel, and ultimately boring.

Truth is I knew lots of people just like them at Ohio State. They, too, kept anyone who didn't fit their definition of cool at arm's length, considering them a natural inferior. After a while, I observed that the ones who take the most pains to set themselves apart, with strange haircuts and bits of metal in their faces, are the most creatively bankrupt; they were always the ones in the workshops who fed off the others' ideas, soaking up the imagination nature hadn't given them.

I ignore their looks. At least I have to give Byron credit: I just don't see him striking up an affair with one of them, some girl with green hair and tattoos on her neck.

The Language Arts Department is tucked away in the back of the campus. It's the least interesting building, as if the architects were running out of ideas and saved all the good ones for the departments that matter: fine arts and visual arts. The way I see it, the Language Arts Department is better off this way. The plain façade has trees surrounding it, maples that are turning red and yellow and orange, leaves shivering with raindrops. It feels warm and familiar somehow.

The door is heavy, and I struggle with my umbrella. A spray of cold drops dots my skirt. A girl rushes past me in a huff, all but shoving me out of her way. The door clatters closed behind her, leaving me in the warm, dry silence of the department. Fittingly, it feels like a library. Not an interesting, old library with moldings and arched doorways, but still.

I check my phone—six fifteen, no new texts or emails. The department is quiet at this hour so I go straight to my husband's office. I pass through a short labyrinth of halls to find myself in front of his door.

It's shut. I knock and then jiggle the handle to no result. Confused, I raise my hand to knock again but reconsider.

Instead, I take two more turns through the maze and find the Student Services desk, where a bored student is perched behind Plexiglas, ready to help with any pressing language arts matters. Today is a different one from last time, no longer the girl with the dreads and painful-looking barbell through the bridge of her nose. This one has mousy hair in a weird bobbed style, and a lip ring she keeps playing with. She's reading a book. Not on her phone or another device—a real, big, old-looking book. I can't tell what it is because the cover is lovingly wrapped in brown paper to preserve it.

"Excuse me." I almost feel bad to pull her out of it, back into boring reality. "Is Dr. Westcott here?"

"He's only in until six," she says on autopilot. I notice that her bangs are too short and look uneven, like she cut them herself. "Office hours are over but you can make an appointment."

Appointment. Add that to the ever-growing list of indignities I've suffered on my husband's account. *Does anybody here even know he's married?* "I'm supposed to meet him after work. I'm his wife," I say, pettily emphasizing the last sentence. "Claire. Westcott."

Not only does she look up from the tome, she puts it down altogether. "Oh. Sorry. I had no idea he had a wife."

My mouth opens in a silent O of humiliation. *Excuse me?* I'm about to blurt but then steps echo behind me, loud, hurrying, and the girl is now looking past me, over my shoulder. I turn to follow her gaze, and there he is, hurrying toward me. Byron. His hair looks mussed, droplets of rain still peppering it like tiny beads.

I know it's silly to get flustered at some obnoxious coed, because after all, I'm the one married to him. I'm the one with the ring (replacement ring, but still). But as soon as he comes close, I get on tiptoe and kiss him, throwing my arms around his neck. His body stiffens a little, and he meets the kiss—although his is much more chaste and less Bacall and Bogart.

"Honey," he whispers in my ear, "please. I'm at work."

You weren't in your office, I want to say. What were you doing outside? But that would make me look insecure in front of the coed, whose pointed stare I can feel on the back of my head. It's probably my own fault because of the public display of affection.

"Sorry I'm late," I say instead, even though I'm not that late and not that sorry. "Let's go?"

For the next little while, it's like old times. He holds his umbrella over my head as we run to his car; he puts on the jazz violinist I like. He already bought the tickets to a special screening of a classic black-and-white movie at the indie theater in Columbus where we used to go in the beginning. We're nearly alone in the cinema, rows and rows of those old-fashioned maroon velour seats all to ourselves, and we huddle over the bucket of popcorn, the warm buttery smell wafting in our faces. I let myself have more than I normally would, even though after three bites my fingertips are slick with grease. I can feel it pooling in my belly, coating my insides. We mouth along with the dialogue we know by heart.

When we emerge, it's late, and the rain has stopped. The street is gleaming with reflected streetlights, and spare drops still fall on my arms and into my hair, out of nowhere.

"A bite to eat?" he asks. I want to say I'm full from the popcorn—I certainly should be—but for the first time in weeks I realize with surprise I actually have an appetite. Not just an appetite—a hunger for life I thought was hopelessly in the past. I want to throw the diet to the four winds and stuff my face, and then I want to stay up late and open a bottle of wine and make love till three in the morning, to hell with having to get up. So I agree, and he starts down the side street.

When I remember what exactly is just a block from here, from this theater, it's too late. The greasy spoon's front is lit up green and yellow, just like before. The popcorn churns in my belly.

"This?" I say, trying to sound casual. "Really?"

"I don't want anything pretentious tonight. I just want a damn hamburger, and this place makes great ones." His eyes gleam, his grin is impish, and for a moment, I let myself imagine that maybe, just maybe, he forgot and forgave. That the ancestral ring, gone from the family forever because of me, is not such a big deal. He'll never be able to give it to his daughter now—not that he's likely to ever have a daughter anyway, the way things are going with my stubborn uterus.

"I just— It's kind of heavy, isn't it?" I know how painfully transparent my attempt is but I go ahead anyway. "I'm in the mood for something fresher."

"So get a Cobb salad," he says, shrugging. His eyebrow twitches, etching a deep, dark line on his forehead. "Claire, please don't start your killjoy routine right now. We're having such a good night."

I draw a breath of damp air, all my words dead on my tongue. If I say I'm sorry now, that'll only make it worse. The only thing to do is to carry on like nothing happened, like I messed up a line in a play. The worst thing I can do is acknowledge it. The show must go on.

The smell, the light, the color scheme—everything conspires to make me queasy but I grin right through my nausea. As soon as the girl comes up to us, I order a bourbon, before she has a chance to open her mouth and try to sell us the specials. Byron gets a Jack and Coke.

"Really going for the trashy concept today, huh?" I say, working hard not to sound spiteful.

His grin almost makes me forgive him. "What? I've been Mr. PhD in Literature all week. Do you know how hard it is not to lose face in front of all these cool, hip types who come to my lectures? If I slip up, they'll never respect me."

What I don't need right now is to be reminded of all the cool, hip types, especially like the one with the pretentious vintage tome. I bet she wasn't even really reading it, just showing off.

"And you could also use some greasy French fries, if you ask me. You're all bones."

Self-conscious, I hug my shoulders to realize he's right. I did lose some weight; it always goes from my face and upper body first so I can't always tell by how my jeans fit. My already nonexistent tits dwindle to nothing but my sharp-boned facial structure becomes more refined. I turn heads either way, and I know it. He would know it too, if he ever paid attention. He's the least jealous guy I've ever been with, and I used to think it was a good thing.

He has never criticized my appearance either: thin, not so thin, makeup, no makeup, inch-long brown roots—he's never made so much as one ambiguous remark. Now that I think about it, this is the first time he seems to have noticed my body in a very long while.

He waves the waitress over and orders us some fries to share, a hamburger for himself. To spite him, I do get the Cobb salad, even though the salad in this place is beyond disgusting.

The fries arrive almost immediately, the basket sitting between us, filling the emptiness with a savory smell so thick I feel myself getting fat by just breathing. I gulp my bourbon. Then catch myself twisting the replacement ring nervously around my finger. Byron reaches over and puts his hand on top of mine, like he does whenever I have one of my little neurotic tics.

Any second, I half expect him to bring up the ring. At certain moments, he tilts his head just so, licks his lips, and I think, *There it is, on the tip of his tongue, and any moment now it'll slip out and ruin everything*. It would be so easy. But I know he won't. Of course he won't.

I finish the bourbon and get another one just as the food arrives. I'll have puffy eyes and the mother of all headaches tomorrow but who cares? I gulp from drink number two, staring wistfully at Byron's plate—not a chance I'm touching mine. The mound of wilted oily lettuce shreds, the grayish boiled egg, the pale, watery tomato slices—it's enough to make me want to hurl.

I know I must say something to break the infected silence punctuated only by the sound of Byron chewing, his jaws working with determination.

I polish off the rest of the bourbon. "We should try again," I blurt. "Seriously this time."

He doesn't stop eating. He only gives me a look over the handful of hamburger. That look.

"Interesting how you mostly want to when you're hammered. You realize you'll need to lay off the wine for nine months?"

That's a lie, so blatant I should be insulted. It's not that I'm wishy-washy in my desire to have a baby. It's just that my infertility fitted so neatly with Byron's disinterest in raising children.

"You said," I start, words jumping over one another in a hurry to get out, "you said, as you got older, you started to think about it. To want to leave something behind."

"Thinking about it isn't the same," he says, lowering the burger. Meat, brown and pink, crumbling, a mess of ketchup and mayo spilling over onto his plate. "And besides...Claire, you know how much it'll cost. Not just the IVF. Everything. Clothes, schools. Our savings won't last forever, the way we're going. We'd have to make serious cutbacks."

I pretend to think. I have a solution but he won't want to hear of it, of course. Nor will he want to give up his gourmet coffee and Scotch.

"I know," I say acidly. "Trust me—I know. It's so much

better to leave behind a Great American Novel than another human being with your genes. But that's not working out so great, as you know."

"You don't have to go there." He wipes his hands on a napkin and then balls it up and tosses it into his plate. Byron's own rejected novels, from a time when I was probably in kindergarten, are still gathering dust in some drawer. We never talk about them. Just like we no longer talk about mine, the big shiny novel that sits like a brick on my hard drive and will probably never leave it.

Byron sighs. "So that's it, then? You want a baby to give your life meaning?" His mouth twists with disdain. "How about— Have you been looking for a job, Claire?"

I sit up straight. It feels like I've been slapped. My head is spinning, ringing hollowly. Although it could be the bourbon.

"I have to go," I say in carefully measured syllables. I get up, pull my dress around my thighs, and storm to the bathroom. Not until the door swings closed behind me does it hit me—this is it, this exact dingy, dirty washroom, where it happened. The ring.

I slam the door of the stall and make sure the latch is turned. Hastily, I pull off reams and reams of brittle toilet paper, throw it on the floor, position my knees on top of it so my skin doesn't make contact with the disgusting tiles. Then I lean over the toilet and, without hesitation, stick two fingers down my throat.

And watch it all come back up, this whole wretched day.

# CHAPTER FIVE

*Your wife didn't even notice her keys were gone.*

*I wish I could say I'm such a meticulous planner that I masterminded the whole thing. But no. My plan had been much simpler but just as effective. Once again, luck was on my side.*

*She was at the public library near campus, where she goes every Friday, waiting for you to be finished at work. As usual, before she goes browsing, she stakes her claim on her favorite chair next to the window—see? I do know her. And you. Maybe better than you know yourselves.*

*She puts her coat and her purse on the armchair, coat thrown over purse as if it will fool anyone. Thinking the sort of people who go to the library are surely above swiping a wallet. I am above it, even though God knows I could use the money. And she—she throws her trendy bag with the glittery logo around like it's nothing.*

*But I wasn't going to risk ruining everything over a few bucks and a cute purse. I waited for her to disappear in the reference book section and then simply came up and rummaged through the purse like it was my own.*

*She has a mess in there, your wife. Lipsticks in three different colors, empty lip balm, gum wrappers, loose change clanging around the bottom. I couldn't resist—I pocketed a lipstick, an unassuming shade of pink not so different from the color of her lips. That tube just looked so sad in there, and she'll never notice. I opened her wallet. She had a bunch of credit cards, crumpled receipts stuffed in the cash compartment, but no photos. I rifled through the receipts and put them back as carelessly as she had, taking mental notes. It was tempting but I didn't touch the cards. The time would come for everything; I just had to be patient.*

*But I did take her house keys and put them in my coat pocket. While she flipped through this or that coffee-table book, I ran to the quaint little shoe-repair place across the street and had copies made. Within fifteen minutes, the house keys were back in your wife's purse, and she never knew a thing.*

*Getting into your house—well, that was another matter altogether. I waited for two more weeks, biding my time to be sure I hadn't messed up, that she really didn't notice anything. Once I felt safe, I could go ahead.*

*I skipped class that day, the day I knew for sure she'd be out of the house. I drove out to where you live. It's such a generic McMansion; I'm surprised at you. How can a spirit like yours feel at home there, be happy there? I've heard you speak. Your mind can soar into the stratosphere and bring along everyone who's listening.*

*I pictured you living in a beautiful Victorian that looks like it might be haunted or, maybe, in a historic ranch, tending to your own horses in your free time. Is it dumb of me to still have idols in our day and age, to imagine a life for them that transcends the boring trappings of domesticity?*

*It's a beautiful house, sure. It projects the right things: money, stability, respectability—the usual garbage I know you don't really care about. It's so impersonal. None of it is you.*

*When we're together, we will sell it and move. To another city, or another state, because why not? We'll go someplace where you'll be inspired, a place worthy of you, a place that will nourish this great mind of yours so you can finally fulfil your true potential.*

*As for me, I don't dare suggest I'll be your muse—I can't be so presumptuous—but at least I'll do everything in my power to make sure the domestic sphere doesn't distract you from your work. I'll make you breakfast in the morning and then fuck you on the kitchen counter.*

*That first visit was just that, a visit. Reconnoitering. I didn't take or touch anything—I swear. Well, I did touch some things but I put them back the same way you and your wife left them. And, all right, I admit that I lingered longer than necessary in front of your bookshelves. I always wanted to know which books you keep at home. Which ones mean so much to you that you picked them out of millions and millions of titles and brought them into your inner sanctum, granting them the coveted spot on your personal shelf. You like obscure British novels from the fifties and sixties; you're a John Fowles fan. I could tell because you have more than one edition of all his books. Other things weren't as surprising: Jay McInerney, Tama Janowitz, Hilary Mantel, and, endearingly, a whole shelf at the very bottom filled with Swedish crime novels, mass-market paperback editions that look like they came from an airport.*

*I picked up a heavy, beautiful tome from the center of the shelf where you put your most precious possessions on display. The gilded spine spoke to me:* THE MAGUS. *I sat cross-legged on the floor and leafed through the pages, breathing their heady smell, my fingertips alight with their texture. I slipped my hand into my underwear, touched myself, and marked it—just the corners of the title page, christened by my wetness. When you next pick it up, you won't notice a thing but your subconscious will rear its head like a wolf scenting fresh blood. And when I'm ready to show myself to you, then you'll know me on a primal level. Your body and your blood will know that I'm yours.*

*I have now been able to fill in the blanks in my picture of you. I know your favorite coffee, your brand of cereal, your alcohol of choice, the DVDs on your shelf. I know your drawers are organized, and your wife's closet somewhat chaotic. I know her shoes are one size smaller than mine, her bra size is 34B (statistically average), and that she has more thong panties than regular ones—surprising, because she looks like such a prude.*

*Isn't it magic when you finally meet that person, the one*

*you're meant to be with? It's as if they know everything about you instinctively, and all their wants and needs and likes and dislikes align with yours. And that's when you know fate brought you together and you're meant to be.*

*In time, it will happen. For now, it's almost as if I already live here, with the two of you. Immaterial for now but growing closer, realer, more solid every day. Like becoming a ghost in reverse.*

# CHAPTER SIX

Another morning waking up alone in our bed.

My head is pounding, my eyes are swollen, and my breath could kill a crocodile, all of which is to be expected after yesterday. Before I attempt to make myself coffee, I go to the bathroom and take an aspirin. Next, I jump in the shower, blasting the water at the hottest setting. I scrub my skin until I'm lobster red and the steam is so thick the fan can't clear it.

When I get out, refreshed and revived, I finally realize I forgot to be sad that he didn't wake me to say bye. It's Friday, and the weekend is looming in front of me, vague but menacing. Great. I just can't *wait* to spend two days stewing in mutual resentment.

I make toast but realize I can't stomach so much as a bite so I let it sit in the toaster. With my cup of coffee and my laptop, I take up my usual spot in the living room.

My fingertips tap on the edge of the keyboard nervously as I open my emails but no more strange messages from dead people have cropped up.

However, there's an interesting email in my writing account. Dear Claire, I'd love to read your novel. Please send me the manuscript to . . .

I have to look up the agent because it's been so long since I emailed her—and written her off as a nonresponse. She's based in the UK and has some reasonably well-known authors on her client list. I format the manuscript per her guidelines, and the moment I hit Send, another email pops up in my regular inbox.

I take one glance at it, and everything—the manuscript request, my dread of the upcoming weekend—evaporates from my head.

Re: Artwork for sale

Good morning Connie, I saw your add and I'd like to see the Colleen May. Is their a time and place we can meet?

Best, Rea

Dubious grammar aside, she didn't leave contact info except for her email address. My skin starts to tingle, my hands trembling with excitement. *I am actually getting away with this!* At the same time, shame makes my face flush. *Can I really, seriously get away with this?*

Yes. Yes I can. I will present Byron with the fait accompli when it's too late to turn back. He'll be happy. He can't *not* be. It's just a painting stashed away in the storage room like some old blanket we never use. And it could help me—it could help me so much, more than anyone can imagine.

It could cover a round of IVF. Or more, depending on how I play it.

Licking my lips, I write a message to this Rea. Real name? Who knows? And who cares, as long as she can pay. Besides, look who's talking. "Connie" was a last-second precaution in case any prospective buyers get too Google-happy.

Either way, I can't very well invite her over. Where do you live? Can you drive down to Cleveland? We can meet at a coffee shop and discuss.

The moment I hit Send, I hope it doesn't scare her off, make her think I'm trying to defraud her. I tell myself it's not an unreasonable request. It's a valuable painting, after all, and aren't you supposed to be at least a little wary of strangers on the internet?

My doubts turn out to be in vain. A reply arrives minutes later. !!Sure! It's not a problem, I live a half hour from Cleveland. We can meet at a coffee shop by the waterfront. So excited!!

We agree to meet at a Starbucks, anonymous enough yet out in plain sight. It's a long drive for me, almost two hours, but I'm not chancing it by meeting in Columbus or, God forbid, here in town. I'm not doing anything wrong, yet I still feel like a criminal.

The painting is in one of those cardboard sleeves, rolled

up neatly. I roll it out just to be sure. It used to hang in the bedroom but having it there was too much for me, and even Byron agreed. The line had to be drawn somewhere, and a painting of a naked couple above our bed, a couple that was, beyond all plausible deniability, my husband and his first wife, turned out to be it.

If this Rea only knew I'd be glad to give it away for free.

Wasting no time, I get ready. I put on a plain T-shirt and jeans, my hair up in a ponytail, and a baseball hat on my head, which clashes furiously with my cream wool fall coat. Normally I wouldn't be caught dead in public looking like this. I know it's silly but I'm still a little paranoid someone might recognize me so it makes me feel reassured. With my purse slung over my shoulder, I carry the cardboard sleeve to my car and put it in the trunk. I throw glances at the windows of the neighbors' houses from under the bill of my hat but they're all dark and empty. Everyone is at work; there's no one to observe me. That persistent feeling on the back of my neck can only be my own guilt.

By the end of the drive, I almost manage to relax. My favorite music from my iPod pouring from the speakers, the sunny weather, the lack of traffic—I take it all to be good omens. Maybe I'll even take a long walk along the waterfront after. Or go shopping. Or buy myself a mimosa at a café to celebrate.

No, no. I'm supposed to be getting used to not drinking.

Much to my consternation, Rea is late. I fidget on my uncomfortable Starbucks chair, my skinny cappuccino untouched on the table, and can't stop checking on the cardboard sleeve, which is leaning on the side of the chair next to me. As if someone might grab it and take off with it. Every time the door opens, my head snaps up, and my heart starts pounding.

Finally, a woman enters, gaze searching distractedly until it alights on me, then on the sleeve. Her face illuminates with tentative recognition, and she advances toward me, uncertain.

I get up and give her my sunniest smile. "Rea?"

"Yes!"

We hug, and she gives me two kisses, one on each cheek. It's like an awkward Tinder date, and I'm sure that's what everyone thinks. Rea is maybe five to eight years older than I, and, even though I hate to pigeonhole someone based on their clothes, she's kind of a granola hippie. She's wearing those flowing pants and a tank top, a magenta-and-gold wrap in her dreadlocked hair, bracelets clanging on both her wrists. Byron's university students would probably lambast her for cultural appropriation. But as long as she has ten grand in cash to pay for a Colleen May painting, who cares?

"So," she says as soon as we sit down and the entire coffee shop stops staring at us, "can I see it?"

"Um," I say. "Of course." I throw a glance around, at all the people sitting mere feet from us, and I'm not so sure this is the place to unroll a rather frank nude painting. Rea gets it.

"We can go to the bathroom," she says eagerly. I start to get up but she catches my wrist. Her touch makes me squirm. Like I'm a teenager selling pot, and I expect her to turn out to be an undercover cop and to bust me any moment.

"Wait. Do you mind if I ask you something?"

"Go ahead."

"How come you have a Colleen May? I mean...where did you get it? She's not that well-known—I mean, not that mainstream." Beneath her healthy bronze tan, she blushes noticeably. What she meant to say, clearly, is that I'm not cool enough to know who Colleen May is.

I don't exactly see myself telling her, Oh, I'm her husband's new wife, and I snuck it out of Colleen's own house without him knowing.

"My mom bought it," I say. I'd thought of the story before I even placed the ad. "Years ago. At some little gallery thing, I think. I must have been, oh, twelve or thirteen years old. It wasn't a big deal then—I mean, she wasn't famous yet. But my mom passed recently, and—"

"Oh, I'm so sorry," Rea interjects on cue. I move my hand away, dodging her attempt to put hers on top of it.

"And I was going through the stuff she left me and saw this thing. It's quite...striking. You'll agree once you see it. So I googled the artist, and it turns out it's worth more than I thought."

Rea nods along. To my relief, not only is she buying it, I'm noticing a look of glee she works hard to hide. To her, I'm the naïve little girl who put the rare painting on Craigslist like an idiot, and this is something Rea thinks she can take advantage of. Next, she'll say it's not that impressive, part of the less acclaimed period of Colleen's work, and oh, look at this crack in the paint right here, and try to bargain down the price.

Well, she has another think coming.

For some reason, that makes me feel better—about my-self, about this whole venture. I have the upper hand. I know something she doesn't. I feel daring, and not wait-ing for the feeling to pass, I open the cardboard sleeve right at the table.

"Have a look," I say, and grin in the face of her hesita-tion. I slide out the canvas, tilt it so only we can see, and unroll it as far as I can.

"Whoa," says Rea. The smug look is gone, replaced by that of awe. "That's . . . intense."

"Yes."

"Her early work. It has a rawness to it."

*Rawness* is an understatement. "Magnificent, isn't it?"

"How much did your mother pay for it?" She's still un-able to take her gaze off the painting.

"I have no idea." Figuring I had teased her just enough, I roll the painting back up. She bites her lip, her eyes following the canvas until I put the cap back on the card-board tube. "Can't have been that much."

"Lucky her."

"Lucky me," I say, grinning again.

"Are you sure you want to part with it?" She meets my grin with her own uncertain smile. "I mean, I know I'm sort of shooting myself in the foot here, but . . . it's so beautiful."

I sigh, pretending to think about it. "What can I do?" I say. "Student loans."

We share that shaky, slightly forced laugh of two strangers bonding over mutual mundane struggles. Just as I'm ready to move on to the next phase—price negotiation—Rea leans in.

"So how much do you know about Colleen May, exactly?" she asks. I didn't expect this question, and it makes me fidget under her curious stare.

"Well, that she was sort of famous. And that she died."

Rea nods. "Eight years ago. Of course, the paintings' value soared. The fact that it was such a sordid story sure did help."

I can barely hide how incredulous I am. The gall of her! Then I remember: Rea has no idea how closely I'm connected with Colleen. She's just hoping to snag a painting for a bargain price and sharing juicy gossip.

"She committed suicide, right?" I ask. I'm aware that my posture becomes too straight, my facial expression too forcefully neutral. But I'm confident Rea won't notice. People generally don't notice awkwardness and flaws in others because they're too busy thinking about themselves. She is no exception.

"Oh, there's more to it than that. I read this article online that said—"

"An artist who commits suicide," I interject. "Not the first time that happened."

But my heart is starting to beat awfully fast. When I pick up the cold cup of cappuccino, my fingers are trembling just enough for it to be noticeable.

Byron told me he was once married and she died, on one of our first dates. He didn't tell me about the suicide until much later. I was a little hurt that he would keep something so big from me when we were supposed to have no secrets from each other, but I tried to be understanding—it's not something you want to lead with when you're starting a brand-new relationship.

"Yeah, but there's more to it than that," Rea says. I blink at her.

"Really," I say hollowly.

"I know! At first, they investigated it as...how do you say it? Foul play?"

"Yes. Foul play." I gulp, feeling a little nauseous. "Why did they think that?"

She shrugs, her dreads rolling along her shoulder, bangles going *clink clink*.

"You didn't know? She drowned. Jumped in the harbor. Except, get this...They never found the body."

I don't see what's so special about that—chances are it might happen when you drown in a body of water that size.

Rea leans in conspiratorially. Her eyes sparkle with unhealthy interest.

"And her husband at the time? He was some kind of failed writer who now teaches literature. And for a while there everyone thought it wasn't suicide at all. Everyone thought he did it."

# CHAPTER SEVEN

I tell Rea I have to go to the bathroom, grab my coat, my purse, and the painting, and go lock myself in a stall.

As I struggle to catch my breath, clutching the cardboard sleeve hard enough to crush, I can't make my thoughts flow in order. I want to call Byron, right this second, from this narrow stall stinking of cleaner. My hands leave sweaty prints on the cardboard. I want to shred this stupid painting and flush it down the toilet, ten thousand dollars be damned.

I resist the urge to call. His phone is on Do Not Disturb during his lectures anyway. But I do compose a text, my fingertips trembling. Honey can you call me please?

I don't even know what I'd say. I just want to hear his voice.

As I exit the stall, the phone dings, the sound sharp and

sudden. I give a start and nearly drop my purse as I scramble to get it.

> Hey! I was just about to text you actually. Em and Andrew are coming over for dinner, can you scare something up? Doesn't have to be fancy. I'll pick up wine on my way & they're bringing dessert.

Betrayal, hurt, and anger boil over, as sudden as they are intense. I throw the phone back into my purse with violence. Scooping up my coat, I grab the painting with my free hand and push open the door.

Rea—oh God, I managed to forget she existed—gets up when she sees me rushing toward her.

"Oh, by the way," she says, "I didn't want to bring it up right away, not that I don't trust you and everything, but maybe we should have that painting appraised first. I know a . . ."

Her expression changes as she glimpses my face. I walk right past her as if she were a ghost and continue toward the exit.

"Connie!" she exclaims behind my back. "I'm sorry! What did I say? Wait—"

The door of the café swings shut behind me, cutting off her voice midsentence. A girl about to go in stumbles out of my way, indignant. Does she look familiar? Everything swims in my vision because I can't blink away the tears—if they escape and run down my cheeks, they'll be real. I run to my car, throw the painting in the trunk along with my coat, and slam it shut with a heavy feeling of finality, like a gunshot.

*     *     *

Outside the house, I sit in the car for a while. Instead of settling my nerves like I hoped, the drive made everything worse. I spent the better part of the two hours ruminating, going over every word in my head until everything has spun completely out of proportion.

If it were me, if I got into an accident on my way home, got hit by a drunk driver—a stretch of the imagination in the early afternoon, but still. If I died on the spot, would my husband be over it in a week? *You are being awful, Claire*, I say to myself, although even that sounds like Byron's voice. *How do you manage to make everything about you?*

But there's a difference, a big difference. Isn't there? I thought about it countless times before, more than I like to admit. He knows that she chose to leave—did it on purpose. The ultimate betrayal. If someone did that to me, would I spend the rest of my life trying to atone, clinging to their memory, wondering if I did or said something to cause it? Or would I hate them for the rest of eternity?

This is what I used to think, anyhow. But this…this opens up entirely new possibilities I previously haven't considered. *Foul play.*

They can't have seriously thought he had something to do with it, can they? I wonder if it's what's making me so angry or the fact that he never told me.

The dashboard clock says it's four thirty. Which doesn't leave me much time to keep ruminating, because Byron's sister Emily and her husband will be here at seven.

I leave the painting in the trunk. I can't stand to even look at it right now. Inside, I take two Tylenol for my aching head and pour myself a glass of the wine I only normally use for cooking. It's acrid, with an obvious undercurrent of ethanol. I wouldn't be caught dead drinking it in front of Byron, who may not be one of those obsessed people with the enormous wine cellar but who prides himself on being able to tell the difference between a merlot and a pinot noir by smell alone.

I wince but drain half the glass nonetheless while I go through the fridge, tossing everything that went bad in the last week. At the end, I'm staring at half-empty shelves, this close to panic. I'm too buzzed to get behind the wheel and drive to the grocery store, and the only thing within walking distance is a bodega. Finally, I decide to throw together a pasta dish. Thankfully, there are some shrimp in the freezer, and the Parmesan cheese hardly ever goes bad . . . does it?

I'm in the heat of it, draining the pasta before adding it to the shrimp sizzling in butter on the stove, and I don't hear the front door. I only notice Byron is back when he's standing in the kitchen doorway.

In the first moment, I forget I was mad at him. He puts two bottles of a very nice red wine on the counter. "Smells good," he comments. "Pasta again?"

The comment stings, just a tiny bit, and I try not to think that it was meant to. I haven't felt motivated to make elaborate recipes in the last couple of weeks. He already commented on the recycling bin being filled with empty sauce jars once. I huff silently as I dump the contents of the colander into the frying pan.

He comes up behind me and puts his arms around my waist, which immobilizes me with my arms awkwardly halfway down. The pan's contents hiss and sizzle. Time to stir.

"Please let go," I say.

"What, I can't kiss my own wife?"

My mouth tastes sour from the bad wine. It really is bad, and the buzz is worse, making me sleepy and exacerbating my headache at the same time. If I kiss him, he'll smell the wine on my breath.

"Food is burning," I point out, and he slinks away. I turn off the element, bend to get the lid to keep the pasta warm, and when I stand up again, my head starts to spin like mad. You're not supposed to mix wine and Tylenol—it's bad for your liver. Or maybe it's Advil?

"Can you help me set the table?" I call out, but my husband is already in another room. I hear him clinking, fumbling with that stupid mixology kit I bought him last year for his birthday. Like a child with a chemistry set. Making another overmixed drink with a million kinds of sugary liqueur that hits you like a sledgehammer.

Fine, then. I open the top cupboard, the one containing the nice set of dishes, the one that still matches because not enough have broken yet. Four plates stacked in my arms, I walk over to the dining room—a room we've used exactly twice since Byron and I have been married. Once upon a time it must have conveyed suburban respectability, hosted family gatherings on major holidays or parties with both spouses' friends and colleagues attending. Now its main purpose seems to be gathering dust. I have no family that I'm close with and no colleagues, and Byron stopped inviting anyone over a long time ago. Except for his sister, of course.

The plates land on the table with a clang.

"Here?" Byron's steps approach, and he appears in the doorway. "I was thinking we could just eat in the kitchen. Not like it's a special occasion. I mean, it's just pasta."

I blink, exhale, and pick up the plates again.

Next thing I know, Byron is by my side, holding up my arm, which is the only thing that prevents the dishes from sliding onto the floor to shatter. "Claire, are you all right? You seem off."

Am I all right? Considering that you didn't tell me you were a suspect in your late wife's death. Considering that—

I mumble something under my breath.

"Sorry?" Byron looks confused.

"It's not *just pasta*," I repeat. "It's linguine alla gamberi. With white wine, garlic, and herb butter. And we're not eating it in the kitchen."

After a pause that makes my ears ring, he starts to laugh.

"Of course." He leans over and surprises me with a clumsy kiss on the lips. I don't have to worry about him tasting the wine—he's already reeking of brandy and some kind of orangey liqueur. "That's why I love you. Such attention to detail. Everything is special with you. Want a cocktail?"

I have no choice but to acquiesce.

Emily and Andrew are the kind of people who always

arrive ten minutes early, and they do today, without fail. A box from a bakery, tied with a ribbon, changes hands— I already know what's inside because it's always the same thing: éclairs. Byron and Emily's childhood favorite, a story I've heard countless times. Kisses on both cheeks are exchanged; excuses for smeared lipstick are proffered.

I never managed to understand how the family that produced someone as passionate and complex as Byron is also responsible for someone as dull as Emily. Named after either Brontë or Dickinson—I could never keep it straight—Emily is utterly devoid of the dark fire that consumed her namesakes from within. From what I know about her, every single thing she's ever done in her life was because she was supposed to. And it's not because she had clichéd, heartless parents who forced their artistic child into a socially acceptable mold until she broke. I heard the stories of Byron and his sister growing up in their eccentric family of book lovers, with a mother who liked her sherry and pot as much as she liked her modernist poetry and a musician father who skipped out on them with an undergrad when Byron and Emily were kids.

I concluded that her near-compulsory normalcy was, in fact, Emily's version of rebellion against this unconventional childhood. I can picture her, awkward teenager (in my mind's eye, she always has poufy bangs, even though in pictures her hair is relatively sleek by eighties' standards) embarrassed to invite her preppy, pretty friends to her house because she doesn't want them to see how she lives.

Fast-forward to present day: Emily is a psychologist with an office in Columbus, married to Andrew, who's a notary, and mom to Mark, age nineteen, whom I met only once at my wedding. Shortly after, he left for college, at the other end of the country somewhere, prestigious, although not an Ivy—I get the feeling the main criterion was for it to be as far as humanly possible from Emily and home.

Not that I dislike her, because disliking someone requires a certain amount of mental labor, passion, and intensity. And she's never done anything to me to warrant all the effort. It's impossible to tell what she's thinking when you look at her—or whether she's thinking anything at all.

Apart from her husband, Andrew, only Byron knows what's under the façade. He talks to Emily on the phone every other day, and not just a quick call to ascertain everything is still as placid in her life as it was two days earlier and two days before that. Real conversations: Byron tells her about work, laughing with her about the lengths to which lazy students will go to avoid doing the assignments and about the petty rivalries between other professors. Stuff he stopped telling me about months ago, and when I try to ask, he just shrugs.

The evening progresses. The red wine Byron brought turns out to be quite good. Emily praises my pasta, and I accept the compliment graciously. Andrew chimes in politely; Byron takes a swig of wine and declares, *I always said she was a phenomenal cook. She can make a feast out of thin air.*

I sip from my glass, doing my best to pace myself even though the pinot noir is like velvet on the tongue, none of the tannin-laced bitterness I usually hate about red wines. It doesn't seem to be working: I feel myself getting tipsier with every tiny sip. I gulp greedily from my water glass, refill it, drain it again. The water carafe is empty so I get up and take it to the kitchen to refill it from the filter.

The kitchen is spinning gently. I set the carafe down with a clang, lean on the counter, and let myself rest. After the din of cutlery and conversation, my ears ring with the silence, and I realize I'm even more drunk than I thought. When I close my eyes, everything sways, nothing gentle about it anymore. My eyes snap open just as Emily walks in, her gait uncertain. I jolt back into action, throwing open the fridge door in search of the filter, only to realize it's empty.

"Let me help," Emily says. Without waiting for me to acquiesce, she takes the filter from my hands and fills it from the tap. Then she does the same with the carafe, winking at me.

"I know, he's such a perfectionist," she says, slurring the words a little. Her eyes are shiny. I've never actually seen her drunk, I realize. "But he won't notice. He had two-thirds of that last bottle all by himself." She giggles, another never-before-seen. With her face flushed, she's pretty. She looks too much like Byron for her own good; the same features that render him so handsome only weigh down her smaller, more delicate face. The tautly pulled-back hairstyles she favors reinforce the austere impression but now her bun has loosened, and wavy ash-colored hair frames her face, giving her a Renaissance-portrait look straight from one of Byron's art books.

She opens and closes the freezer and then starts rummaging through the cupboards. "You must have real liquor in here somewhere. I told B. I'd go fetch another bottle of wine from his reserves, but I need something stronger tonight. Oh! Here we go—the good stuff."

No one is more surprised than I when she emerges with a bottle of bourbon. Two tall glasses appear, and she splashes two fingers of Maker's Mark into one and then gulps.

"Oh damn. Sorry." She hands me the second glass, with a much more generous splash of liquor sloshing around the bottom. The smell races up my nostrils. She clinks her glass against mine.

"I like you, Claire. I do. I mean, sure, you're young enough to be his daughter, but . . . " She gives a theatrical shrug. Shame makes blood rush to my face, setting my skin on fire. Without thinking, I upend the glass of bourbon into my mouth.

"Oh no. Shit. Sorry—I didn't mean it like that. I upset you. I can be so stupid sometimes."

I'm not mentally ready for a heart-to-heart with a drunk Emily. Had I made that rookie writer's mistake, reduced someone to a stereotype and forgotten about their hidden depths, the ones everyone supposedly has? Although that's only in books, isn't it? In real life, people may have hidden depths, but 90 percent of the time, they're as cliché as they come.

"I like you better," she says at last, with as much gravitas as she can muster with that much alcohol in her system.

"Better?" I echo.

"Better than Colleen. Sorry, I know, no speaking ill of the dead and all, but I never liked her." She tops off her glass and then mine. I drink without thinking twice. "Good painter, maybe. Although, even then . . . " She points with her eyes at the doorway, through which I can see yet another one of Colleen's framed creations hanging in the hall. It's autumn trees reflected in a lake, image flipped upside down, all reds and yellows and aggressive oranges like the whole thing is on fire. This one I actually like, despite it being Colleen's. "Let's just say that's debatable. So pretentious. I never liked modern art."

I'm yearning to change the subject to something, anything else. But the bourbon softens the edges, and all I do is blink and listen.

"Good painter, bad wife. She didn't care about him. He wasn't top priority to her, you know? Hell, he wasn't even in the top ten. Who wants that?"

From what I know of Emily, she's the kind of working mom who had her son raised by various nannies, then day cares, then boarding schools, and who, last time she was over at our house, humble-bragged to me about the "healthy but gourmet" meal delivery service she had just signed up for. Hearing this from her is odd, at the very least. Then again, enough alcohol will wring the truth out of anyone. Especially an uptight and probably overworked forty-nine-year-old empty nester with a predilection for skirt suits.

"I always liked you so much more. You remind me of myself, in a good sort of way."

I'm taken aback.

"I just wish I'd done what you're doing. Focused on my family. You're so...old-fashioned. Oh, I'm sorry, at twenty-five you probably think that's an insult." She hiccups.

I shake my head vigorously, which is enough to reassure her that no, I don't think it's an insult. I don't correct her that I'm actually twenty-seven. It's probably all the same to her.

"But I mean it as a compliment. Not dowdy. The opposite. You're...classic—that's what I meant."

"Thank you, Emily." I realize I have trouble making my mouth form words.

"That's what he needs. A classic woman. That's what he deserves. I know you'll take good care of him. And of your kids, when you decide to have them. Right?"

This is too much. She crossed a line. I make a clumsy motion to pass her, to go back to the other room, to Byron, but she blocks my way—on purpose or not, I can't tell.

"Oh, don't go. Let's have another drink. Where do you keep your wine, anyway?"

Seeing a way out, I nod at the doorway, over her shoulder. "The...the corkscrew. I think it's over there."

"Hey, B!" she bellows over her shoulder. "Come here. We need your help uncorking the bottle."

I start to turn around, but the room turns around me instead, faster and faster. And then it turns on its side and rushes, rushes toward my head.

"Claire!" The image of Emily flashes before my eyes, the sound of my name reverberating inside my head. "Oh, Claire. Byron! Help!"

It could be my imagination but I see her toss the contents of my glass into the kitchen sink, her movement small, precise, and razor sharp.

# CHAPTER EIGHT

*It was weeks before I used the key for something, finally. Until then, I only watched, your personal guardian angel. I studied—you would have been proud of me, your most involved, hardworking student you never knew about. I learned about both your schedules; yours I already knew by heart but now I learned hers as well.*

*She was trickier because she works from home. Works—ha. If you could call lounging around the house all day working. But I found out when exactly she leaves, how long she's gone. I found out her favorite brand of soda and what orange juice she likes (the pulpy kind—what normal person likes juice with pulp?). She drinks wine from the fridge, saving the stuff that's on the wine rack in the dining room for special occasions. Your special occasions. I picture you with her, sipping wine, smiling, laughing, kissing, and my heart hurts so much I could die.*

*My patience is challenged. I could take that whole plas-tic container of pills, all ground up, and mix it into the juice container, where she wouldn't taste it underneath all the sugar. Even if she took one glass—and she drinks sev-eral a day—it would still be enough. She would collapse and die, choking on her vomit. Just like that, gone.*

*But taking it slow is my cross to bear. And besides, I am not ready yet, not ready to be Mrs. Westcott. I am but the caterpillar, who first needs to become a pupa and only then emerges as a butterfly, ready and iridescent. You wouldn't want me as I am now; the chasm between us is too big, the age difference, the social standing.*

*So, while she spirals slowly, inevitably downward, I will rise to your level.*

*That day, I went into your house while she was out. I changed some things up, things neither of you will notice. I put a couple of ground-up pills into the wine in the fridge and shook it until it had mixed in flawlessly. In the bath-room, I emptied her natural supplement capsules and filled them with the insides of a different sort of capsule. That is all, for now. I took stock of her other medicines, what the pills look like. I'll come back another time and take care of those.*

*She's duplicitous, your wife.*

*She's lying to you about so many things. And now I have proof. Oh, if only I could just tell you everything I know now . . .*

*But I won't. I don't want to get you this way. My way may be harder, may take longer, but that's okay.*

*Everything worth having is worth waiting for—isn't that how it goes?*

# CHAPTER NINE

I'm sick through the weekend. I hardly even realize it until I float back to consciousness.

The air in the bedroom is stuffy but somehow I find myself shivering under the blanket and the comforter. The only light is coming from the bedside lamp on Byron's side, set to the dimmest setting.

My head spins but I prop myself up on one elbow and look around. I faintly remember doubling over, my insides twisting as I vomited my heart out. My chest and back are sweat-damp, and I'm wearing one of Byron's pajama tops. It sticks to my skin. The bedside clock reads 8:02, and I genuinely have no idea whether it's a.m. or p.m. I call out weakly for my husband but he's nowhere in sight.

As I swing my legs over the edge of the bed, fighting the nausea that creeps to the top of my throat, I realize

I lost more than just time: I seem to float inside my husband's already oversize pajama shirt, my hip bones jutting, my stomach concave. A half-empty glass sits on my nightstand. The liquid in it is cloudy and pinkish white, smelling strongly of artificial berry flavoring that makes me want to retch.

"Electrolytes," Byron says from the doorway. My head snaps up.

"Drink, drink. It's to replace the minerals you lost from all that vomiting."

Without taking my eyes off him, I sip. It's not that bad, and I find myself finishing the last dregs in seconds. "What . . . what happened?"

He shrugs. "Food poisoning? Must have been a bad shrimp."

"*You're* not sick." Was he? Truth is I wouldn't have remembered if he had been.

"Emily said she threw up too when she got home."

Emily drank enough cheap bourbon to float a ship, I almost say. Instead, I just glare at him accusingly, although I'm not sure what exactly I'm accusing him of.

"How long have those shrimps sat in the freezer?"

"You're saying it's my fault?"

The effort of speaking is too much. My head spins. All I want is to lie down again but I fight the tug of gravity and sit up straighter.

"I'm not saying that. I'm saying we got food poisoning from bad shrimp. There's a difference."

"What time is it?"

"Sunday night. You slept through most of the weekend."

Alarm shoots through me but is soon carried off on another tide of nausea.

"Don't worry about it. You're going to be fine. Do you want some more?" He nods at the glass I'm still holding in my hand, my fingers sticky.

"Electrolytes?" I agree with a barely perceptible nod, and he vanishes from sight before reappearing moments later. Did he have the glass all ready and waiting for me? He hands it to me, and when I peer over the rim, the little flecks of pink electrolyte powder still spin and spin in circles in the center, like he just stirred it.

"Drink," he's saying, his voice growing closer and then distant again, like the sea crashing on the shore. "That's right. Good girl."

\*     \*     \*

When I wake up next, it's like the weekend never happened. It's Monday morning, the same as most Monday mornings lately: I'm in bed alone, it's bright outside, and the light falls through half-open curtains onto Byron's side of the bed in a brilliant river. No sign of Byron, who, according to the clock, left for work more than two hours ago.

Surprisingly, I feel fine. Except for my thinness, my skeletal wrists and protruding ribs, there's nothing to remind me of the illness that consumed two days of my life. I don't feel the slightest twinge of dizziness or nausea when I get up, still a little weak but stable.

It takes me some time to get my bearings. I go down-

stairs, make a coffee, and pop a couple pieces of bread
into the toaster because my stomach is rumbling, but in a
good way. While the coffee machine hisses, I go upstairs
and fetch my laptop. I spend five or ten minutes mindlessly browsing, wondering if I'm supposed to be doing
something else, something important. But it seems all the
stuff I had to do has evaporated from my head.

Then my inbox dings. When I click over to the message,
I feel nothing but disorientation, but then the name at the
top sets off the chain reaction of memory, and panic races
up my spine.

> Hi, this is Rea, I know it's the second message but
> I'm sorry if I said anything to offend you! I'm still
> interested in the Colleen May painting. If you still
> want to sell it, I'd love to make a competitive new
> offer. Thank you, best,
>
> Rea

Just as I am, in a bathrobe over pajama pants, I run
outside. The dash from the front door to the car in the
driveway takes the little energy I have left, and by the time
I stop and plant the palms of my hands on the sun-heated
hood of the car, I'm panting, my heart thumping a fast and
dull tattoo. I lean on my arms, catch my breath, and only
then retrieve the keys from the pocket of my robe and unlock the trunk.

It opens with a soft click. For a moment, I stand still,
staring at it, not understanding what I'm looking at. Yet.

The trunk is empty.

There can be no mistake. There's no trace of the cardboard sleeve with Colleen's painting in it. My coat, the one I threw in with the painting, is gone too.

The sun beats down on the back of my neck. It's the end of September; how can it possibly be this hot? The air comes off the asphalt rippling. Or maybe I'm just losing my mind. I slam the trunk shut and start ambling back toward the house, sweat running down my back.

Like a mindless robot, I shut the door behind me and plunk the car keys into the bowl by the entrance. Then it occurs to me—did Byron bring my things inside?

That thought should make me sweat more, if anything, but somehow, it seems less disastrous than having lost the painting altogether. And it's impossible. I can't have lost it. I remember clear as day—

Rea. Could she have followed me?

And opened my trunk how? With a crowbar? Hardly. I would have seen the dents, the scratched paint. The alarm would have gone off.

Besides, had she done that, she probably wouldn't be sending me sycophantic emails.

Just to be sure, I check the coat closet and the hooks by the entrance: no sign of my cream-colored fall coat that I loved so much. And the painting . . . Byron would have put it back in the storage room, with all the rest of her things he can't bear to part with. I race across the living room, my bare feet slapping the floor, and skid to a halt in front of the door to the basement. Drawing in a deep breath, I try to turn the door handle.

It doesn't budge. The door is locked.

Any guilt I had been feeling drowns in a tide of anger. He did go through my trunk. He found the painting, put it back, and decided to lock the door too. To discourage me from pilfering any more of Colleen's things.

And somehow, the worst part is how normal he acted about the whole thing. Knowing him, I'd have expected a confrontation, a scene, lots of fury and rage and flying spittle—and with makeup sex hot on its heels, usually the same evening. That's exactly what happened the few times I'd brought up the possibility of selling anything of hers. Or moving out of the house.

But Byron wants to have his cake and eat it too. Or, more precisely, to live in his late wife's house, yet to make love to his flexible twentysomething new wife passionately on their bed at the same time. My mother always did say men aren't monogamous creatures...

The thought jolts me out of inaction. Anger surges, and I grab the first thing within reach—a copper vase from a decorative table—and throw it. Blindly, without aiming at anything in particular, without intending to do any real damage. But damage usually happens anyway, whether we intend it or not. Dread fills the pit of my stomach when the vase hits the glass top of the coffee table with a pin-sharp, characteristic *crack*.

Tiptoeing up to it—as if it were a wild animal—I assess the damage. The elegant little table is beyond saving: a web of cracks radiates from the point of impact. Great, another thing of Colleen's that I've wrecked.

I cast a glance around the open space. Through the

archway to the kitchen, I see the cold toast sticking out of the toaster, the no-longer-steaming coffee cup under the spout of the coffee machine. My laptop is where I left it, on the couch.

I know exactly what to do.

I start across the living room toward the couch, and sharp pain drives itself into the pad of flesh below my big toe, drawing a yelp from me. Hopping to the couch, I twist my foot to see a shard of glass sticking out of the roughened skin, thin and glinting.

I pull on it, and a tiny little drop of blood forms, a red pearl.

# CHAPTER TEN

My foot has been coated with Neosporin, Band-Aid affixed neatly over the puncture. The floor has been swept thoroughly, although I didn't find any other bits of glass. Finally, I curl up on the couch, my injured foot tucked under me, a fresh cup of coffee in hand.

All things in order, in their own time. I remember what Rea said about Byron. The police, she said. They thought he was involved somehow. Is that how she put it? Just to be sure, I google Colleen once more but the row of links is so familiar I think I could recite them by heart. Hardly surprising, seeing how she's been dead for eight years. So instead, I google my husband.

After I type his name into the search field, pages and pages of results come up. That's to be expected, considering his first name. The first three or four links are official.

The college's site with his profile and professional organizations. I click through them, just to be sure I'm not missing anything. There's a head shot of Byron, a good ten years younger, and information I already know in neat columns of text.

The link right below those is an interesting one. RateProf.com.

As soon as I click on it, I wish I hadn't.

*PinkiePie13:* Prof. Westcott is awesome. Yeah he's tough, and he won't pass you just for showing up, and if you're taking his class prepare to read . . . a lot. But it's all worthwhile. That, and it doesn't hurt that he's hot. 😜 There. I said it.

*BrooklynBaby:* He's one of those who make a really boring subject sort of interesting. But watch out, he's a tough grader! If you wanna do well, pay attention, do the readings, and DON'T SKIP CLASS!

*Bholmes:* Westcott sucks. I took the class as an elective, and he could show a little effing understanding. I'm an artist NOT A WRITER and I may not have been officially diagnosed but I AM dyslexic, yet when I told him that's why I can't read twelve books in a single term, he was a total dick about it. Wouldn't round my grade up TWO LOUSY POINTS now I have a C and my GPA is fucked. Asshole. 0/5.

*AsherBeckett99:* LOL @ Bholmes. You know this guy plays favorites right?? He only goes easy on the girls. The hot girls. Which is like ¾ of the whole group, so yeah, if you don't have tits, you're fucked.

*MaddieDoll:* You guys, stop it. Teachers actually look at this thing. He's a good teacher. That's all. No need to get salty because you slacked off all semester and he failed you. Just saying.

I scroll past page after page of this. And then something catches my eye. At first I think I imagined it but when I scroll back up, there it is. Glaring at me from the screen.

*Notyourmothersfeminist:* Hey. Does everyone not see a huge problem with a guy who was accused of murdering his wife and is still allowed to teach?

Here, I'm posting a link to an article about what happened to his wife, feminist painter Colleen May. She used to teach here too, years ago, and shortly after she quit she died under strange circumstances. Here's another link about her in the Canvas:

I can't help but roll my eyes a little. The student newspaper at the college is called *The Canvas*. The pretentiousness of it.

For the link-phobic: May's death was ruled a suicide despite a near-total lack of evidence of this. Her body has never been found, which of course makes it hard to prove that there had been foul play. But here's the kicker: I have it on good authority that they did consider Westcott a person of interest, if not an actual suspect. I spoke to someone who's doing her master's, and she knew someone who was questioned about Byron Westcott back in the day. He was cleared—I don't have the info on why exactly—and went on teaching as before. BUT DON'T YOU THINK BEING A SUSPECT ALONE SHOULD BE GROUNDS FOR DISMISSAL??? The fact that it was hidden from the public was bad enough!!! Students have a right to know this. He's in a position of authority over vulnerable young women. That's . . . alarming. #patriarchy #rapeculture

*TateTheMate:* So . . . what, no due process? No innocent till proven guilty? Guy's wife kills herself, we have to fire him from his job too?

*Ramonathepest:* Oh my god. That article. All that evidence and the guy walks free? Disgusting.

*Notyourmothersfeminist:* Ugh, here we go. The valiant defenders of the poor defenseless menz. It's very possible the guy got away with murder. And I think young women's lives should come before his little material comforts. Check your privilege Tate.

**Ramonathepest:** Sounds like he should be in jail.

**WokieMcWokeface:** We should stage a protest. Like a massive walkout of one of his classes. I'll post about it in the group.

**Ramonathepest:** Yeah. Good luck with convincing all his little fangirls.

**WokieMcWokeface:** Women participating in #rapeculture are so disgusting.

**Notyourmothersfeminist:** BYRON 👏 WESTCOTT 👏 SHOULD 👏 BE 👏 FIRED.

It goes on like this for a while, and the whole thing breathes such vitriol right through the screen that it makes my eyes water. I check the dates on the posts: a year ago almost to the day. Yet I can't recall anything out of the ordinary happening—or maybe it did but he never told me. Clearly, it went nowhere or I would have heard about it one way or another.

I open the links in new tabs. Then I copy and paste the screen names into a note, to search later.

I find myself wishing desperately there was someone else I could ask—discreetly—what exactly went on. I men-

tally go over the few friends and colleagues Byron brought
over to the house since I've lived here. There is, of course,
Emily, but the thought of seeing her one-on-one fills
me with primal dread. Just thinking about her makes
my stomach squeeze painfully, a phantom tide of nausea
threatening to spill over.

Friends, then. Byron's friends. Even in the age of Facebook, *friends* is a word loaded with many different mean-
ings where Byron is concerned. At first, I attributed his
lack of meaningful connections—except for Emily, who
is family—to Colleen. Perhaps after she passed, mutual
friends distanced themselves, deliberately or not. And after you've been married as long as Byron and Colleen,
most of your friends are mutual. But that would be more
normal for a divorce, not a death. After a death, you'd
think the contrary would be true—the friends would reach
out to offer their support.

Of course, Colleen's death was anything but ordinary,
which explains a lot.

It's not like he doesn't have any friends. Every holiday
so far, he's gotten plenty of invitations and accepted most
of them. That, he told me, is just how things are done at
the college: You have to mingle, you have to fit in, especially if you're hoping for tenure one day.

One thing isn't there, however—the real connection. He
always reminded me of myself that way. At first, I found
it endearing, a sign that he was too complicated and pro-
found for most normal people, with their predilection for
sports, reality TV, and small talk.

Then I started to notice a tendency that didn't bother

me much, at first. Every time, after the party was over, once we were in the car on the way home, he would start to dissect the hosts in a kind of joking, not really mocking way. Everything from appearance to what they said. *God, can you believe that guy? Forty-two is too old to have long hair, especially when you've got a bald spot the size of Texas on top of your head. Did you hear Myra talking about modernist poetry all night? So you've read some W. H. Auden—hardly cancels out the fact that the rest of the time you subsist on airport paperbacks.*

It makes him sound mean, except for the fact that he was always spot-on and observant, pinpointing things I'd noticed subconsciously but couldn't articulate. And it made me laugh too. Not because I'm such a bad person, but because it made me feel like we had something together, a complicity.

Now, as I mentally go over the not-so-long list of his contacts, I can barely remember their names. Only the little nicknames Byron gave them behind closed doors. Byron doesn't have a Facebook account—he thinks social media is a futile waste of time—and I don't have one either. Not because he would disapprove, but because I don't need one. No one to keep in touch with, no one to brag to about my supposedly perfect life. But his colleagues sure do. Derek Hollis, a film studies professor from the college, is the first one I come across. I click on the Message icon. You must log in or sign up to do that, Facebook informs me smugly.

Okay. Fair enough. I create an account as C. Greene (my maiden name), intentionally leaving everything blank.

I can deal with it later—I suppose I'll need this account again, and I might want to keep it anonymous for now. Then I write Derek a message.

Hi, it's Claire, Byron's wife. It was nice seeing you—

Here I have to pause and try to remember exactly when was the last time I saw him in person. Right—he and his boyfriend, at the Fourth of July party of another one of Byron's friends.

—at Renata's party. Sorry to reach out like this, at random, but I wanted to talk to you about—

Another pause for thought.

—a surprise for Byron. Message me here or give me a call on my cell, here's the number.

Best,

Claire Greene Westcott

I hesitate a long time before hitting Send, knowing there won't be any turning back after that. Then I realize there is no turning back anyway.

Once the message is sent, I take a deep breath and go make myself another cup of coffee. When I get back to the computer, I do a Facebook search for the names I saw

on the forum. It doesn't take long to find a girl named Ramona who goes to Mansfield Liberal Arts College. I send
her a friend request, then search the other posters from
the forum by handle: Sure enough, most of them turn up
at the click of a cursor. I send requests to all of them. By
the time I'm done, Ramona and one other have already accepted.

Nervous, I check the inbox. Nothing. The message
hasn't been read yet.

I click over to the other windows and reread the links
posted on the forum. But I've read this brief article from
the local newspaper many times in the past.

POLICE CLOSE INVESTIGATION INTO ARTIST'S DISAPPEAR-
ANCE; DROWNING RULED A SUICIDE

Mansfield, OH—Local police have announced that
they're closing the investigation of the suspected
drowning of 37-year-old painter Colleen Westcott,
known under her artist name, Colleen May.

Roland Hewson, chief of the Mansfield police force,
has stated that no concrete evidence of foul play
has been discovered in the probe. Hewson also
stated that evidence in the form of what might be
a note from the victim has convinced him that the
disappearance of Colleen Westcott is a suicide.

Westcott disappeared on April 11, 2010, and her
car was found parked near the waterfront in Cleve-

land two days later. The ensuing weeklong search yielded no results, and her body has never been found. However, a leather coat identified as belonging to Westcott washed ashore half a mile from the pier where her car was parked. Westcott was declared dead by the authorities in 2011.

I close the window, annoyed. These things never have enough detail. "What might be a note"? What on earth is that supposed to mean? It either is or isn't.

They think Colleen is dead or they think she disappeared. There's a difference.

Apprehensive, I click over to the next window.

The Mansfield College Canvas, reads a large, flashy header. Here's an article that didn't show up in my earlier searches.

STUDENTS OBSERVE DAY OF MOURNING DEDICATED TO BELOVED PROFESSOR

Today, April 11, 2011, from noon until one, a performance art piece will be held in the main atrium to commemorate the one-year anniversary of the death of fine arts professor Colleen May. (The student newspaper, it seems, didn't bother with Westcott.) Although Dr. May hadn't taught in two years before her disappearance, she marked this campus in the best possible ways. Her students, many of whom have moved on to advanced degrees and made their names as artists, remember her fondly.

There are more details about this "performance art

piece" but I really can't be bothered with it. It seems like it's not so much about Colleen than the ones who plan on milking her death for extra exposure—and possible bonus points on their grades. I close the window. Nothing useful here.

My phone rings, jarring me away from my thoughts, and when I pick it up to look, it's an unknown number.

# CHAPTER ELEVEN

In the warm, bright room skewered by sunlight pouring through the windows, I feel cold, with a prickling feeling on the back of my neck, like I'm being watched—or like I did something bad and am about to get caught. I'm overcome with a sensation of vulnerability, alone and exposed in this airy room like a goldfish that becomes aware of her tank for the first time.

I wipe my hand on my shirt and try to calm myself before I pick up the phone, telling myself it's probably Derek. But when I do pick up, the only answer to my slightly breathless *hello* is empty static.

I open my mouth to say hello again, three, four, five more times—but no sound comes out. I already know it's pointless but I listen to the silence, unable to muster the will to hang up.

When the voice comes, it's female, low, muffled somehow, as if she's speaking through thick glass.

"Where is it, Claire? What did you do with it? Tell me
where it is."

"I . . . I'm sorry?" I stammer.

The click is short and sudden, and I realize I'm listening
to silence once more—real silence this time. The connection has ended. Dumbstruck, I look at the phone and then
put it down carefully. With sweaty hands, I thumb through
the call log—there it is, twelve seconds long, although it
felt much longer to me. Number unknown. But I didn't
dream it up.

My breath leaves me in a long, shuddering sigh. A
woman. A real, flesh-and-blood woman on the other end
of the phone. She's not just in my head. She emailed me.
She took the painting out of the trunk of my car.

*Colleen*, breathes a ghostly voice. It spreads under my
skin like ice water. It's Colleen.

But Colleen is dead.

A soft little chime from the computer makes me jump
and knock over the coffee cup with my foot. Coffee splat-
ters all over the surviving low table, leaking treacherously
under the art books. Cursing, I jump up and snatch the
books away too late; the back covers are wet, dripping on
the floor and the couch. It takes the better part of twenty
minutes to deal with the mess, and by the time it's done, I
almost manage to forget what caused it in the first place.

Right. I pick up my laptop again, and my heart jumps
happily when I see I have a new message.

Hi Claire, **Derek Hollis** writes. I want in! Let's meet up and talk. My lunch break is from two to three thirty today. There's a coffee shop close to campus. Just be warned, that ol' bastard can't be surprised.

And a winking face.

*That ol' bastard can't be surprised.* Something about it seems sinister. Or maybe it's the day I'm having, with all the creepy nonsense.

I check the time—I have plenty—and write back. He replies practically in real time. Cool! It's a date. See you there.

*     *     *

Derek Hollis is not the type of person to meet at a Starbucks, unlike Rea. I'm not surprised when I get to the address: It's one of those fair-trade-organic-vegan places. When I get a latte with regular milk instead of soy, the two heavily tattooed girls behind the counter, cashier and barista, don't say anything but wrinkle their noses throughout the transaction, as if my credit card has a bad smell. Since I never ended up eating any breakfast, I also find myself forced to get one of those strange dry things that pass for a date square. I carry my plate and coffee to a more or less secluded table in the corner.

At this hour, lunch rush has passed but the place remains fairly busy. It has to be a question of ethics and not taste—when I pry a piece of date square away with my fork and pop it into my mouth, it's pretty much just ground-up dates and walnuts. My stomach starts to churn before I've finished chewing.

Luckily, that's when I spy Derek, lingering by the counter with his back to me as he studies the menu. I spit the date square into a napkin, ball it up, and stuff it under the rim of the plate just before he turns around and notices me. He waves, and I wave back.

He orders an herbal tea, then comes over to join me, setting the mug on the table.

"Claire! It's been a while." I agree with a nod, and he goes on, telling me I look nice (I look haggard and frumpy, and I know it) and asking me how Byron is doing, how my novel is doing, and what on earth is that surprise, since Byron's birthday is in March.

I look at him, wide-eyed, slack-jawed, struggling to come up with something to tell him—something I really should have thought of before, on my way here, back home, any other time than right now. But my brain is sluggish, and I can't think of a single thing.

And finally, I can't take it anymore. I crumble, my eyes screw shut, and tears burst forth, too powerful for me to stop them. Sobs shake me to the core. I paw blindly for the napkin, except it's balled up with a half-chewed mess of dates in the center, and they only gave me the one.

"Here." Derek Hollis presses a clean napkin into my hand. When I finally dare to open my eyes a crack, I have no idea what look I'll see on his face—shock, surprise, awkwardness. But he just sits there, looking concerned.

Derek Hollis doesn't look like he belongs in this hippie-dippie café, or on the Mansfield campus, for that matter. In defiance to all the clichés, he has the tall, blond, clean-cut look of a former jock who did well in life and didn't let himself go. His close-cropped hair recedes a little but is thick and healthy, and he wears a clean, ironed button-down shirt that fits like a glove over his well-toned upper body. In another life, he might be that dream guy all the girls gravitate toward, a shoulder to lean on. Except, of course, for the fact that he likes men.

He slides the steaming mug of herbal tea toward me. "I haven't touched it yet. Have a sip—it's chamomile."

I'm not enthused at the idea but I do it anyway. The tea burns my lips, and the bitter, hay-like taste of chamomile fills my mouth, making me shudder. But I realize Derek is right. The tea warms its way down into my stomach, instantly calming me. At least calming me enough to be able to talk again. "Thank you."

He heaves a discreet sigh. "I was afraid of this. It's not really about any surprise, is it?"

I only look at him blankly and blink. And gulp.

"What's happening?" Derek asks. His blond brows furrow. "What did he do?"

I'm becoming aware of the strangeness of the situation. Of his calm, his lack of surprise. The question only cements it.

"Why are you assuming it was something he did?"

He gives a weary chuckle. "It's pretty obvious, Claire. We barely know each other. Why else would you suddenly get in touch?"

At all the parties and gatherings, I always gravitate to him and his partner to make small talk and chat about the recent Oscar-bait films that came out. Probably because he and Greg (well, especially Greg) are closer to me in age than anyone else there. I did my best to try to bridge the gap between acquaintance and sort-of friend so to hear him say that kind of stings.

"You message me out of nowhere, wanting to meet, and it sounds urgent. I figured there weren't a million things it could be."

I don't know what moves me but I put my hand on top of his. My fingers are icy and clammy in contrast to his dry, warm hand but despite all the awkwardness of the moment, he doesn't pull away.

"Things aren't good, Derek. Not good at all."

"Tell me all about it." His eyes are blue and honest, and I hear no ulterior motive in his voice.

Telling him about it is the last thing I should be doing. Not because I think it might get back to Byron—something tells me it won't. But complaining about a man to his friends—or even his coworkers he's sort of friendly with—is just not something a good wife does. Not something Claire Greene Westcott does, anyway.

But the fact is he's here, and he's looking me in the eye and listening. Which is more than I can say for Byron for the last while. So I don't stop myself.

"He barely seems to know I'm there." I pull my chunky-knit sweater tighter around me. "In the last few months, I feel like I'm a ghost. We hardly ever even—" I cut myself off.

"He loves you, Claire. He talks about you all the time." But when he says it, the words are flat with no real conviction behind them. "He was crazy about you when you got married, remember? I've known him for a decade, since before I finished my master's. I've never seen the guy this happy." I'm not sure which one of us he's trying to convince. "At least, not since before..." He trails off and avoids my gaze.

"Colleen," I say. The syllables cut me as they roll off my tongue. It's as if the din of the café dies down right at this unfortunate moment, and her name resonates like a glass shattering.

"That's what I wanted to ask you about," I say, and watch the look on his face shift. He's wincing, like he knew this was coming but still hoped against hope that it wouldn't.

"Is it true?" I lean in and lower the volume of my voice but keep it firm. He hesitates but doesn't pull back. "Did Byron...Was he a suspect? Did the police think he actually had something to do with her death?"

"Where did you hear that?" he asks, eyebrows furrowed. Under his gaze, I squirm—I can't tell him about RateProf.com; that's just embarrassing. But to my relief, he doesn't wait for the answer. "It was gossip," he says firmly. "Yes, the police investigated but it was because Colleen had disappeared, and no body was found. That was normal. Standard procedure. They questioned Byron, of course, and people on campus..."

"Why would they question people on campus? She hadn't been teaching for years at that point."

He says nothing. The pause lingers, growing heavier with every millisecond. "People," he says at last, not without reluctance, "who knew Byron. They just wanted to establish the timeline of things. But of course, some students got wind of it, and the rumor mill got grinding. You know how it is."

No, I don't know, I almost blurt, self-righteously. *I* never participated in gossip or spread rumors, not in high school, not in college, where I tended to keep my peers at arm's length. Thankfully, I manage to keep my mouth shut.

"But then they assessed all the evidence and concluded it was suicide. By drowning," Derek says. "I mean, there was even a note. And I think, deep down, everyone knew it was true. So no one harassed Byron further, thank God."

"They knew it was true?" I ask. "How?"

He leans back in his chair, and his hand slips out from under mine, leaving it hovering awkwardly over the table. I set it down by my side like a stiff, dead thing. He stretches, running his fingers over his close-cropped hair.

"Because Colleen," he says, "well . . . she might not have been teaching for some time, but still. Everyone knew she had . . . issues."

I know I should tread carefully now that he's finally opening up. But I can't help it. "What kind of issues?"

At first I think I've done it—pushed too far. Derek sighs with frustration. "Oh hell," he mutters under his breath. "Claire, listen. There's something I must tell you, and maybe it'll make you feel better or maybe it'll make you feel worse—I don't know—but I'm going to take a chance."

I brace myself, mentally praying for him to go on, to not change his mind.

"One thing is for sure. Byron...you guys might have your problems, but trust me—it's nothing compared to the hell he went through with that woman."

I'm taken aback. I expected something earth-shattering, for sure, but not this.

"Yeah. Colleen really did a number on him. I know you're not supposed to speak ill of the dead, and Colleen has her flock of rabid admirers who are ready to jump down your throat the moment you utter so much as one un-flattering word about their idol, so..." He trails off, waves his hand dismissively. "I've done my best to keep my mouth shut about it, especially back when she...when she passed. But now you're here, and you're asking, and I feel like I can't keep it inside any longer."

I draw in a sharp breath.

"The woman was crazy. She was a crazy, evil, manip-ulative bitch who put Byron through hell because the relationship was falling apart and she couldn't let go." He lowers his voice to a deeper, angry pitch as he leans to-ward me on his elbows. "You have absolutely nothing to be jealous of. He's well rid of her. I was happy for him when he met you. You're good for him."

"Falling apart?" I echo. I barely heard what he said after that; my mind latched on to the words, turning them around and around, trying to understand. And they refuse to fit with everything else. With the paintings, and the house, and everything Byron himself has told me.

Derek sighed. "You can keep this a secret, right? I mean, Byron told me this in confidence, and I never repeated it to anyone. Don't get me wrong: If I thought there might be cause, even the slightest reason, to tell anyone—the police or anyone else—I would have, but there wasn't. Because he didn't do anything wrong."

"Of course," I repeat hollowly.

"They'd been having troubles for a while. The normal sort of troubles, rough patches like everyone has—he was about to be given tenure, she was travelling all over the country showing her paintings in galleries, too much work, too much stress. She cracked under the pressure.

"There was a party at their house. At your house," he corrects himself, a little too hastily, and his gaze avoids mine. "He threw one every year after the last class of the summer semester but it was my first one, right after I started teaching my first class at the college. I was pumped—I mean, they were the power couple, you know? Flashy, fun, sort of famous even. She started to sell paintings for tens of thousands apiece, and she had recently quit teaching to paint full-time. Aka the dream, right?" He chuckles. "Back then, it was, what, ten, nine years ago, the house had a backyard. I don't know if you knew?"

I shake my head. "There's still a backyard," I say, uncertain what he means.

"Yeah, but this was before that giant ugly deck was built. They had a garden there. Colleen loved it. She was primarily the one taking care of it too so, after she died, it grew over with weeds and the neighbors complained. So he had to do something about it, you know? In this case, it was to pour concrete over most of it and build that deck-slash-gazebo-slash-veranda thing."

I nod. Now all that's left of the garden is the thin border of lawn and some flower baskets that Byron pays one of the neighbors, an older man two houses down, to keep maintained. We've held barbecues on that veranda once or twice with Emily and her husband, bottles of rosé, and mosquito-repellent torches that filled the air with the sickly sweet lemony scent of poison that never quite kept the bloodsuckers at bay. With Byron manipulating skewers of chicken (the only meat Emily eats) and vegetables on the giant, clunky barbecue that spent most of its life rusting under a heavy tarp cover.

"It was different then. Just a picnic table, some chairs; we'd lounge around among all her plants and flowers. So I arrived there, bottle of wine in hand, nervous because everyone else there was a good decade older and had, you know, real careers." His smile still has an incredulous tinge to it, tainted though it is with bitterness. "So maybe I drank a little too much, out of nervousness. When I realized I really overdid it, I went inside to find some water, or just a quiet corner I could curl up in until I'd sobered up and could be sure I wouldn't end up puking on someone's shoes. Outside, Colleen had hung up all these lanterns and those little outdoor lights that look like Christmas lights, and the yard was lit up like it was still day even though the sun had already set.

"So I go indoors, and the house is empty. And dark, and . . . cold, like they let the AC run too low for too long. I don't know—I just got a chill right then and there. It felt hostile. I don't know how else to explain it. And then I heard them talking in the next room. I felt bad about

eavesdropping but it was too late—I was stuck there because I was too drunk to sneak back out quietly without
being noticed. All I could do was stand there behind the
doorway to the living room, try to be still, and hope they'd
go back outside.

"But they were fighting. I understood right away, before
she even started yelling. They spoke in hushed tones but
their voices just hummed with anger. It was the anger I
heard more than the words themselves but it wasn't hard
to guess what they were.

"He told her to calm down and not make a scene,
that their friends were right outside. *Fuck you and your
friends*, she snapped. *It's not the time or the place*, he
said, and he sounded almost supplicating. *It never is*,
she replied in this sneering, hissing voice. *You just walk
around silently blaming me, and everyone can see that.
I'm not an idiot.*

"He said, *You're not yourself right now. What did you
take this time?*

"That's when she raised her voice, protesting violently.
*You're drunk*, he said, *but that's not all, is it? What did you
take? I thought I flushed it all down the toilet last time.*

"Then she mumbled something, in the voice of a lost
child on the verge of tears. It got under my skin. She
just kept whimpering, and he just kept asking, voice ris-
ing higher and higher, *What did you take, Colleen? Are
we really going to do this again? They'll lock you up this
time.*

"She murmured something, he asked her to repeat it,
and she said, *I hope they do.* That's when I decided I

needed to get out of there, no matter if they saw me or not. I started to move but that's when she screamed. This hair-raising scream that froze me in my tracks. And I remember word for word what she was screaming. *Stop punishing me*, she yelled. *It's not my fault I lost it.*"

When I can finally bring myself to look at Derek's face, it's frozen in an expression bordering on horror, eyes glazed, as if reliving the moment inside his own head.

"I saw Byron's back, partially, from where I was hiding. I was stone-cold sober now. She threw something at him, a glass or wineglass I think, and he barely dodged it. Broken glass went flying everywhere. Then there was a plate, then some kind of cutlery.

"Byron tried to subdue her. He said something too soft for me to make out, and then I just remember her sobbing. That's when I backed out past the entrance to the living room and went back outside where all their friends were tipsy and someone had put on eighties music and someone else was singing along out of key. I stood there at the patio door, probably looking like a ghost, and there they were, having a great time."

Derek focuses his gaze on me. His shoulders droop a little, like he's embarrassed. "Yeah, that's what I saw. A half hour later they reappeared. Colleen's hand was bandaged. She told someone she dropped a glass and cut herself. I could be wrong at this point but her pupils were like saucers; she looked like she was high. That's all. Actually, no. That's not quite all."

What else? The words are on the tip of my tongue but I'm afraid to speak them out loud.

"I never dared really confront Byron about it. It's kind of personal, isn't it? But later, someone at the college told me something, and I connected the dots, so to speak."

"What she lost," I say, my lips numb.

"Yeah. They'd been trying to have a baby. It was Byron's idea. She wasn't entirely on board with it."

I already figured as much, but still, it's like taking a bullet. My shoulders turn inward, and I pull my head in between them. I'm thinking about the painting that was no longer in the trunk of my car. About the doctor's appointment next week that I'd optimistically made, that I'd have to cancel because now I had no way to pay for it.

Derek may have thought he was telling me this for my benefit. But I feel a million times worse.

Byron had wanted a baby. With her. With a woman who had no interest in such cliché, traditional things, who chose her brushes and smearing about toxic paints all day. With a woman who . . .

"And the same person told me—"

"Wait." I hold up my hands. I can't take any more of this, not all at once. Derek looks apologetic. "Who exactly is that other person?"

Derek studiously looks away, and surprising even myself, I feel a surge of a wholly different emotion. No longer fear or anguish, but anger, bright and clean. "It's too late to be coy at this point. Who was it?"

He rubs his eyebrow, his posture and body language signaling his unease. A couple of people in the background look up from their Mac laptops for a split second.

"Her name is Isabelle Herrera. She's not at Mansfield anymore." Derek looks like he's wishing he could fall right through the floor. His forehead and cheeks turn that blotchy pink of only very fair-skinned people, making his eyebrows and stubble look even blonder.

"She was an assistant. She and Byron were . . . involved."

# CHAPTER TWELVE

I sent an email to the address Derek forwarded to me—
I made him do it right there in the coffee shop, from his
phone, so he couldn't make more excuses, bow out, and
then vanish. I checked my new Facebook account too,
and a couple more of the posters from RateProf.com
have accepted my friend requests. I still haven't decided
how I'm going to go about approaching them, what
story I'll cook up. But I have time to think about it.
For now.

The next thing won't wait.

I arrive at the Ova Clinic a good half hour before my
appointment. I'd called and badgered the secretary to get
Dr. Hassan to see me today. The secretary was apprehensive but finally bleated something about Dr. Hassan having
a cancellation this afternoon so perhaps, as an exception,
she might see me. I know there was no cancellation, and

considering what the clinic charges per visit, they can very well make time for me.

I park my car in the small lot next to the clinic, and by the time I step into the lobby, all my furious energy has deserted me, leaving me drained, my head heavy and my bones achy. They have the AC going on full blast, and the bone-dry, icy air of the clinic envelops me, smelling softly of lilac-scented air freshener. All it does is make me sick to my stomach, or maybe it's the date square aberration or the recent food-poisoning-that-wasn't, but most likely, it's psychological. Psychosomatic, as Emily would say with that self-important air. It's really just the memory of the bad news I received here, all these months ago.

*Is that when everything started to go south?* I wonder as I sign in at the security desk. A pure formality; they never once checked my ID. I'm just being crazy. Byron can't have grown cold to me because it turned out I'm infertile—no, "reproductively challenged" is the preferred term. If only because he hadn't known we were *trying*, strictly speaking. Believe it or not, I was going to make it a surprise. Quit the pill almost two years ago now, shortly after we got married. I still had that stupid idea in my head, an idea my university friends would have sneered at. The idea of marriage and on its heels the baby and family vacations and maybe a dog.

The first time I visited the clinic, Dr. Hassan said that it can take up to a year for the pill to really leave your system and for things to go back to working normally. But the year came and went, and my period kept arriving precisely on the third of every month. And that was well before my husband stopped showing the slightest interest in me. Back then, we had sex every day. We were in that honeymoon phase everyone says doesn't last. I should have believed them.

One of the things I like about this clinic is the absence of tackiness: no storks, no larger-than-life toothless, grinning baby posters plastered all over the place. You wouldn't know you're in the waiting room of a clinic at all. The colors are tasteful, the flowers on the end tables are real, changing with the seasons (fresh-cut tulips in the spring, and now the giant orbs of dahlias), and there are no scuffed-up, dog-eared parenting magazines from ten years ago. It's more like a spa, I tell myself every time I come here. It's not like my future will be directly affected by what waits in the office beyond the door on the other end of the room. I'm just here for a manicure or a facial, nothing more.

Today, though, it all drives me nuts. The jazz pouring softly from the speakers under the ceiling might as well be elevator music, and the calm blue of the walls sets my nerves on edge. I check my phone to find that my appointment time was actually two minutes ago. Any minute now, I tell myself. Any minute.

I heave a patient sigh tinged with resentment (for whose benefit, I don't know—the receptionist is on the other side of the arched door, too far to hear it) and turn my attention to the apps on my phone. All the students have now accepted my friend requests. Good. I start a new message and loop them all in.

Hi. My name is Claudia (I feel ridiculous typing it but I

don't want to risk using my real name either). I read what you wrote about Prof. Westcott on the forum and I agree completely. I've had my own bad experience with Prof. Westcott in one of his classes, two years ago. I wanted to talk about it and possibly devise a plan of action. This can't continue! He can't victimize even more women!

I draw another deep breath to settle my nerves and then hit Send. A whoosh, and there it is, out in the universe, no take backs.

I look at the little white circle with the check mark in it that means my message was delivered but not yet read, for what feels like an hour. But when I check the time again, it's only been ten minutes. Twelve past my appointment time.

Impatience gets the best of me, and I get up and start pacing, unable to contain the nervous energy in my legs. When three more torturously long minutes drag by, I think I'm justified to go talk to the receptionist.

"Excuse me, Lucy?" She looks away from the sleek, flat Apple computer in front of her. I crane my neck, unsubtly, to see what's on the screen—what has she been doing this whole time? Playing solitaire? Watching cat videos? "My appointment time was a quarter of an hour ago." That way it sounds less trivial than fifteen minutes.

Lucy blinks at me and says, with her signature flat affect, "Dr. Hassan will see you shortly. Feel free to go grab a seat." I bet this line is taped to the edge of her desk for reference, because it never changes, like the fucking jazz track they can't be bothered to replace.

"I already have. I'm waiting for—"

"Dr. Hassan is very busy. She'll see you as soon as she's available."

"I'm the only one here!" I snap. That barely gets a re-action out of Lucy B., per her name tag. She's buttoned up in a white blouse, mousy blond hair pulled back in a skinny ponytail, but there's a residue of yesterday's eye makeup around her lash lines, bluish and unhealthy look-ing. And her voice has a fried note to it. Out partying late, no doubt.

When I came here for my first appointment, I tried to make small talk with her while she printed my receipt for the consultation fee. She asked me what I do for a living. The nerve. But I told her I was a writer—what else was I going to say? She asked me what my book was about.

"It's about a man and a girl who are in love but she dies. And their love story replays itself generation after gener-ation, until one of them figures out how to stop her from dying and break the cycle." The man is heavily based on Byron but I didn't tell her that, of course. Not that my book was any of her business to begin with.

Lucy B.'s gaze flicked to me from the computer screen for half a second. "Wasn't that, like, some movie or some-thing?" And then I had to laugh politely and say something asinine like, *You know how it goes; there are only six sto-ries under the sun and everything is a variation.*

I immediately knew what kind of person this Lucy B. was. She probably doesn't even read.

And now she's looking at me with the same glassy bird-stare. "Ma'am, please have a seat."

"I just told you. I—"

In my back pocket, my phone gives a short buzz, then another and another. I pull it out and am taken aback to see Byron's name and picture flashing on the screen. Incoming call. What the hell? Did Derek say something to him?

Oh God.

"I need to see Dr. Hassan," I say, and my voice wobbles as my throat closes, tears not far behind. The sheer humiliation of crying in front of this girl only makes it worse. I thumb Decline, and my phone goes silent, finally.

When I look back to Lucy B., she's staring at something over my head. When I follow her gaze, I see Dr. Hassan herself, standing in the doorway of the waiting room.

"Ms. Wilson?" She measures me with a quizzical glance. She and Lucy B. exchange that look, lightning quick, thinking I can't see. Dr. Hassan nods while Lucy's eyes ever so slightly roll.

I decide then and there that I hate her.

"Follow me."

I obey, following Dr. Hassan into the office, and close the door behind me. I pull on the hem of my shirt, tuck the stray strands of hair behind my ears, and wipe under my eyes with the pads of my fingers. Now that she's here, looking calm, I start to wonder if I'd overreacted. I clear my throat and say a polite hello.

"Lucy made it clear this was quite urgent," Dr. Hassan says gently. I imagine she must be used to handling highly emotional women in here, and she must have her techniques. She's one of those women you know are in their forties or older but who have smooth, ageless faces and natural-looking hair that may or may not be dyed. Her warm brown eyes gaze right at me, and I feel myself blush.

"Yes." I exhale. "My decision is made, and I want to start as quickly as possible."

"Start . . . ?" Dr. Hassan prompts.

"What we discussed last time." I don't want to say the words, out of some weird superstition.

"Okay." She motions for me to sit. I take a step toward the armchair but stop halfway.

"I have the money," I say, even though that's not technically true yet. But there are other paintings, and I will find a way. "So we can start with the hormones and everything."

"The money is not the only issue, Ms. Wilson," she says, in that careful, slightly slowed tone she has. "We discussed this. The success rate—"

"The success rate will have to be good enough," I blurt, to stop her saying it—because if she does, it will definitely become real.

"Are you sure you wouldn't consider alternative means? Such as a surrogate, or maybe even—"

"No." The word comes out a little louder than I intended. So much louder that we both sort of jump. I get myself under control once again but she's already giving me that look, the look I absolutely can't allow. The look that will lead to her doing things like calling security, or throwing me out, or even looking up Ms. Connie Wilson and her lawyer husband, Bertrand.

I gulp. "I'm sorry to get so emotional about this. But I have to at least try first—do you understand? I have to try and have my own baby before I consider...alternatives." I let my gaze drop, staring at the toes of my shoes. Alternatives are not an option—this has to be my baby, mine and Byron's, with our genes, carried by me. Otherwise...it doesn't feel real. Our family doesn't feel real. And if it doesn't feel real to me...how will it ever feel real to him?

A tear creeps out of the corner of my eye at the thought, a real, genuine tear. I let it trail down my cheek until it drips from my chin.

When I look up, she nods, understanding, and I know she ate it up. "Very well. I can give you the prescription for the hormones. You can get a nurse here at the clinic to give you the injections or—"

"That's okay," I say. "I know how. I can do it myself." I give a close-lipped smile. "My mother was, is, diabetic. I'm not afraid of needles."

Her gaze lingers on me for a moment too long, and my skin starts to burn, but just as soon she's nodding, agreeing, scribbling something on the prescription pad. Within ten minutes, I'm out of there, practically sauntering past Lucy B., unable to resist giving her a final triumphant, condescending glance over my shoulder.

In the parking lot, I walk toward my car, taking note of the other two cars there—one a silver Mercedes SUV that belongs to Dr. Hassan herself and a mid-2000s Honda at the end of the lot. When I get close to it, there's a Hello Kitty air freshener dangling from the rearview mirror. That has to be Lucy B.'s.

I make a mental note before I get in my own car and start the engine.

# CHAPTER THIRTEEN

I drive until I come across a drugstore at least fifteen blocks away from the clinic, and only then do I stop. While I wait for my prescription to be prepared, I check my phone again.

There's a new email, and it's from Isabelle Herrera. In carefully chosen neutral words, she agrees to talk to me. There's also a message on Facebook from one of the girls I messaged as Claudia, whose words are a lot less careful and less neutral—she's pretty much foaming at the mouth in emojis, jumping at the chance to get Byron fired or worse. I can't help but wonder if Byron failed her for spending too much time in class on social media.

Speaking of Byron, he didn't leave a message. But I do have one voicemail—which is odd because I never heard my phone ring or vibrate, not during the appointment with Dr. Hassan or while I was driving. I put the phone to my ear. Static, and then the familiar voice, like fingernails on metal. My sister.

Maybe the events of the day have been too much, and I simply can't handle her after everything, so I hang up without listening to the end. I'll deal with her later. Maybe tomorrow. Or the day after that.

I haven't spoken to her since before Byron and I got married. Along with most of my college acquaintances. I cut them out of my life like unnecessary dead weight—just more people who didn't understand what I saw in a man so much older.

When I think about them, my stomach knots, and my throat tightens again, like I'm about to cry. I haven't missed any of them, or at least I was able to convince myself that I didn't. And a treacherous thought sneaks to the front of my mind: Maybe they weren't so wrong after all.

I won't let myself think that. That's not true, and not fair to me or to Byron.

"Ms. Wilson?"

The voice sounds inquisitive, and as I turn around, I realize the man behind the counter has been calling me repeatedly. I'd zoned out. I hastily apologize and go to pay for my prescription, which is astronomically expensive. Good thing I made the trip to the ATM right before. The cash changes hands; the small white paper bag with the pharmacy logo does too. I glance inside and see the syringes in there, wrapped in plastic and looking so harmless. It wasn't a lie, what I said to Dr. Hassan, but it wasn't the whole truth either. Despite ample experience,

I'm quite nervous around needles. Especially after everything that happened when I was growing up.

I drive home, shaky and exhausted, my stomach rumbling. Somewhere along the line, I've managed to find
my appetite again—perhaps the whole day of not eating
helped or maybe it's my much-improved state of mind.
The prescription hidden at the bottom of my purse gives
me new faith in life. So I stop at the grocery store and
stock up. Then, at home, I whip up a dinner like I used
to make in the good, early days. Three courses and with
homemade dessert. I decant the bottle of red wine I
bought and set out the nice glasses.

Just past six thirty, the table is set, the first course of
bocconcini salad is congealing in its dressing at the bottom of the salad bowls, and the only thing missing is
Byron. Now I think back to that call I let go to voicemail,
alternating between remorse and alarm. I pull up his number on my contact list and stare at it wistfully, letting my
thumb hover over it without tapping the phone screen. I
debate texting him but the idea of him not replying burns.

I find myself, like in the early stages of our relationship,
overthinking and overanalyzing everything, afraid to miss
a phone call, a text—or even so much as a word, a look,
a twitch of the lips, or a glimmer in the eyes that might
reveal what he's thinking. Hanging on to these little details desperately, as though if I only could decipher the
ultimate meaning behind them, I could have the key to his
heart and soul and, most importantly, mind. I remember
that feeling so well, infuriating and pathetic at the same
time—feeling like a stupid child trying to figure out the

thought patterns of someone so much older, more experienced, more sophisticated.

Colleen could read him like an open book, I think, replaying Derek's words over and over in my mind. Colleen not only knew him; she could pull his strings.

That thought, an unwelcome intruder, taunts me, refusing to leave me alone until it finally sends me fleeing to the kitchen. There, I mindlessly check on the lamb dish simmering in the slow cooker—a wedding present from Emily, smart and practical and expensive like all things Emily, of course. And just as lacking in soul. The stew is too liquid; the sauce that was supposed to thicken—according to Moroccan Kitchen Everyday at least—is still runny and oily with a weird gamey smell. Cursing under my breath, I rummage through the cupboards for the cornstarch, and the whole time, the little nagging voice of self-doubt keeps buzzing in my ear like a fly I can't swat. I can't find the starch. Dammit. Who runs out of starch?

As I turn to check the pantry one more time, the clock catches my eye, and I realize with a start that it's nearing seven o'clock, and still no Byron. I turn off the slow cooker, watery sauce be damned. Not that it matters, buzzes the little voice.

He's probably fucking some twenty-two-year-old coed right now.

I throw the stirring spoon into the sink with a deafening clatter and throw open the fridge. The bottle of wine I use to cook rattles in the rack inside the door. I snatch it out and pour myself three-quarters of a glass, from which I take two or three deep gulps.

It's enough to settle my nerves. At least it's a start. I go to the living room couch and settle in, the pillows accepting my body in their soft embrace. I take another sip and go to put the glass down, only to realize there's nowhere to put it. I'd destroyed the coffee table, Byron's one-of-a-kind glass coffee table that he bought on God knows what exotic trip with Colleen—of course with Colleen, always with Colleen—and there's my laptop sitting at the foot of the couch. Did I leave it there this afternoon? The battery must be dead by now. Wasn't I doing something, something important?

I open the lid, and it greets me with the password window. I type it in and have to do it twice because my fingertips are trembling. I have a whole slew of messages on Facebook, and a rejection in my work email. The glow of the screen makes me headachy, which in turn makes me nauseous, and I close it. I can deal with it another time.

One more sip of wine—it dribbles down my chin and leaves a few damp spots on my shirt. Wow, it's really hitting me hard. I'm drinking on an empty stomach. I shouldn't do that. Wait, my hormones. I think I'm not supposed to mix them with alcohol. Oh God. I should have read that material the pharmacist gave me. But it was three pages long, and I didn't bother. I figured Dr. Hassan already told me all about the worst of the side effects, and I thought I remembered. The paper is still in my purse. I should go hide it, put it with the hormones and the syringes in my hiding place. But the walk to the hall where I left my purse on the hook is too daunting. I'm just going to close my eyes. Just for a moment.

There's noise, thundering that I understand to be steps. Something clangs in the distance, followed by the sound of cursing, and the combination of it all steadily pulls me out of my sleep.

Wait. Sleep? The entire evening fell through the cracks of my memory. When did we have dinner, when and how did I get to bed? Then I become aware of the aches and pains, starting with the killer crick in my spine. With a groan, I try to sit up. In front of me is the large bay window of the living room, dark now, shrouded in the tulle curtain.

I'm not in bed at all. I'm on the couch in front of the destroyed coffee table, my wineglass sitting on the floor next to my laptop, and everything comes back with a flood of panic.

How on earth did I fall asleep? And for God's sake, what is that smell? Burnt toast? For a moment, I'm absolutely certain I have a brain tumor, and that's the real reason for everything, and I surprise myself by giggling. Relief. What I'm feeling is relief. This is an explanation. Closure.

Then I realize I don't have a brain tumor, and the burnt smell is very much real, as is the smoke—oh no. Gray smoke fills the living room. I scramble to get up but my head spins, and I have to hold on to the back of the couch.

"Jesus Christ, Claire!" Byron bursts into the room so suddenly that I spring back, startled. "What the fuck?"

The word, coming from my cultured husband, is like a slap.

"What do you think you're doing, taking a nap with the oven on?"

"What?" He must see the genuine confusion on my face, because for a moment, his angry expression softens. Only for a moment.

"The stove top and the oven are on. And whatever was in there is now coals. If I'd gotten here ten minutes later, it would have caught fire. And meanwhile, you decided to take a doze? What the hell were you thinking?"

His hair is disheveled, he's wearing his work shirt but no jacket, and there's a towel scorched with burn marks slung over his arm.

"I turned it off," I say, my voice muted and hoarse. I remember it clearly, which is more than I can say about everything that came after, but still. This part I do remember, and I'm not lying. I remember turning off the stove. Yes, the stove. And the oven? I'd turned it off before that. Once I finished baking the lava cakes. Didn't I?

He sees my hesitation before I have the good sense to hide it. Anyway, I'm far too drunk and disoriented to make sense. His shoulders sink. "For fuck's sake, Claire."

Before I can say anything in my defense, he disappears back into the kitchen. I follow on his heels.

It's hard to breathe in here because the smoke is so thick and black. The lava cakes I'd made—or rather, what's left of them—are in the sink, charred remains fused permanently to the baking dish. The slow cooker is open, dried-up remains of stew stuck to the bottom.

"I don't know how—" I start, but he spins around.

"I think I know how. How much did you drink? That bottle was nearly full yesterday. Now there's not even half a glass left."

My gaze travels from his furious expression to the bottle of cheap wine that stands on the counter like an accusation. He's right; it's almost empty. Except when I poured myself a glass, it wasn't. I could swear it.

But what can I possibly say in my defense? Someone broke into the house while I was asleep, poured a full bottle of wine down my gullet, and turned on the stove? Even I realize that's ridiculous.

"Is there something you want to tell me?" His voice snaps with irritation. "Is there a problem I should know about? What exactly do you do here by yourself all day when you're supposed to be writing?"

I'm aghast. Bringing my failed manuscript into this? It's adding insult to injury. Mean and unnecessary. "I'm cleaning and cooking," I say slowly. "For you."

"I can damn well see that."

"Look, I don't know what happened," I bleat. I glance at the clock. It's nearing ten p.m., and what I should be asking is why he's coming home so late, but how can I, faced with this mess? "I swear. I was tired and dozed off. And maybe—" I'm scrambling here, making things up. "Maybe I thought I turned the stove down to minimum but I actually cranked it to maximum instead. I was distracted. I can help you clean."

"Just go to bed," he growls. "Please."

That's about all I have the energy to do. I go upstairs and collapse onto the bed fully dressed, burying my face in the satin pillow, breathing in the smell of detergent and fabric softener and his shampoo that suddenly seems completely alien, unfamiliar, and evil.

*　　*　　*

*I hope you'll forgive me for what I've done. It was a bold move to drug her wine. But if she actually ever cooked with it, I never would have. I would never risk any of that ending up in your food. But I know she nips into the stuff all day long. I sniffed it before I mixed in the crushed pills, and it was so sour and disgusting. She only pretends to have good taste around you, to fool you. Deep down, I suspect she's trash. Like me, perhaps, you could say. But don't worry—not for much longer.*

*Anyway, it's not even the worst thing I've done.*

*I hope you'll forgive me one day. Something tells me you will.*

# CHAPTER FOURTEEN

The next day, I feel good, relatively speaking. I fell asleep pretty much instantly and woke up naked, tucked neatly under the covers—which almost brought tears to my eyes except, when I examined the bed, I could have sworn that Byron didn't sleep in it. There was nothing, no note. The only reminder that any of that was real are the charred dishes sitting by the sink, filled with an inch of nauseating, soapy water.

When I peer into the living room, I see bundled-up sheets and a pillow on the couch. Just like I thought. Yet for some reason, the sight still causes near-physical pain.

When I remember what I have planned for today, I groan inwardly, and I'm this close to writing her a message to cancel. The last person I want to talk to right now is Byron's one-time sort-of girlfriend. But at the same time, I know I can't do that. I set this thing in motion, and for the first time, it occurs to me that I might not be able to stop it.

I'm not even sure I want to stop it. Not after yesterday.

It's not that I think Byron had anything to do with what happened to Colleen. But the more I replay the scene in my mind (and I do, many, many times over, pausing over each little detail), the more the eerie mental image becomes vivid. This same scene, eight years before. Husband yelling accusations at his furious, frustrated wife, who doesn't know what to say.

I don't know what to think. I need to know more. And that's why I need Isabelle Herrera.

We agreed to talk on the phone since she now lives in Minnesota. I googled her, of course. Her Facebook is locked under privacy filters so I had to get creative. Luckily, she friended my dummy account back after a few hours. Her profile picture is of her with a group of friends, her face out of focus. Isabelle appears to have a nice, comfortable life, a husband, but all of it is somehow quaint, too mundane, as if she is making the most generic choices on purpose. As if, unlike most people, she is trying to be unremarkable.

She calls me at noon sharp, like we said in our emails. My phone says No ID Available, but I know it's her, good and punctual.

I pick up, my heart doing backflips. My hand is sweaty when I bring the phone to my ear.

"Hello?" says a pleasant voice, lower pitched than mine but velvety somehow. Still, all that smoothness can't hide how nervous she is.

"Isabelle?" I ask, unnecessarily.

"Yes, it's me. I'm on my lunch hour. You must be Claire?"

I tell her that yes, this is me. Byron's wife, I almost add, in a petty moment of jealousy.

"I'm happy to talk to you." Something in her voice tells me it's exactly the opposite, and her little nervous laugh confirms the lie. "I mean, you must not be that happy to talk to me. But believe me, I have nothing bad to tell you. I haven't so much as spoken to Byron in years. I live in Minneapolis now, and I'm quite happy here."

Good for you, I think.

"Oh, it's not that," I say, with an awkward laugh of my own. "I wanted to know— My friend Derek—" I'd rehearsed this in my head about a thousand times over but when I desperately scramble for the words, they're gone. "He told me you knew something about Byron and . . . and his first wife." I can't bring myself to say her name, like she's Bloody Mary.

There's a silence on the other end, soft breath and softer static. The silence lingers, and it gets heavier with every millisecond.

"If that's what you're thinking, he did not cheat on his wife with me," she says in a low, half-whispered hiss, and I wonder if she's not alone. I know she works in the office of a telecom giant, a twenty-story tower in the downtown center. Where did she hide away on her lunch break? Are her coworkers eavesdropping?

"I never thought that," I reassure her. Truth is I thought all that and more. But that's not how I'm going to get this skittish woman to take my side. "I just— You knew them both. You were close to them when they were married. I just wanted an insider perspective."

"Wait a minute." Suddenly her voice is sharp, angry. "Are you press?"

I'm taken aback by the question. "What? No. I'm—"

"I wouldn't put it past some so-called investigative journalist to pose as his wife," she hisses.

"I'm Claire," I say levelly. "We got married two years ago. I'm not a journalist. Why would you think that?"

A heavy sigh. "Shit," she mutters under her breath. "Sorry. It just makes me jumpy, you know?"

I don't know what to say so I let out an empathetic *hmm* and then let a pause linger, waiting for her to follow the natural impulse to talk it out.

"I mean, when she . . . after she went missing, they called me into the police station and made me give a statement. It was the first time I'd ever been in a police station. Can you imagine?"

So that's it, I think. This is what Derek was really telling me about. Those campus rumors started with her.

"That's awful," I say. I'm really thinking it, if perhaps for different reasons.

"Then you probably already know," she says with firm resolve.

"Know?"

"That I was the one who . . . how do I put this? Oh God, I sound like I'm on a bad crime show. I was the one who alibied him. Byron."

I inhale deeply.

"Yeah. So, just on the off chance you *are* a journalist, for the record, it's true, and I'm not taking it back—I was with him the day she disappeared, all day, and he didn't do it. God, just listen to me." Another shaky chuckle. "I have no particular reason to defend him either; I have no horse in this race. I haven't seen him in years and never will again."

The cold certainty of her words sets me on edge.

"I just wanted to know," I blurt, "what they were like. Together."

She huffs. "If Derek told you that story with the glass, then you probably have a pretty good idea."

"He's the one who suggested I talk to you," I say.

"Look, I don't know what to tell you. You probably think I'm some despicable slut, the other woman, the kind of girl who sleeps with married men. And you probably won't believe me but here's the thing: We never slept together."

"I never said—"

But she interrupts me.

"We might have. Eventually. But we were just flirting, okay? If he cheated on her, it was only emotionally. We'd eat lunch together, go get coffee. We had fun. We understood each other. He wasn't happy with her, at least not anymore. He told me they used to be so happy before but she'd . . . she'd changed. She was having some problems. He was happier with me but he wasn't going to cheat on her. I don't think so."

"I know," I find myself saying. "He's not like that."

Her chuckle is the answer. For a while she doesn't say anything.

"I don't know if I'd say as much."

"What do you mean?"

Another sigh. I can tell she's wrestling with her conscience.

"Look, Claire," she says forcefully, and I know which side won. "I know no wife wants to hear this about her husband, and you're free to just hang up on me. Either way, I don't care. And maybe he's changed, and I hope so for your sake, but back then, Byron wasn't a good man."

She catches her breath after this tirade. I'm holding mine, just barely. "Brilliant, yes, damaged, certainly. But a good guy? No. I think that's what drew me to him originally. I'm like that—well, I used to be. Attracted to fixer-uppers." A self-deprecating laugh. "But he could be so selfish it was scary. One moment he's the most caring, understanding, empathetic man in the world, and he gazes at you with those blue eyes like he alone can understand you. And the next, it's like you don't exist. And if it's ever between him and his comforts and you and your needs, you will never win. He could be cruel when he wanted, and in contrast to that other him, it stung even more.

"At first, I could relate to him, the whole thing with his wife being on drugs, and he even thought she was cheating on him—but then I realized how callous he was about it. Like, as soon as she stopped meeting his needs, she became disposable. That's not love . . . you know? I don't have anything concrete to use as an example, I don't even remember the exact things he said, but it was just . . . a feeling. A strong feeling. That's when I started to pull back, without realizing it yet."

"What exactly happened?" I whisper. My left hand is clenching and unclenching, and my feet tap on the floor.

"The evening she disappeared, we went for drinks with some others from the faculty, and after everyone left, we stayed behind. We drank and flirted all night, and then we kissed in the parking lot. We were both too drunk to drive home so we shared a cab—or tried to. He ended up at my place. I know people were talking shit after but nothing happened! He was drunk and fell asleep on my couch. That's all. And in the morning, he realized Colleen never made it home either.

"But let me tell you something, Claire." I decidedly don't like the way she says my name. "If I hadn't been with him all night, if I hadn't seen him myself, I don't know what I would have said if the police asked me whether Byron was capable of doing harm to Colleen. I don't know."

"But you *were* there," I say pointedly.

"I was there," she echoes, her voice hoarse and bitter. "But all I can tell you is this. I'm not the only one who saw that side of him. Look up his other girlfriends. I did. I'm not going to repeat what Sarah Sterns told me—you can ask her yourself. And when I tried to get in touch with Melissa Donnelly, here's what I found. Melissa supposedly moved away to the West Coast somewhere, but the fact is she hasn't been seen or heard from in four years."

# CHAPTER FIFTEEN

It takes me the better part of an hour to compose an email to Sarah Sterns. I keep backspacing, the cursor devouring word after word, gobbling whole sentences. And what can I possibly say to her, anyhow? Hello, I'm Claire Westcott, and I'm trying to figure out if my husband is an undercover sociopath. Could you help me?

That makes me sound pathetic. And Claire Westcott isn't pathetic. Claire Westcott always has manicured nails and her clothes never clash and she makes the perfect beef bourguignon. Claire Westcott has a perfect life with her perfect husband.

In that moment, I find myself hating Byron with an anger as fierce as it is petty. I hate him for making me look like this in front of complete strangers, his ex-girlfriends no less. For making me feel like this, all because of a

woman who died nearly a decade ago and who, for all in-
tents and purposes, sounds horrible.

I exhale, letting my hands rest on either side of the keyboard, and let myself think of our first meeting, almost
three years ago. On the first two anniversaries of that date,
I got twelve roses and a dinner out. Something tells me
the third one will come and go unnoticed, and pride won't
let me bring it up.

For our second wedding anniversary, he gifted me with
a bracelet, made reservations, everything proper—to anyone observing from the outside. Only I could feel the shift
in him; only I could feel the cold between us. Or worse
yet, not even cold—just emptiness, a vacuum. Where our
minds used to be one, there was now a chasm.

I stared at him from across the table of the chicest tapas
restaurant in Cleveland, sucking my stomach in to avoid
straining at my silk shift dress, my high-heeled shoes
pinching my toes, and I might as well have been looking
at a painting of my husband, not the real him. I had no
idea what was going through his mind. His conversation
was polite and generic. It was like an awkward second
date neither of the parties really wanted, except for the
replacement emerald ring on my finger and the real gold
bracelet in the velvet box in front of me. I feigned the re-
action he no doubt expected while inwardly I wondered
why he'd suddenly splurge on a thing like this. He drove
us home and said he was too tired to have sex.

I got my answer about the bracelet a few days later.
Looking at old photos of Colleen, I saw an identical
one on her wrist. He regifted Colleen's bracelet to me—

a bracelet she probably only wore that one time. It's delicate and beautiful and precious, all things she would have hated.

That sounds tacky as hell, not at all like Byron to repurpose gifts to an ex—except it's *different*, isn't it, because she's not really an ex. They never got divorced—she died. She will never be the ex-wife.

I close my eyes, turning the replacement ring on my finger, over and over and over again.

Byron and I met at an open house event at Mansfield College. I was considering going in for my master's or maybe earning another degree that had better job prospects than my creative writing one. I wasn't in my best mood that day: The novel I was frantically submitting to anyone with an email address brought in rejections by the shovelful, all the short story submissions I mailed to every literary magazine in existence vanished into the ether without a response, and the next novel I'd begun writing to take the edge off waiting had stalled, victim of the hundred-page slump. I was twenty-four, with an honors degree and supposedly a whole future ahead of me, but that future became foggier with every not-so-reassuring email that landed in my inbox.

At Ohio State, I managed not to make a single real friend in all my four years there. I didn't have cute tattoos of birds and feathers, and I wasn't interested in happy hour at the local student pub. I felt like I was going through the motions, turning in assignment after assignment, essay after essay produced with almost mechanical fervor, vigorously proofread, references ironclad. I wasn't the life of the party but I didn't feel like I was missing out on anything. I was the darling of the teachers. Claire is brilliant, Claire is capable, Claire always turns in the most polished work. Claire is the one of the whole bunch who actually has prospects in the field.

But the others graduated and moved on to different things, some jumping into their master's degrees right away, some moving on to work at small publications, and my "prospects" never materialized. I wondered if I'd wasted the so-called best years of my life by not bar-hopping with the other girls in my classes, by sticking to the straight and narrow because I thought it might get me somewhere. But returning to the huge, impersonal, over-crowded campus of Ohio State felt like crawling back with my tail between my legs, and, at least until recently, I had my pride.

I'd researched Mansfield, and it seemed like the small, intimate place where I might find myself, finally. Have that famed, mythical "college experience" everyone always talks about with such fondness. The brochure had program descriptions that piqued my interest. Either way, I felt like I had nothing to lose by going to the open house.

I knew I was in the wrong place pretty much the moment I set foot on that campus, the forbiddingly angular postmodern buildings looming over me, spelling my doom. On the website, the pictures made the place look sleek and edgy, but in person, it was hulking and hideous, an assemblage of abominations. But I was already there, and I don't know why but I decided to give it a chance, at least until the end of the tour.

I remember the feeling that overcame me when I stepped into the English Department for the first time. It was, as odd as it sounds, a feeling of hope. Maybe this wasn't such a disaster after all. The building, cool and kind of dark even in the middle of a blazing-hot afternoon, embraced me like an old friend. Sweat that had broken out along my hairline and on my upper lip began to cool, and I felt like myself again.

It was just me—all the other potential applicants had dispersed amid the flashier, artier departments, and my steps echoed in the emptiness. I examined the artwork on the walls, the printouts of articles and the award certificates, and let myself wonder if perhaps I should apply for my master's degree here after all. Then I turned down a hallway lined with doors, and I could see through the glass inserts into one of the offices behind them— exactly the way I imagined an English professor's office should look, bookshelves lining the walls, a mix of well-loved paperback and hardcover editions and fancy gilded spines. A desk with one of those old-fashioned lamps, stacks of books, a slightly outdated desktop computer, and a leather chair that looked so comfortably worn that I wanted to plunk down in it and spin like a small child.

"Can I help you?"

The voice made me turn around, feeling like I had been caught snooping. A man was standing at the entrance of the hall, where I had just come from. The big window was right behind him, and I couldn't see his face right away, but his voice—I loved his voice. Deep and pleasant. "You're not in any of my classes, are you?"

"No," was all I managed to stammer. He came closer, and I could see him. It was hard to pinpoint his age; anywhere between thirty and forty-five—that was my first guess. I just knew that I liked his face, his eyes, his dark-blond eyebrows—everything about him. And as silly as it sounds, it was as if a little bell went off in the back of my mind: This is fate.

"Didn't think so. I remember all my students by name. Pride myself on it."

"I'm here for the open house," I said, mentally checking all the things that were wrong about me: my body language (awkward), my appearance (sweaty), my clothes (shouldn't have worn this dress two days in a row—oh God, do I have sweat stains in my armpits?). But I bravely pinned my arms to my sides, glued a smile on my face, and persevered. Because I couldn't not.

He gave a chuckle. "Wow. Is it bad to tell you you're the first one?"

"Can't be," I said, and I think I was genuinely surprised.

"Yeah. English is sadly overlooked at this school. Sorry, shouldn't have said that. Now you won't apply for your BA."

"I hate to disappoint you but I already have my BA."

"Oh darn," he said, and snapped his fingers. "Woe is me. Soon no one will enroll in my classes anymore, and they'll throw me out."

"I have a hard time believing that." Now my grin was as real as it gets—something about an utterly charming and handsome man being self-deprecating made it impossible not to smile.

"Well, if you're going to apply for the MFA, you might

end up working as one of my assistants. And I can see few downsides to that."

I realized I was standing there grinning like an idiot, all hardships of this day forgotten. I had to say something before he thought I was some dumb, mute sheep. So what I said was, "My name is Claire."

"Prof. Westcott. Or for those who aren't my students, Byron."

"You've got to be kidding me," I said. I think I laughed and barely managed not to snort.

He gave a theatrical sigh. "Unfortunately, it's true. Feel free to laugh; I know my students do."

"Good thing I'm not one of your students."

He gave me a private tour of the campus that day, leading me past one hideous building after another, telling me anecdotes about each one. "And this one has been featured in *Architecture Today*, considered a wonder of modern design—world famous, no less. Too bad that not a day goes by without at least one elevator breaking down, and the world-famous design did not foresee stairs except for the fire exit." And on and on. So I laughed.

By the time we were done, the sun was setting. I was shocked when I saw the orange sky—where did the day go? How did five hours get away from me? Byron invited me for a bite to eat. "And a glass of wine, if I'm so lucky. I managed not to scare you away yet. Didn't I?"

I told him no, he didn't scare me away, and I was down for a bite to eat and the wine too.

After, he asked for my number, and I gave it to him. It would be a week before he called. But he did call.

Six months later, my ideas of an MFA were forgotten, and I had an emerald ring on my finger and my future finally rolled out in front of me, looking as cloudless as ever.

Never once did he mention the wife who killed herself.

# CHAPTER SIXTEEN

I still wonder what he saw in me that day. On the other hand, what wouldn't a man in his forties see in a conventionally pretty, blond twentysomething who was clearly too awestruck by him to speak coherently? But I never wanted to think of him like that, and I still don't. It dirties a thing that was pure from beginning to end.

This much I know: It wasn't delusion or wishful thinking. It makes him sound like a lecherous old man that he certainly wasn't then and isn't now. He was a gentleman. Not only that, he was cautious at first, distant for a reason I could never pinpoint. It was a riddle. He was clearly attracted to me—physically and on every other level. Our conversation sparkled; for the first time I felt that my creative writing degree was useful for something. I wondered whether everything I'd ever done had been leading me here, toward him, like the proverbial red string of fate. I wasn't just another blond in a slightly rumpled sundress wandering around campus. I'd read fifties existentialist literature. I could maintain a conversation about late Victorian poetry or early twentieth-century Gothic novels as the foundation of the suspense genre as we know it today and not be bored.

Even though I was self-conscious, worried that someone so much more experienced might find my little opinions trite, Byron actually listened to what I had to say and looked interested. He watched me with the kind of fascination every girl wants to see in the eyes of the man she really, really likes.

And yet somehow, even after all that, he took a whole week to call me. I had exhausted myself with regret, over-analyzing every word and gesture, trying to figure out where I had disappointed. Up until the phone rang.

"I put that shirt in the washing machine," he had said, his hot chocolate–and-brandy voice in my phone, not in the slightest distorted by the crackling connection. "The card you wrote your number on was in it. Only about a third of the ink survived, and feel free not to believe me, but I spent the week trying all the possible numbers I could discern in that mess. I lost count of the times I made an utter fool of myself. Looks like I finally hit gold. Will you forgive me?"

I forgave him. Even though it was a lie, it was a cute lie. But then he was just as reluctant to sleep with me for the first time. All my signals seemed to fall on deaf ears so I figured he was just being chivalrous. It was another six weeks of dating before he invited me over.

He was everything you'd want in a lover. He knew what he was doing and never let it end without an orgasm for me. Looking back, there was almost something textbook about that first time: He went down on me beforehand, he had a condom at the ready and never made things awkward about putting it on, and it went on for a respectable twenty minutes—no weird requests or strange positions. After, he got up and got us glasses of sweet wine.

"You know," he said, pulling me close to him, "I was worried. I wanted you the moment we met. But..." He sighed and took a sip. "Well, first, I didn't want to be presumptuous or have you think I'm some pervert who's only after one thing."

"Are you?" I asked, to be playful.

"Oh, no. I'm after all the things." He kissed my neck, and I spilled my wine, three or four sweet, sticky drops on his pillowcase. "Also, I have terrible luck with women. Just as things start to get interesting, they either disappear on me or start acting strange."

"I can't imagine why." I was still being coy but he got that faraway, sad look in his eyes. I waited for him to continue, to elaborate, but he never did, and in the end, I decided to take his words at face value. "Well, you don't have to worry about me disappearing."

"I sure hope not. It's the long weekend next week, and I was thinking of a getaway. A little chalet somewhere. What do you think?"

I agreed, happy enough to change the subject. He never brought up any of his former flings again, which was just as well, as far as I was concerned.

Now, as I send my email to Sarah Sterns after nearly an hour of hesitation, I hope in the back of my mind that she never answers. Then, despite my growing consternation, I open Facebook in a new tab.

My little message window has had time to turn into a veritable arena of hatred. My breath catches when I see the number of new messages from the other girls in the conversation.

Hey Claudia, **one writes.** I'm so so so sorry you had to go through that. Have you considered filing a formal complaint?

**Another one chastises her below:** Don't victim-blame Claudia. You know what happens to victims who report.

**Another:** I know someone who takes one of his classes. Victorian Literature. She says he never harassed her personally but he's always acting suggestive to girls he thinks are pretty or whatever.

**The ringleader intervenes. She even types her messages in a deep-bloodred font.** We need proof. We need material if we're going to file a complaint and get this asshole fired.

**The Victorian Literature girl:** I know someone who had a whole email exchange with him, over some essay. Apparently it got pretty heavy, pretty much outright harassment. He suggested stuff like she should come by his office after hours to "talk about it." Can you believe him?

I can barely keep myself from rolling my eyes. For the first time in days, I'm reassured. Colleen might be one thing, whatever Isabelle Herrera thinks is another, but so far, I see no indication that anything untoward is happening with Byron and his students.

How is he still allowed to teach???

Claudia, do you have anything?

The bloodred font glares at me demandingly. My fingers hover over the keyboard. I'm this close to changing my mind, just closing the laptop and forgetting about the whole thing.

I was in one of his classes, like I said, I type. He would flirt with me nonstop. At first it was kind of flattering but then it got to be too much. I was dreading going to class by the end.

I hit Send and groan. That's all my writerly imagination could scare up? But it turns out this is all they need.

Ugh. That's unacceptable. No one should have to deal with that in a place that's supposed to be for learning.

What a pig.

I know, I type. And I mean, it wouldn't be so bad but he's married, right?

Answers pour in, in real time.

Oh so it's not so bad because he's not fat or bald? If, say, Prof. Whitmer did that, it would be worse?

Don't try to excuse his behavior Claudia.

How do you know he's married?

I blink and lean back from the screen. My face flushes. Suddenly this whole situation is flipped on its head, not so innocent now.

I think I heard that he is, I type, but don't dare to send.

**The ringleader beats me to it:** It doesn't matter whether he's married or not. It's not the point. The behavior is inexcusable.

I heard there was something going on with him and a grad student, types one of the other girls. Her profile picture shows neon-pink hair and cat-eye glasses.

I heard something like that too, types another.

Yeah, I know which one, a girl chimes in, the same one who asked me whether I'd considered filing a report. Mia, she works at the desk in the English department.

I have a brief flashback to the girl behind glass, watching me attentively over the cover of her heavy tome.

Ugh, women who betray other women are the absolute worst.

I realize I'm not needed in this discussion. What really interests them is not firing Byron or even his supposedly inappropriate behavior; it's gossiping about other girls and who they're sleeping with. Same old routine under a new banner.

But I got something out of it, even though it's not much: Mia. A grad student. Jealousy, stifling and ugly, grips my insides. I mustn't do anything crazy, not until I find more. I clench and unclench my sweaty hands, struggling to calm myself. I've never let myself be rash, be stupid, act on my baser impulses, and I'm not going to start now. It gets you nowhere. Especially with men. Girls my age— hell, even women twice my age—don't understand this but a man must never wonder what to do about the crazy woman. Men never stay with the crazy woman. They stay with the woman who makes things simple. Byron may have thought he was different—exempt from this rule— but look at him and Colleen.

Then again, I never made things anything but simple, and it didn't stop him growing cold. And the worst part is I don't even know why. I can practically hear my sister in my head, laughing at me. Chrissy always thought I was a freak of nature, a throwback, pathetic. I wasn't sad to cut her out of my life when I got married. Look who's pathetic now, I thought, as I stood in front of the mirror in my beautiful, tasteful off-white silk dress, my emerald ring matching my eyes, about to marry the man of my dreams. And now everything is crumbling, just like she predicted— and I'd dismissed her as bitter and jealous. What would she think if she saw me now?

The thought alone is enough to give me a physical pang. I don't even know where she lives now, what she's doing. For all I know, she could be married too; she could be a single mom; she could be dying of cancer. I haven't spoken to her in more than two years and haven't seen her in person since not long after Mom died. Mom wouldn't have liked it. She would have wanted us to stick together, help each other like sisters are supposed to.

But it wasn't me who started it. Chrissy turned her back on me first, long before I cut her out of my life. The moment she turned eighteen, a year before me, she took off, packed only the necessities into a duffel and was gone. She said she couldn't stand to be in that house anymore. She's the traitor, not me.

And now all I have is the voicemail she left while I was at the doctor's. *I'm in town. Call me. I know what you're doing, and you need to stop before it's too late.*

# CHAPTER SEVENTEEN

The next morning, I wake up alone and don't realize until I'm standing in the shower that I barely even made a mental note of that fact. Maybe it's the nausea that grips and twirls me before my feet hit the floor—oh yes, those side effects on that printout the pharmacist insistently pressed into my hand. I really should have read it. Not that it would have made a difference. I've decided I'm doing this so I am.

In the mirror, my face is puffy, my eyes dull green marbles pressed into a mass of bread dough. I splash massive amounts of toner onto a cotton pad and wipe my face but it doesn't help. The sting and smell of alcohol wakes me up a little though. And already it's time for another shot, I think, cringing.

I hid the syringes and the vials of hormones in the safest place in the house, where no sane man would ever venture: inside a tampon box. I covered them with the paper insert that comes with the box—the TSS info sheet—and closed the flaps. Still, I inspect the box up close to make sure nothing has been tampered with. I inject into a discreet spot on my thigh, wincing when the needle digs into my skin. And done.

For a short while, I manage to convince myself that things are improving. The day is sunny and warm, and light pours into the living room through the bay window, livening up the cold lilac walls. I avoid the disaster area in the kitchen, where dark rings on the counter still remind me of the burned, ruined pots and pans. I start the coffee machine and pop two pieces of bread into the toaster. I might be nauseous but I have to keep up my calorie intake. I will need the extra energy soon. I focus on that thought and catch myself smiling, my first genuine smile in a long time.

I stack the burned pots in the corner. I'll be more careful in the future—I'll know better. I'll stop drinking altogether, not even a sip of wine while cooking. After all, I'll have to stop for at least nine months and then however long it takes to breastfeed. Buoyed by the idea, I scoop the two open wine bottles out of the fridge and, while the coffee is brewing, pour the first one down the sink. The sour smell wafts up, making me cringe. Alcohol is gross anyway, when you think about it. We don't drink it because it tastes good, do we? I don't need any of that toxic stuff in my bloodstream.

The contents of the second bottle finally spiral into the drain with a hollow glugging noise, and I wait as the last drops trickle out. They're lush and purple—the grenache that Byron likes. It occurs to me he might be mad that I poured out his favorite wine that he likes to sip after work.

Whatever. He'll get over it when I break the good news to him, I think with glee, shrugging as I twirl around and slam-dunk the empty bottle into the recycling bin.

The toast pops out of the toaster, startling me. I swing my arm and manage to knock over the first empty wine bottle. My reflexes seem to be running in slow motion, because I barely have time to draw a breath before the bottle shatters on the kitchen tiles. Green glass goes flying, and I find myself standing in the middle of a disaster area—barefoot, naturally.

Cursing, I tiptoe for the broom, and by the time I'm done sweeping and making sure no stray shards lurk under the furniture, the toast is cold, and the coffee barely lukewarm.

Not the best start.

I gather my breakfast on a tray and carry it outside, vainly trying to steady the tremor that seems to have permanently taken hold of my hands.

It's a beautiful September day. I settle in on the veranda, my tray on the deck table, my feet curled up under me in the comfy chair. The sun slants just right, so I'm warm enough but still in the shadow. It's a mistake to think the sun is less potent in the fall. And besides, tans are vulgar. I've always thought so. I came of age at a time when the trend was already on its way out, and it was more of a Chrissy thing anyway. Like many other girls at our school, she'd go to the salon every couple of weeks and spend what I thought was mad money to use the tanning bed.

The thought of Chrissy gives me a tiny, inward shudder. I glance nervously at the silent, black screen on my phone, sitting on the tray next to my plate. Under the pretext of swiping toast crumbs off the surface, I press the button. I have no new alerts.

After I'd listened to the voicemail one last time, I finally deleted it as I should have done right away. Yet it stuck with me, lingering like a bitter aftertaste. I spent half the night tossing and turning, stumbling through shadowy dreams of our old house, of our old room that she had turned into two separate ones by hanging up one of those heavy plastic shower curtains with the weights in the hem.

Even at home, Chrissy felt the need to separate herself from me, as if that undeniable whiff of failure associated with me might cling to her if she spent too much time in the same space. It would stick to her like the deep-fryer smell from my after-school job, and her cool, popular friends would pick up on it, as teens always do, detecting uncoolness with the precision of bloodhounds. And then maybe they wouldn't let her hang out with them anymore—a fate worse than death when you're in ninth grade.

So she pulled that weighted curtain closed and left me on the other side. She never brought people to the house. If they saw the room, the curtain, our dented couch with the beer cans at its foot, no amount of shoplifted clothes and brand-name sneakers would save her. She was only waiting for the chance to get out. As soon as she could, she did.

If she thinks I'll let her barge into the life I've painstakingly built for myself with hard work and dedication—if she thinks she can try and sabotage it, out of sheer jealousy or envy or whatever drives her—she has no idea how wrong she is.

I sip my coffee as the sun creeps slowly but surely across the deck table toward my hand. I'll have to move my chair soon, and I don't feel like it. For once, I want to sit and soak up the warm rays, skin cancer and premature aging and tan lines be damned. That's what Colleen would do, I'm sure.

I banish the thought of her before she can take up any more space in my head. Instead, I look out over the flower baskets, over the slice of the neighbor's manicured backyard that I can see from the veranda. They have a garden with a layout that used to mirror ours, until the deck was built. I wonder occasionally whether I'd enjoy maintaining a garden, the real thing, not just a couple of boxes of geraniums. All that digging around in the earth, planting seeds, watering, and then pruning and weeding. Again, something Colleen used to love. For that reason alone, I love this veranda. I smile to myself as the sun finally reaches my elbow and relish the heat of it. Screw the garden. I'm glad it's gone.

My phone gives a short vibration that blows the moment apart. I don't move, not outwardly, but every muscle in my body stiffens. Slowly, I turn my head and see the alert right before the screen goes dark. In a slow, controlled movement, I reach for the phone and pick it up.

It's an email from Sarah Sterns.

Dear Claire, I read. Thank you very much for contacting me. She writes in an old-fashioned style, in too-long sentences. Which usually means she overthought it, agonizing over every word. I can picture her, chewing on the inside of her cheek, her pale face bathed in the light of her screen, composing through the better part of the night. Then she'd sleep on it and, having made sure that every word was still in place, send it in the morning.

Why so much effort for the wife of an ex-boyfriend from years and years ago?

> Isabelle messaged me about you so I was expecting your email. We've spoken several times over the years, not just about Byron but also about Colleen. I know this must sound pretty strange—

No kidding.

> —but it's not because I'm obsessed, or because Isabelle is. And it's not because either of us had any trouble letting go of our relationships with Byron Westcott. So please don't be threatened or alarmed.

I forget that I'm sitting in the middle of a sunny September morning. I had stopped feeling the sunlight, which is now working its way up my arm. Its heat mingles with the chill that settles in my bones.

I've often made up theories about Byron and his relationship with his wife. I note the "wife" with a twitch of jealousy. *I'm* the wife, I think pettily, and want to reply to her just to correct her. Colleen was just the starter wife. And I must say I've never even come close to anything that might explain what went on between the two. But it must have been pretty unique, a deep connection, the kind that changes you. No wonder no other relationship can match that for him.

Thanks for the reassurance, I think, seething.

But, without further ado, I should probably answer your question before I go off on tangents. Byron and I started dating five years ago. We met at an alumni event at the college. I did my graphic design BA at Mansfield almost twenty years ago, and I had just moved back to Columbus to take care of my mother. I won't bore you with the details but it was tough, leaving my whole life behind in Buffalo, and I needed to find a job fast, too, to keep up with the medical bills. That invite arrived in my email at just the right time, and I thought it was— I know it sounds stupid in retrospect—serendipity, or something like that. Fate.

For some reason, the word sets my teeth on edge.

I thought a little networking couldn't hurt, anyway. So I went, but instead of finding a new work opportunity or reconnecting with old friends, I found Byron. Or he found me.

It was a little intense, how he just seemed to zero in on me. Truth be told, I only realized that looking back. At the time, I was flattered—not just flattered, dazzled. He was handsome and fun to talk to, but at the same time, he never monopolized the conversation like a lot of men do. He wanted to know about me. Before I knew it, I was spilling the whole story, right there at the alumni banquet over a glass of prosecco and some canapes. About my mom's dementia, and my work troubles, the whole thing. I must admit I was a tiny bit drunk by then. Later, when I sobered up, I was sure I'd never see him again. Talking to men about your problems is the fastest way to make them vanish into the ether, isn't it?

I stare at the screen coldly. What, am I expected to relate? I never made my problems Byron's problems. Not at the start, not after we were married, and even now, I'm doing my damned best.

So imagine my surprise when he messaged me the next day—on a professional networking site, no less. I never left him my number but he found out my full name from someone at the event and took it from there. Again, that should have been a red flag. Or maybe I'm paranoid. But in light of how things ended, you can hardly blame me.

Once again, I hold back an uncomfortable shiver. Isn't that what I'm doing right now—looking for cracks in Sarah Sterns's character so I can rationalize her away as yet another crazy woman who was rejected and couldn't cope? So I can sweep this whole thing under the proverbial rug and keep ignoring the things happening right in front of me, writing them off as any marriage's inevitable terrible twos?

I turn my attention back to the email.

We messaged back and forth for the rest of the week, and on the weekend, we went on a date. I was a little surprised when he suggested a place so far out of the way, almost an hour's drive from the college, in the middle of a ramshackle neighborhood—the kind of place I wouldn't walk alone at night. The restaurant itself seemed like a hole in the wall. But he said the place was the city's best-kept secret, and I took his word for it. He ordered drinks, and the food was surprisingly good! He drove me home afterward, didn't suggest coming up, the perfect gentleman.

Then we went on another date, then another. We kissed, and I could tell we had chemistry, yet still he made no attempt to invite me over. In fact, I got the feeling he was trying to keep me as far as possible from his house—as if he were trying to hide me from someone.

For just a moment, I manage to forget I'm not reading fiction, and my breath catches. But then I glance at the next sentence, and Colleen's name brings me back to earth in a heartbeat.

> I made a couple of inquiries with some old acquaintances at the college, and the story of Colleen came out. I have to admit I wasn't as alarmed as I should have been. If anything, I found it intriguing, and almost endearing. I mean, poor guy, right? I thought it explained a lot. He wasn't fully over her, he was afraid of getting hurt, all the typical horseshit. And of course I filled my head with the usual delusions: that I'll be the one to bring him back to life, to heal him. How stupid was I, you're probably asking. But at the time, I really believed it. Besides, it sort of gave me perspective on my own problems, which didn't look so serious in comparison. So I attacked the task of bringing Byron back to life with all the energy I could muster. I pushed and pushed until he finally gave in and asked me over for a drink after one of our dates.

I can't help but flinch. She is writing about having sex with my husband, after all. Even though at the time I was little more than a clueless undergrad adrift in life. And since he's twenty years older than I, obviously, there were other women—many of them.

The moment I walked into that house, it became so clear. It didn't look like a single man's house. It looked like a couple still lived there. Like she never left. And the paintings—I'd looked up her paintings online and recognized the style immediately. After I saw that, I wasn't sure I could have sex with him at all. It felt wrong. Perverted, you know?

I, of course, hadn't questioned any of it, too dazzled by Byron (in Sarah's own words) to bring it up. I was so wrapped up in the marvel of it all, this exciting new relationship with the alluring older man. Did I deserve what I got, stumbling boldly into the middle of someone else's sordid history? I was barely twenty-four at the time, a child from his perspective. Sarah, on the other hand, had to be in her early forties. Did she pick up on things I ignored? Did Byron realize that? What if he did...and didn't like it?

So, I'm not exactly proud of what happened next but please bear with me. He offered me a drink, and I took him up on the offer. Did I ever. He had this whole bar in the living room, and he made us some kind of cocktail I'd never had before, super-bitter and strong, not my kind of drink normally, but that evening, I was only too happy to down one after another. And it went to my head, like I hoped. Hard and fast. Everything is actually kind of blurry afterward but I remember enough snippets to put the picture together. We were on the living room couch. It was intense—we were tearing off each other's clothes—and I guess I was drunk enough not to pay attention to his dead wife's paintings all over the house.

I didn't see the one in the bedroom until the next morning, when I woke up in his bed. I can only assume you've seen it. It dawned on me right then and there, through the pounding headache of my hangover, what I was up against. And that was before I realized I was alone in the house.

I stop reading and squeeze my eyes shut. The sun bathes my face, and all I can see through my closed eyelids is red, red, red.

He just left me there. At first, I thought he was downstairs in the kitchen, but no. Here I was, disoriented, barely able to stand after everything I drank the night before, alone in the house. There was a note on the counter, scrawled carelessly on a shred of paper torn from a notebook, saying there was some kind of emergency and he had to leave for work and to please help myself to anything I needed. I made myself a coffee and found some aspirin in the bathroom. I drank my coffee perched at the kitchen counter, feeling like a pathetic mess. I was going to wait for him to come

back, if you can believe it. But then they called
from the care home and told me my mom had
taken a fall, so I had to go. In retrospect, it was
probably for the best—saved me a pretty humiliat-
ing conversation. Because later that day, he broke
up with me. On the same networking site. I still
remember every word: I was so humiliated I think
it's branded into my mind forever.

*Dear Sarah*, it said, *I'm sorry but we can't see
each other anymore. I'd appreciate it if you didn't
contact me again.* That's all. I understood that I'd
made a fool of myself but I didn't think I deserved
that. I should have just left it at that, cut my
losses, and moved on. But in the heat of the moment, my head still aching, my mind in disarray,
I wrote back immediately, saying I was sorry, the
drink went to my head, and so on.

I find myself smirking, my heart light with relief. I really
thought it would be a lot more sinister. What I'm reading
is the old story of a woman who behaved like a drunken
mess, screwed up on a date, and needs to blame someone else. I should tell her to contact her local AA chapter,
really.

Then I remember the disaster the other day, and my
face flushes painfully. Pressing the cool back of my hand
to my burning cheek, I keep reading.

The problem is, it didn't end there. I got three more messages from Byron over the next few days. Nothing outright threatening, but they made my skin crawl. The first one was on the networking site. I saw that he had viewed my profile dozens of times in one day, and then I got a short missive saying that he was sorry but he found drunk women extremely unattractive and there was nothing to be done. That was a couple of days after the whole disaster, and I was so embarrassed that I deleted it before it occurred to me to take a screenshot.

Then I got another one on Facebook, a private message saying that he was sorry for his harsh words but after what he went through with his first wife, he simply couldn't deal with that again. I never replied. It explained things, sort of, but it still left a bad taste in my mouth. If so, why ply me with liquor? Or let me crawl all over him when I was dead drunk. Sure, what man would ever turn down sex when it's offered, but... He didn't seem like the type. Then again, I was starting to realize Byron Westcott was not what he seemed.

I got a third message a week later. In my email. It said simply: *Dear Sarah, you clearly have a problem and you need help.* Messed up, for sure, but

what made it worse was two things: it was right after I'd gone on a job interview at a design firm not
too far from campus. That, and I never gave Byron
that email address. He shouldn't have known it.

Needless to say, I didn't get a callback from that
interview. Am I being paranoid? Maybe.

I did my best to forget and move on. I deleted
him from my social networks and my phone. Not
only did I not contact him again—I did my best
not to think about him at all, as if just thinking of
him might summon him again, like some demon.
Things resolved themselves a few weeks later. My
mom passed away. I sold her house and moved
back to Buffalo.

I managed to almost forget about the whole incident, until Isabelle Herrera contacted me out of
the blue . . .

I lower my phone. Is there any point in finishing? I
know where it goes from here.

The question is whether it's all believable. A lot of
things seem contrived—as if she was making connections
where there were none. But with everything else . . .

A small cloud pulls over the sun. The dregs of coffee in
my cup are cold. I gather everything on the tray to take indoors but I barely have time to pick it up when the phone
dings with a voicemail.

Crap. Why didn't it ring? I pick up the phone and listen, my heart speeding up unpleasantly.

"Hello." I recognize Lucy B.'s annoying vocal fry at once. "This message is for Connie Wilson. Dr. Hassan would like you to come in for an appointment as soon as possible."

# CHAPTER EIGHTEEN

My peaceful morning blown to smithereens, I race to get dressed. It's not until I'm already driving away from the house that I remember I'm supposed to be impeccable Connie Wilson, lawyer's wife, and my outfit of T-shirt and jeans doesn't suit at all. Whatever. I don't want to waste time, and they probably won't even notice.

When I walk two blocks from where I parked, I see Lucy B.'s car in its usual spot, in the lot next to the clinic. It takes five minutes to find a pay phone but once I find one, I call the towing company and let them know that a car is parked illegally in the parking lot of my establishment and then hang up and take my time walking back to the clinic.

Lucy looks at me unsuspectingly as I walk in, and I return the condescending smile she gives me before turning her attention back to the screen of her computer.

"Excuse me," I say in the most saccharine tone I can

muster, "I just saw a car being towed from the lot. Little blue Honda? Is that the car of one of your patients, by any chance? You should probably warn them."

I hide my grin as she turns back to me, blood rushing away from her face. "Oh my God," she groans, stretching out the vowels unnecessarily like she always does— *gaaaaawd*. "Oh no. Shit." She realizes she swore out loud and looks at me with a panicked expression. "Sorry. One minute. I'll be right back."

She gets up in a rush, making her desk chair clatter, and runs out of the office. The door swings shut behind her, and I wait for another two beats before I get up too. Dr. Hassan hasn't noticed she left yet, and I figure the car business will take a good five minutes to sort out. Without wasting another moment, I walk over to her desk and peer at the Mac screen.

Sure enough, she's been browsing Facebook. Her full name, it turns out, is Lucinda Burke, and her profile picture is of her on a beach—how trite. She's grinning and holding one of those tacky drinks of every color of the rainbow, an alcoholized sugar bomb with an umbrella sticking out of it.

On the desk itself, there's one of those bobblehead figures of a character from a popular TV show, a pack of gum, a stick of lip balm, and—jackpot!—a wallet. I pick it up and rifle through her cards in search of her ID and then put the wallet back just as I hear her thundering steps in the hallway outside. By the time she bursts through the door, furious, tears streaking her face, I'm already sitting primly in my chair. Waiting to be seen.

\*   \*   \*

"Why did you call me in? Is something wrong?"

There can't be any new developments—I'd done all the tests months ago, their conclusions not very reassuring. But I knew that already. Could something new have turned up?

Dr. Hassan sits behind her desk, hands folded. "Not at all. I just feel like we need to get some things taken care of up front," she tells me in her velvety, tactful voice that she probably reserves for giving people bad news.

"This is about money," I say, and my own voice falters. My contentment about my coup earlier evaporates at once, and I feel dumb and petty for even bothering with such childish games. "I have it. I just need to—"

"It's not just about the money," she says firmly. "I rushed things with you last time, I'm afraid."

"What is that supposed to mean?" I ask, wary.

"You were emotional, and you clearly needed to feel like things were moving forward—"

"Well, yes," I say. And is it any wonder? She's been stringing me along for months now.

"But I'm afraid there are some necessary steps we need to get out of the way before we can proceed further," she says gently. My heart clenches. "There are some forms for your husband to fill out before we can begin."

"Forms? We already filled out the forms, didn't we?" Or, rather, *I* filled them out, artfully forging "Bertrand's" loopy signature.

"There are more. Pertaining specifically to your husband's health. My secretary was supposed to give you those some time ago, but there must have been some kind of mix-up."

"But I already started with the hormones." I'm already suffering the nausea, mood swings, and hot flashes like I'm about to go into menopause, and she's yammering about forms?

"Then the sooner you return these to me, the better. There's a health questionnaire, and of course, he's going to have to come in in person."

"Why? All he has to do is jerk off into a cup," I snap. A look close to shock crosses Dr. Hassan's face, and I'm instantly horrified with myself. How crass of me. That's not like me at all. It's something I should have left in the very, very distant past, the words of another person, someone I am no longer. That person is very much gone, and good riddance.

It's true though.

"Sorry," I murmur, unable to help the fact that I'm not sorry. What does she want from me? More importantly, under what pretext am I supposed to drag Byron in here, and how to explain why he's now Bertrand Wilson, the lawyer? He'll think I've completely lost the plot. "It's just I want to get this underway as soon as possible."

"Connie, we talked about this. You will need patience. And your husband has to take a blood test, among other things. In order to be successful, we need to be thorough."

"You never said anything about a blood test."

"I did. When we first started discussing your options."

I have no memory of this. She sighs patiently. "It won't

take more than fifteen minutes of his time. And I'm sure you both want a healthy baby, don't you?"

"I— I'll see what I can do," I murmur. I'm utterly thrown by such a loss of control over the situation. I don't know what to say or how to act. God, I just want to leave.

"Have him give Lucy a call at reception and schedule an appointment," she says, smiling, no doubt trying to be reassuring. "Then we can settle the financial matters and move forward. Finally. Which is what you both want, no doubt."

Numbly, I nod along. She has no idea, no fucking idea how far those two seemingly simple things are out of my reach. Struggling to contain my emotions, I thank her and shake her hand.

I'll think of something. I'll find a way. I'm me, dammit, and I got this far.

As I leave the office, Lucy B. is hammering something angrily into her keyboard, and she doesn't even look up. Thank God—at least I'm spared the humiliation of having her see my dismay. Tears fill my eyes, blurring my surroundings. I barely make it to my car, and only then do I cover my face with my hands and let the tears flow.

It takes me nearly a half hour to calm down. When I inspect myself in the mirror, my face is a fright, my eyes swollen, my nose red. And I can't go back home without a solution. All kinds of crazy ideas race through my mind, each more improbable than the last, until I realize there's not a thing I can tell Byron that won't give away the whole game.

Asking him flat out is simply not an option.

I will think of something, I say to myself. Out loud, to make the words a reality. I will think of something. And then there'll only be the money to worry about, and I can handle that.

The painting. I make a mental note to get the key to the basement so I can search for it. I'll turn the whole house upside down but I'll find it.

My phone buzzes in my purse, making me jump. With increasing dread, I dig for it, not daring to guess who it might be. Not my sister again. She's the last person I want to talk to right now.

Dread changes to shock and confusion when I see Byron's number on the screen. And confusion, in turn, gives way to fear. *He knows*, flashes the panicked thought in the back of my mind. He knows I'm here! He found out.

"Hi," I say, answering the call. My voice is shaky.

"Hi, honey." He sounds distracted. "How are you?"

I tell him I'm all right while I scramble to figure out why he might be calling. What day is it? Nothing special. I didn't forget any special date or anyone's birthday.

"What are you doing right now?" It's a question the old Byron would ask, the Byron who was still head over heels in love with his young wife. Those sexy conversations while he's at work—so not something I would do with anyone but him, but with him, it was a turn-on. It was naughty and sexy and playful, not slutty. But judging by his tone, it's not one of those conversations.

"I'm in town," I say, doing my best to sound nonchalant. "Doing a little shopping. Why?"

"Our anniversary is coming up," he says. "This week-end." Not the wedding anniversary but the day we met.

"I know."

"I was thinking that I can take Friday off, and we can have ourselves a little, impromptu long weekend. What do you say?"

I'm too astonished to speak, not daring to believe it. "Friday? I . . . I guess Friday is—"

"Friday is perfect," he says. "I'm looking at this romantic little cabin right now. On the lake. The forecast says the weather will be great. You'll love it."

"Byron—"

"Just agree," he says, voice pleading, like a child begging for candy. "Please? It's been so long since it was just us."

It's just us every single goddamn day, I want to say.

"What I mean is we could really use the time off. Just to relax and unwind."

"Okay," I say. A little tremor in my voice gives away my excitement despite my best effort. Okay. It's all going to be okay.

Before I drive off in the direction of home, I find Lucinda Burke on Facebook and copy and save her profile picture into my phone. Staring at that grin of hers and the tacky drink, I almost feel forgiving, magnanimous in the light of this latest happy development.

Then I remember her rolling her eyes at me. I email the picture to myself, put my phone back in my purse, and then drive home.

# CHAPTER NINETEEN

*You have no idea what a snake you have married. How horrible and deceitful and untrustworthy she is.*

*She thinks no one saw her going into that clinic. She even used a fake name. But I was watching. I saw her go in, and I counted the minutes she was inside: forty-three minutes total, in and out, like she was going for a teeth cleaning. I can't help but wonder what other lie she will concoct to cover up what she's done. I'm filled with fury on your behalf just thinking about how she manipulates you. She knows you'll be happier if she lets you go but she won't. Instead, she schemes to have her way, to trap you in your loveless, miserable marriage forever.*

*But I saw her. I know what she's up to, and I know her true face, the liar that she is.*

*In the time I've been watching you both, I've begun to understand her. And to understand you as well. You're a*

*romantic, Byron, as your name would have it. You seek
things in people that aren't there but you want to see
them so badly that you imagine them. You think you married a beautifully complex soul, whose troubles stem from
the same place as her creativity. That's what attracts you
to women: You mistake the fact that they're troubled for
depth. But she isn't deep. Hell, she hardly ever creates to
begin with: She lounges around at home, binge-watching
cable shows and snacking all day. Only when you're about
to come home does she rouse herself, get dressed, throw together a dinner, and pretend she's spent the day in artful
contemplation. She fooled you but she doesn't fool me.*

*She goes behind your back, Byron. She schemes. This
stunt with the clinic is merely the latest of many, and many
more to come. You won't be happy until you're rid of her.
You won't be free until she's gone.*

*That's when I think I finally made my decision. Enough
observing. It was time to do something, finally. Something
real. Something drastic.*

*That day, when she left the clinic, I trailed her all the
way home, and she never noticed. And then, through that
bay window to your living room, I watched her collapse
facedown onto the couch and weep her heart out.*

# CHAPTER TWENTY

We leave for the cabin on Friday morning. It should be
ready for us by noon, Byron says as he loads our bags into
the car. I'm listless, doing my best to look forward to it but
for some reason, I feel on edge.

The description doesn't mention Wi-Fi so I fear the
worst. For the whole weekend, I'll have my phone as my
only connection to the world, and who knows whether I'll
have any signal out there in the wilderness. Byron actually seems happy at the prospect. "It'll be great," he says.
"Sometimes it's nice to look up from the screen for a few
minutes and look around you."

"A few minutes," I say pettishly. "Not three days!"

"Oh, Claire." He shakes his head but his expression is
that of endearment and not annoyance. "I forget. You're of
the internet generation."

"And you're of the rotary dial generation," I parry, but I

can't help but grin. He's managed to tease happiness out of me, in spite of everything. In moments like these, my love for him takes me by surprise, with a feeling like I'm being flipped upside down on a roller coaster: It takes my breath away, the memory lingering long after the moment itself has ended. But it's that same love I felt the moment I saw him, even though I didn't realize it yet. It's that love that kept me going for the last little while since he became cold, just the promise of it enough to get me through day after interminable day.

I fix my hair in the sun visor mirror. I let it be natural since I don't want to be the bore who brings her curling iron to a rustic getaway. So today, I let my locks fall flat against my head. My face looks more open, my forehead higher, the delineation of my head more square and austere. Without makeup, I look pale, and the crescents under my eyes are more defined. Subtly, while Byron is busy loading up the rest of the bags, I take a small tube of concealer out of my purse and dab it under my eyes with my fingertip.

As if he can read my mind, he climbs into the driver's seat and looks at me. "You look beautiful like this," he says. "I've always liked you natural." He caresses my cheek briefly, the gesture a touch awkward. He plays with the ends of my hair. "You should let your real color grow in," he says.

I laugh. I know I will never do that, and he probably knows too. It's just the thing men think they're supposed to say, as if it wins them some sort of brownie points. And we're supposed to find it endearing and cute, proof that they love us for the real us and not all the daily effort they can barely guess at. It's a social contract: They pretend to love the real us and we never let that effort lapse, ever.

The drive takes way longer than I thought. It's been two hours, and all I can see on either side of the road are endless forests, with farms here and there, like squares from a chessboard scattered randomly through the woods. Byron stops at a gas station, then buys a basketful of apples from a local orchard and, to my surprise, a bouquet of flowers, a tacky thing of multicolored daisies and echinacea.

I make sure to accept the bouquet with delight nonetheless but I can't help but feel a twinge of discomfort in the back of my mind. Maybe I'm reading into it a little too much but it seems like a sudden change. I tell myself he's making an effort, rekindling what we had, even though the very thought is insulting—what we had doesn't need to be rekindled. We're not that boring, predictable couple whose match was based on simple sexual attraction and who struggle to admit that the spark has gone out. What we have is magic.

Maybe that's why it seems so impossible to let it go.

The apples are mealy and sour so I throw mine out of the window when I think he's not looking. He's cheerful, humming along to an oldies station he finds on the radio—oldies to me, at least. He's being the old Byron. Or at least working hard to look like the old Byron.

The cabin is not what I expected either. He turns off the main road, and after a maze of country roads that go up and down hillsides until I'm borderline nauseous, he pulls up to a private road, the sign next to it reading THE MAN-

ITOU. To my apprehension, he turns down the road. Our bags slide around the back seat as the car lumbers down the dirt track.

The stickler in me wants to point out how wrong the name is, that it's an ancient spiritual concept and that using the word to name a rent-a-cabin is more than a little disrespectful. But in the old days, when we were happy, I never would have been such a killjoy so I let it slide.

The cabin is spacious—a first floor with a vast kitchen, living room, and bedroom, plus a second bedroom up on the mezzanine. But there's a run-down air about it. All the materials are cheap, the doorframes all have gaps that let drafts skewer the entire house, there are cobwebs on the wooden beams under the ceiling, and the kitchen appliances are older than I am. When I peer through a dusty window at the terrain in the back, there's a whirlpool under a tarp. The top of it is sunken under the weight of accumulated rainwater, and there are pine needles soaking in it. It looks anything but inviting.

Byron, on the other hand, seems oblivious to it all. As soon as all the bags are inside, he drops them by the door and makes a beeline for the giant fireplace in the living room. After fifteen minutes of fussing and prodding the damp logs with the poker, a weak fire finally starts.

"This is nice," I say, trying to convince myself more than him.

He gives me an apologetic look over his shoulder. "Sorry—it was so last-minute. And since the weather's this nice, it was hard to find anything better."

"We'll make the best of it," I say. Something I would have said in the happy early days.

"There's a lake out back, right behind the trees," he says. "And there should be a shed with a canoe and all the equipment. We could take the canoe out."

As I recall, the moment I set foot outside the car, mosquitoes the size of hornets had swarmed me, their tinny buzzing filling my ears as they attacked every inch of exposed skin. Taking the canoe out to their natural habitat is not high on my list of things to do. I did pack bug spray, didn't I? If only I could remember where it is.

"We can start a fire in the fire pit," Byron suggests, picking up on my lack of enthusiasm. "It'll keep the bloodsuckers at bay. And we can roast marshmallows."

We end up doing neither of these things. We unpack our bags and the cooler, and Byron starts to curse when it turns out, predictably, that we forgot a number of crucial things— such as salt and a corkscrew to open the three wine bottles he thoughtfully brought along. So we go to the cramped little grocery store in the nearest village and load up on overpriced essentials. The village is so tiny I could walk from one end to the other in a half hour, with no charm, no attractions, and not so much as a dingy coffee shop. Still, I find myself dreading going back to the cabin.

When we get back, the quiet is eerie, even with the crackling of the fire that fills the space with stifling, dry heat. When I go to the kitchen to make lunch, I discover that the water pressure is dismal and the hot water is lukewarm at best, no matter how long I let the tap run. That, and it smells mildly of sulfur.

We eat in silence until Byron gives up and goes to fiddle with the dated stereo system. After the meal, coated head to toe in mosquito repellent, I go down to the lake to check out the facilities.

The damp, mossy ground is soft, absorbing each step of my oversize rubber boots as I make my way down the narrow path and past the copse of trees, until I see the glimmer of water. Then the trees part, and finally I'm sort of glad I came here. It's a beautiful little lake, a robin's-egg-blue jewel reflecting the sky and the yellowing treetops. I can see the whole thing from where I'm standing but the small, rickety dock in front of me is the only one on the entire lake. Nor are there any other houses on the banks. Surely it can't be just us.

Forgetting caution, I advance onto the dock. A shabby little canoe lies upside down next to it. I crouch and then lie on my stomach and peer into the water. It's clear enough that I can see the bottom, the stems of water lilies and mysterious lake grasses, tiny gray fish darting back and forth. I get so lost in the moment that I lower my hand, letting my fingertips skim the surface.

The cold jolts me, taking me by surprise. I pull my hand away but the half second was enough to make my fingers go numb. My whole arm aches, and I sit up and then scramble to my feet, overwhelmed with the need to get away from the water.

"It's not really for swimming," Byron says behind me. I jump and turn around. "There's a cold underground spring that feeds it, or something like that. The website was honest about it. But hey, we always have that hot tub!"

"I didn't bring a swimsuit," I point out.

He winks. There's something grotesque about him winking—it makes him look silly, and silliness doesn't suit him. "It's just us."

"I'm not getting into a rented hot tub naked," I say with a small laugh. "I don't want chlamydia, thank you."

"You can't get chlamydia from a hot tub, you know."

"I thought you weren't that kind of doctor."

He takes my hand—the one that's still numb and cold from being dunked in the lake—and rubs it between his palms, working the heat gradually back into my fingers. Without letting go, he leads me back to the house.

Once we've explored the surroundings, he rekindles the fire in the fireplace while I start dinner. We decided to keep it in the spirit of the thing: two venison steaks we bought at the butcher's before we left, thick slabs of meat the color of black cherries. The gamey smell makes me a touch nauseous as I take them out of the fridge and un-wrap the blood-soaked paper.

It's the meal I made for him the very first time I cooked for him, in the kitchen of our house. I'm surprised that I had forgotten. Venison steak with a port reduction. I take the bottle of port out of the cooler and measure half a cup, using a coffee mug since I left the measuring cups at home.

Then I set about searing the steaks, and while they hiss in the pan, I go get my phone—to look up the recipe for the reduction, I tell myself. Only for that.

Two bars of signal. Much better than I hoped. My op-timism about the weekend renewed, I check something online, impatiently refreshing the browser window.

Still there. Which means she might not have noticed anything yet. But she will, and soon. I let myself smile with only my lips, my back turned so Byron can't see me, and put the phone down on the kitchen counter.

Ding.

It takes us both by surprise. Did it do this on purpose? I glare at it, at the email alert on the screen.

"Claire," Byron says, sighing. "Just put that thing away, please? Can't we just enjoy ourselves?"

"It's my writing account," I hear myself say. "I'll just look at it real quick."

"Your rejection letter will still be there on Monday," he mutters, but I'm beyond getting mad at him. I'm already picking up the phone. Somehow, I have a good feeling.

Dear Claire,

Thank you for letting me read your manuscript. While your writing style is beautiful and your prose is polished, I had some issues with the story that prevent me from offering representation. I found the portrayal of love excessively idealized, and the love interest a little too perfect. Characters in literary fiction must have flaws, and I kept waiting for the other shoe to drop because a character that perfect isn't realistic. As for the protagonist, I found her too naïve for someone who's been reborn every other decade for centuries. You have a great premise, but the characters need major work, so I'm regretfully passing.

"Well?" Byron is asking, but he recedes into the background, along with the room, the stove, the crackling fire in the fireplace. All is replaced by a tinny ringing in my ears. I blink, surprised at the grittiness of my eyes. Then I blink again, and everything is restored into order. The steaks hiss alarmingly, begging to be flipped over. I do that, ten seconds too late: The seared side is closer to charred.

Byron sighs, not having gotten an answer to his question, and goes to retrieve one of the wine bottles from the cooler. Absentmindedly, I listen to him huff and puff as he struggles with the cheap corkscrew we just bought.

Without another thought, I pick up the coffee mug with the port in it and drain it in one gulp. It's so sweet that my teeth echo with a dull pain but it goes down as smooth as grape juice. I refill the mug and take another sip, no longer caring if Byron notices.

He doesn't. He comes up behind me and hugs me, slipping his hands around my waist. "There, there," he says. "What does that woman know, anyway? You're brilliant. Do you want a glass of wine?"

I'm overcome with irrational anger at him. Fiery, searing anger that makes me want to spin around and hit him across the face with the heavy mug I'm holding—just smack it against his jaw, blindly, with all the strength I have. Of course he knew it was going to be a rejection. He never would have married me if he thought I might be threatening to his superiority in any way. No, he gets to play the dejected genius reduced to teaching teenage ingrates, and I'm just his wife, waiting for him with a steak dinner on the table every night. I must never do better than him.

"Yes," I say. "I'd love a glass of wine."

It's that red he likes, way too dark, too bitter, brimming with tannins so strong it's like biting into an unripe persimmon. But it will do.

"Slow down, honey," he says when I drain half the glass.

I make myself smile.

We end up eating slightly overdone steak with slightly runny port reduction. He makes sure to praise it far more than it deserves—if it's a bid to make me feel better, it accomplishes the exact opposite. At least he's topping off my wineglass without missing a beat, and without unnecessary remarks.

"You should have let me read it," he's saying. I have trouble focusing on his words. His face, too, seems to blur around the edges. I'd chalk it up to the wine but the rest of my senses are still sharp as glass. My husband's image shifts and changes before my eyes like a reflection in a funhouse mirror. He tilts his head, and suddenly, his strong jaw looks misshapen and grotesque, his nose long and pointy, his eyes small and too dark, glinting maliciously from beneath low brow bones. He makes the slightest movement, the light falls differently, and he's back to normal again, as handsome as the day I first saw him, the day I met him, and the day I married him.

"I offered, didn't I? I used to critique ten of these in one week for my workshops. I could have—"

My head hurts. Why does he keep blathering on? Can't

he see that I'm squeezing my temples without being subtle about it? He doesn't seem to care. He never notices things that inconvenience him anyway.

And I'd never, ever let him read it. I feel weird letting him read my work but especially this book, with the main character so blatantly inspired by him. By the person he used to be anyway.

Dinner is thankfully finished, and we're on the couch with the TV on, watching nothing in particular on a local channel. The couch is as uncomfortable as it looks. I finish the last dregs of wine in my glass and put it on the floor. Byron is eating ice cream out of the carton, and he offers me a spoon. I accept, more out of compliancy than because I really want any. It's salted caramel, his favorite that I can't stand. By now I'm drunk enough that I can't taste much.

The idea comes to me in that moment of drunken brilliance. I take the container and set it down next to the glass and then make a move right for my husband's lips. To my surprise, I meet no resistance, and our mouths collide with a soft, wet smack.

"Claire," he murmurs. I can taste the salted caramel. "Stop. What are you doing?"

I pull the hem of his shirt out of his waistband and find my way underneath. I still feel the solid wall of muscle but now there's a bit of softness overlaying it, just a tiny bit of flab. When did that happen? I wonder. When I plunge my hand under his waistband, what's there is soft too. He used to get hard from the slightest touch. But now no amount of kneading seems to have any effect.

He mutters my name under his breath, catches my wrist, and removes my hand from where it was.

My lips shape the word *why*.

"You're drunk," he mutters. "Totally shit-faced. You had a whole bottle to yourself. I should have watched you."

"I'm fine," I protest, but when he gets up from the couch, I realize I can't follow him. With a sigh, he leans over and picks me up like a child, under my armpits. My legs hit the floor.

"Come on," he's saying in my ear. "To bed."

That's not how I imagined it. I make protesting noises, which he ignores as he hauls me up the stairs. I can barely stand so he has to carry me, and by the time we're on the mezzanine, he's sweating. I catch a glimpse of his red face as he lets me drop onto the bed.

He pulls off my socks and then my jeans. I go still and quiet but my hopes are in vain. There's nothing sexual about any of it; he might as well be undressing a doll or a child. He tucks the cover under my chin; it smells too strongly of bleach and detergent, and I picture all the other strangers that used it in the past days, weeks, months. The thought brings an unexpected tide of nausea. Closing my eyes, I groan.

"I'll get you a glass of water," he says, and I listen to his steps growing farther away and then down the stairs. The floorboards creak as he paces.

I never notice whether he brought me the water. Next thing I know, I'm waking up but it's not morning. Everything around me is dark, so dark I might as well have gone blind. My head pounds, and my mouth is dry and foul tasting. I attempt to sit up but the slightest effort makes me feel like I'm about to throw up.

I hear something familiar through the thrum of my headache: a series of creaks coming from downstairs. He's pacing again, I realize. Why isn't he asleep?

"I don't know what else to do," comes his hissed whisper.

Then I realize there's a second sequence of creaks, entirely separate from the first. I freeze, incomprehension and disbelief warring with caution. He's not alone.

"Well, this isn't it." The voice is lowered to the point where I can barely hear the words but I'm pretty sure it's a woman. "Make her believe you love her again. It can't be that hard. She's obsessed with you—"

"It's not that easy," he snaps. "What do you think it's like for me?"

"Just do it. Be nice. Be a loving husband. You have no choice. She's starting to suspect something, don't you see?"

"Good," he spits. A stunned silence follows. I hold my breath.

"No. Not good. We talked about this. As far as she's concerned, you're head over heels in love with her, and you have to convince her. Fuck her if you have to."

The word is like a gunshot, nearly tearing a gasp from me. I clasp my hand over my mouth.

"You should leave," Byron says coldly.

"No way."

"Leave," he repeats. "Now, before she wakes up and sees you."

"Okay," she whispers. "But I won't be far."

More floorboards creak beneath soft, feminine steps, and then the door closes softly, followed by the click of the lock.

Then everything goes quiet.

# CHAPTER TWENTY-ONE

For the first time in what feels like forever, I wake up with my husband by my side.

Sunlight pours into the cabin. In its brilliant rays, everything looks different, dustier and shabbier. I sit up, disoriented, trying to untangle the dreams from the memories.

There's a glass sitting by the side of the bed with a couple of gulps of water still left at the bottom. I pick it up and finish it greedily but it's like a drop of rain in the Sahara.

I turn to look at Byron, peacefully asleep in spite of the bright sunshine. Confusion stirs in the back of my mind. Was it real? The eternal question. I pull my knees up and rest my forehead against them, closing my eyes. Red pulses behind my shut eyelids. When I look up again, he's still there. He winces slightly, his mouth twitches, and as I lean closer, he murmurs something too faint for me to make out.

Still, my mind makes its own interpretations. Somewhere deep down I'm certain he whispered, *Colleen*.

Byron opens his eyes.

"Curtains," he says. "Close them. Claire?"

I just blink, as if I've forgotten how to move.

He sighs and sits up. "Good morning," he says with res-
ignation. "It's only seven a.m. We don't have to get up. But
someone has to close the curtains."

"Was there someone else here?" I ask.

He looks utterly confused. He rubs his eyes. "What do
you mean?"

"Last night." I already feel foolish, and it only gets worse
as I watch his expression shift from confusion to annoyance.

"No. I went to sleep less than an hour after you. Slept
like a rock, for once; it must be this air...What do you
mean someone was here? Did you hear something?"

"Did you lock the door?"

"Of course I locked the door. And turned the latch too.
No one could have come in."

"Someone else does have the key. The owner?"

"Yeah, but...listen to yourself. Why would the owner
come here while we're sleeping?"

I shake my head, trying in vain to get rid of the nausea
and headache. "Never mind. I'm going to make coffee."

*     *     *

Byron ends up making coffee while I make breakfast. He
opened all the curtains, and all the windows that have

screens, and I can't help but feel exposed, like a zoo animal. We dance politely around each other in the kitchen, and I keep glancing sideways at him for cues. But he acts perfectly normal, and no matter how hard I listen for anything strange, any steps or creaks that seem out of place, there's nothing but the normal noises of the forest.

Byron eats with enviable appetite while I push my scrambled eggs around my plate. He hardly looks surprised. He doesn't seem to notice at all.

"Was I very drunk last night?" I finally ask.

He shrugs, barely pausing between mouthfuls. "Drunk? You had too much wine. Mixed with the fresh air, it goes to your head faster."

"Did I make a fool of myself?"

Another shrug, but he glances away this time. I lower my gaze to my plate. Maybe I did get drunker than I thought. Maybe I dreamed the whole thing.

I pour myself more coffee and drink it too fast, scalding my palate.

"Careful," my husband says. I look at him and realize he's been watching me, intently, this whole time.

The day passes by lazily. We take the boat out in the afternoon, with me perched on the bench at the front and Byron in the back, rowing. The mosquito repellent hardly works, and I keep slapping at my arms and legs in exasperation. Even the thick wool of the knit jacket I'd borrowed from Byron doesn't seem to be much of an obstacle for the vile creatures. On the other hand, Byron doesn't look bothered at all; it's as if they don't notice him.

The lake is breathtaking, mirror-still, reflecting the sky

and the treetops that have begun to yellow, but I can't focus on any of it. I just want the torture to be over, to be
on solid ground again, hopefully indoors where the mosquitoes can't get to me.

Byron keeps talking about how lucky we are to have
gotten the place at such short notice, and it's too bad it
was at the last minute because he would have loved to
have borrowed some fishing rods to see if there were any
trout in the lake. "I bet they're as big as a dog," he says.
"Have you ever been fishing?"

I shake my head and slap my hand down on the mosquito that just landed on the side of my neck. When I take
my hand away, there's a tiny smear of blood. Itchy welts
are already developing on the backs of my hands and under my sleeves. Great.

"Ever gutted a fresh fish before?"

"Ew," I say with a small laugh.

"No worries—I'll show you."

"I'd rather not."

"It's really simple. I just wish I had something to catch
them. Maybe I can improvise." His eyes are glittering.

"Oh, no."

"Wait. Let me check." He reaches into the pocket of his
windbreaker, the ugly old thing I keep insisting he throw
out. "Hang on. Hold this for a second."

I hold out my hand, and an object lands in it. I grow
still. It's a flat, rectangular velvet box.

"Well?" he prompts.

Holding my breath, I open it to reveal a pair of gorgeous drop earrings. The gems catch the sunlight and light

up from within, with a neon-green fire too intense to have come from a lab. Emeralds. To go with my ring.

"Byron," I say. A smile blooms on my lips, uncertain and shaky, but still.

"You really think I forgot what day it was?"

To be honest, I didn't think he cared anymore.

"I'm afraid I don't have anything for you," I say. "I hadn't realized we were exchanging gifts." And the truth is I had a gift planned for him for months—but thanks to Rea and Dr. Hassan, with her bureaucratic bullshit, that gift is off the table until I figure something out.

"I don't need anything," he says. "And that's the point of a surprise. I wanted to surprise you."

He certainly has.

"Why don't you put them on?"

I'll look ridiculous, dressed in Byron's oversize sweater and my big rubber boots, my hair flat and face plain, but with emerald earrings that skim my jawline. I murmur something to that effect.

"Nonsense," Byron says. "Put them on!"

"I'll drop them in the water."

He doesn't look pleased but lets it go. I look for a place to put the box where it'll be safe from the damp and finally put it in the pocket of the giant, shapeless sweater.

I should be happy but my joy is like a stone stuck in my throat. They're beautiful, just what I like, and clearly expensive. But why did it have to be platinum and emeralds?

Like the ring—the real one, not the copy.

Colleen's birthstone.

Throughout the rest of the day, Byron's mood only gets better. We make a fire outside—it turns out Byron was right; the smoke does seem to keep the mosquitoes at bay—and we have cups of hot chocolate spiked with brandy. He makes lamb skewers on the grill outside. I do my best to say yes to everything, trying not to think about how I'll barely fit into my jeans when we get home, but I'll have a whole workweek to starve myself back to my regular size. Those stupid hormone shots aren't helping. That's when I remember I missed the one yesterday and the one this morning.

Instead of running back to the house to check on the vials I brought with me in the usual hiding place, I ask Byron to pour me some of that brandy. Just a finger, please. I sip it slowly, letting it warm my insides.

It's well past eleven p.m. when we go back inside the house, only to realize it's freezing cold. We left the windows open, unwisely, and the day's warmth slithered away the moment the sun set. The whole place feels and smells like damp.

Byron goes around closing all the windows. "I'll just start the fire again," he says. "It'll get the damp out in no time."

I wish he'd just turn on the heat but in my yes-to-everything spirit, I let him start the fire in the fireplace. My face is overheated, my eyelids heavy. I let myself collapse on the couch. The springs still poke and prod me in the sides but I'm sinking into it, almost comfortable. I watch Byron arrange the logs in the fireplace, crumple up a piece of newspaper, light it. The fire devours it and jumps lazily onto the logs. Heat begins to emanate from them at once.

I watch Byron watch the fire, immobile. And then he half turns so I can see his profile, stark against the flames, and I'm stricken: There's something sinister about it, the outline of his nose and his hard mouth, the tilt of his head.

That's when he says the words, his tone casual yet inescapably deliberate: "So, are you going to try on the earrings?"

# CHAPTER TWENTY-TWO

"I don't believe this," Byron thunders. "How can you not know where you put them?"

"Your sweater!" I blurt, remembering at last. "The one I had on in the boat. I put them in the pocket."

He's facing me head-on now. "My sweater?"

"You saw me, right?"

In the firelight, his features are softer, yet the anger in them stands out starkly, lining his face with deep, dark shadows. His eyes glint with anger.

"And where, pray tell, did you put the sweater?"

I look around. Nothing on the arms of the couch, nothing on the hook by the door. I get up and circle the room with growing frustration, already suspecting, deep down, the sweater will be nowhere to be found.

"I . . . I don't know. I must have—" I'm blabbering pathetically but I can't help myself. The warmth is gone, replaced with a thin shiver that works its way up through my legs and core until it makes my teeth clatter.

"The last I saw you in it was on the boat," he says.

All I can do is shrug.

"Claire," he says, shaking his head. Exasperated. "Those were real emeralds, you know."

Oh, don't I know it. I want to cry.

"We're not exactly rolling in money either." Implying, *Thanks to you and your little shopping sprees when you should be looking for a job.*

"Then why buy them at all?" I snap, cornered.

"Because I wanted to make you happy, dammit!" he explodes. He gets up and starts to pace, like he's trying to crush something into the floor with every step. "You're completely losing it lately. I don't know if it's staying at home so much, or your writing, or—"

"It's not my writing," I say under my breath.

"You got so shit-faced last night you couldn't remember your name," he snaps. "All because of a stupid rejection letter. So don't tell me—"

"It's not my writing. It's you."

The last word rings out in silence. He's stopped pacing. "Me?" He lets out a shaky, disbelieving laugh. "You have to be joking."

"You hardly notice I exist anymore."

"Because I'm too damn busy trying to keep it all together! To keep food on our table, and to keep being able to afford nice gifts for you. Gifts that you see fit to leave all over the damn place."

I cover my face with my hands and groan. My cheeks burn with shame. What have I—

"The sweater," he says, and resumes pacing. "It's probably still in the boat."

"It can't be. I wouldn't have taken it off till I was inside, with all these damn mosquitoes—"

He exhales noisily, struggling to control his anger. "Claire, can you please stop talking and go get it before some raccoon takes off with it?"

I glance at the window with doubt. It's so dark that I can't see a thing beyond the windowpane. "Can't you go get it?"

"I need to stoke the fire. Do you want to stoke the fire, maybe?"

I shake my head. "Fine. I'll get it."

"Hurry, please."

I step into my rubber boots, which are waiting for me by the door. I think of throwing on my raincoat but decide not to. It's only a short dash through the trees.

"Take the flashlight," Byron says. "It's on the table."

Grabbing the flashlight, I step onto the porch and let the door swing shut behind me.

At once, I realize how thick the darkness is. It's almost physical, a living, black mass surrounding me, and all I have is the faint glow of the windows behind me and the thin beam of the flashlight.

I circle the house and find myself facing the copse of trees that separates me from the dock. Except in the dark, it's not just a few elms and skinny birches—it looks like an entire forest, thick and forbidding. The flashlight doesn't seem enough. Its beam looks dim and weak, flickering on and off. I give it a whack against the palm of my hand but it hardly helps. The beam trembles with uncertainty as I take my first steps into the trees.

It's not as scary as it looked. I walk ahead briskly until only a few steps separate me from the dock. My rubber boots make sucking noises with every step, sinking into the damp earth. I almost have time to get used to the darkness when my foot slips in the mud.

Everything reels. The beam of the flashlight draws a luminous arc as it slips from my grasp and drops to the ground. My behind hits the dirt with a dull thud that knocks the wind out of me. My teeth clack together painfully, trapping my cry. My hands land in the unappealing mixture of mud and pine needles. More icy-cold dirt seeps through my jeans. With a groan, I extricate myself. I can see the flashlight's lone beam through the trees, only a couple of steps away, but as I reach for it, it flickers once, twice, and, to my horror, goes out.

I get back on my feet, dizzy and disoriented. Only now I realize I'm tipsier than I thought. But the warmth is gone, leaving behind only the achiness and sour taste on my tongue.

"Byron!" I call out, but my voice, instead of ringing strong in the silence, comes out squeaky and weak. The wind carries it off, far away onto the lake. I try again with similar mediocre results. "Byron!"

I take a couple more stumbling steps and stop in surprise when the lake appears in front of me, seemingly out of nowhere. Here, without the trees to obscure my vision,

I can see a little bit better. The clouds don't entirely cover the thin sliver of moon, and a flat blue glow bathes everything. It's a breathtaking sight that I, a writer, should find it in me to appreciate but all I want is to get away.

I spin around, looking for the boat, which we had moored by the dock. Any moment now, I should hear its edge knocking softly against the post, along with the rhythm of the waves. But all I hear is soft splashing, the hum of insects, and the croaking of frogs.

Where's the boat?

There's no boat by the dock. Did it get unmoored and carried off? I advance toward the very edge of the dock and peer over the water. But the lake is still and mirror-flat, empty.

Turning around, I can glimpse the house through the trees, and the sight gives me some reassurance. The windows glow warm orange, seemingly so close. I contemplate just making the dash, grabbing Byron's sleeve, pleading him to come with me, and I'm about to make the first step when something among the trees moves. A shape darkens the window as it passes in front of it—a human shape.

"Byron?" My voice is a squeak. The shadow is gone—or not gone, just gone still, unmoving, invisible. Home—I want to go home, I think, fixating on the word, aware at the same time just how far away home is. Another thought crosses my mind. *Help.*

A branch snaps, sharp like a gunshot, so close. Too close. I jolt, buoyed by sheer panic. The flat, blue, alien landscape around me spins in the opposite direction. The boards of the dock creak, and to my horror, I feel one of them give beneath my weight.

My boot catches in the gap, and my foot slips free. The sky reels before my eyes as I topple backward, and a moment later, the icy water swallows me up. Cold wraps around me, trapping my scream beneath my skin. A million icy needles bite my flesh. Water roars in my ears.

I flail my arms and kick my legs but the water slows me down, like a fly trapped in honey. My clothes soak it up like a sponge, my shirt turning to ice-cold lead that fuses to my skin. Dragging me down. To the algae and the darkness and the mud.

My feet connect with something...squishy, spongy, grasping at my ankles and pulling me deeper in. I kick with all the strength of desperation, and for a moment, I break the surface. Scalding air fills my lungs, and I begin to cough, but just as soon, the mud pulls me under again, my nose and mouth and ears flooded with bitter lake water.

Help. Help.

My lungs are on fire while the rest of me is slowly turning to ice. I have to find more strength to kick. I'm going to drown oh my God I'm going to drown help me help me help me Byron Byron please—

An invisible force pulls me up, tugging against the resistance of the water. The lake doesn't want to let me go but the pull is stronger, and a moment later, I feel the air on my face again. Water rushes out of my nose and mouth, and I take my first shaky breath. My wet, heavy hair clings to my face, obscuring my vision. All I can make out is the dark figure, grunting as it pulls me with all its might onto the bank.

It drops me there, and like a sack of wet sand, I sink to the mossy ground, gasping for breath and coughing for my life. As if my body only now realizes the danger, it begins to shiver with surprising force. My teeth clack so hard my jaw aches. I clench and unclench my frozen hands but can't feel them.

"Claire?"

It feels like I've been lying here for a year, opening and closing my mouth in mute shock like a fish.

"Claire?"

There's the dull thump of footsteps on the ground, and then Byron leans over me. "Oh my God, Claire. What happened?"

Without waiting for an answer—as if he knows the answer—he grabs me under the armpits and hauls me up. "You're soaking wet," he says, and he doesn't sound all that shocked. "You fell into the lake?"

Yes. I fell. I fell—that's what happened. I fell.

Then who pulled me out?

He did, of course.

But didn't he just now come running?

I close my eyes, powerless, as he picks me up and carries me inside.

Everything else is in snippets.

Byron stripping away my wet clothes, the soaked, ice-cold fabric stubbornly clinging to my skin until I think it's going to come away with it, leaving me red and raw.

Byron again, rubbing the circulation back into my legs,

my arms. The fire crackles. Byron tilts my head and makes me drink something lukewarm and bitter—tea? I sputter but with every gulp I take, my core grows warmer, and then the warmth spreads into my limbs, rushing to the surface of my skin until I'm warm and comfortable and sleepy, oh so sleepy.

Byron, carrying me upstairs, my head lolling against his shoulder. This is nice, I find myself thinking. Like the good times before.

(Didn't he just come running?)

(Who pulled me out of the lake?)

Byron lowering me onto the bed, into warm, clean sheets. He tucks the blanket under my chin. The lights go out.

Just like before.

When I come to next, it's because the bed creaks and tilts. I faintly make out Byron's shape on the edge of the mattress, hunched over as he gets undressed. Then the blanket shifts as he climbs underneath it. His touch is cool on my overheated skin, waking me up a little.

He fumbles, and I can feel his warm breath on the side of my face. On it, I smell brandy—copious amounts of brandy. Enough to make me wince. He doesn't notice. He plants a slobbery kiss on my temple. The kisses travel down my cheek to my lips. I mumble something into his mouth when it closes over mine. *I can't breathe; stop it.*

His hands are everywhere, on my stomach, kneading my breasts, between my thighs.

Hot, boozy breath carries a raspy whisper. "Open your legs. Come on—open them."

*Stop it. I want to sleep.*

"Come on, Claire." He nudges my thighs apart and rolls on top of me. I moan under his crushing weight.

"That's right." The blunt tip of his penis nudges the inside of my thigh. He guides it with his hand, panting heavily into my ear. It goes in, unceremoniously, and that first push is painful enough to jolt me fully awake.

"Shh." He begins to rock back and forth, thrusting. It's dry, uncomfortable, but my flesh becomes used to it and parts obediently. After a few thrusts, there's no more resistance. I don't have the strength to say or do anything so I just relax into it, let myself float under the ceiling. I don't know how long it goes on; can't be that long but I have time to drift in and out of consciousness a couple more times before he grunts, gives a last deep thrust, and I feel the scalding rush of his come on my raw insides.

"There you go. Good. Good girl. Sleep now."

I don't need permission.

I let myself collapse back into the quiet dark, like I never left it.

*       *       *

The next morning, I sit up, confused. It takes me a moment to figure out where I am: What is this shabby place, what is this light? Why does my body feel like it's been gutted hollow, even my bones?

Then memory comes rushing back.

"Good morning," Byron says. He's standing on the stairs leading up to the mezzanine, steaming cup of coffee in hand.

*Don't even think of pretending none of it happened, again.*

"Good morning." I'm appalled at the hoarseness of my voice.

"Did you sleep okay?"

Is he joking? I sit up and feel the soreness between my legs. A little bit of warm liquid slithers out of me and stains the sheet under my behind—a sensation I despise. But it's proof, ultimate proof that I didn't dream it all.

I know I need to keep playing along, keep being the fun wife. I open my mouth to say yes, I slept okay, and how are you, but instead, my mouth twists, out of my control, like that of a child about to throw a tantrum.

"I want to go home," is all that comes out. I want to go home, go home, go home. The words blur, deformed by the sobs that shake me.

Within a heartbeat, he's by my side. "Claire. Oh my God, darling, what's wrong?"

"Just take me home," I whisper.

(Who pulled me out of the lake?)

"Is it because you fell into the lake? It's my fault. I should have gone to get that stupid sweater. I'm sorry."

It's all I wanted to hear yesterday. God, it feels like a year ago. And today, it's no longer enough. "Home," I repeat, like the same obstinate, annoying child. "Home, home, home."

"Claire," he says, stern now but still kind. "It could have happened to anybody. The lake is only a couple of feet deep by the shore anyway. Nothing bad could have happened."

I give a single shake of my head.

And I watch his expression shift and change, the loving look slipping away like it was never there. His lips press tightly together, and the lines on his face deepen, showing his real age, reminding me of that gulf between us.

Without another word, he starts to pack our things.

By early afternoon, we're driving up to the house. I never thought I could be this relieved to see the place. He has yet to say a word.

He gets out of the car, and I notice, finally, that he's wearing the sweater. The same one that was supposedly left in the boat that wasn't there.

He's unloading the bags, and still, I can't bring myself to move. To will my hands to unbuckle the seat belt, to open the door, get out. Go inside.

My phone buzzes. I reach into my purse, too tired to imagine who it might be.

An email. I thumb the screen to open it.

How did you like it, Claire? How did you like to drown?

I stare at the screen in mute horror.

Did you like drowning, Claire?

No no no no, I try to say, but my mouth only forms shapes, not sounds. This isn't right, this isn't right, she didn't drown, she isn't dead—

Sender's name: Colleen.

# CHAPTER TWENTY-THREE

"That's so messed up. Did you see that thing in the paper?"

I pull my gaze away from the surface of my coffee. "What?"

"The article in the online *Star*. Some woman was doxed. They put her address and phone number in a fake escort ad online. Scary stuff."

I blink at him. My brain seems to have forgotten how to process simple information. "What woman?"

"No idea. Some receptionist. Isn't that scary though? What's surprising is that it doesn't happen more often. It's the age we live in." He sighs and shakes his head.

It's Monday morning, and we're having breakfast together at the kitchen counter, like before. Miracle of miracles. But I'm too out of it to appreciate it. Or to appreciate the story of the poor doxed receptionist who got swamped with calls asking for sex over the weekend before finding a fake escort ad with her address and phone number in it. They took her picture from her Facebook profile. She had to go stay at a friend's because she feared for her safety.

"What a time to be alive," I say mechanically, ready to be mocked by him for such stock platitudes. But he barely takes notice that I've spoken, already absorbed in another article on his iPad.

I try to remember what it is I had to do today. I think I had a busy, packed calendar but my mind draws a complete blank. It all feels like part of some other universe, one I am locked out of and have lost the key to. My goals seem so far away and about as realistic as climbing Everest in high heels.

Someone is trying to get rid of me.

There's someone else, another woman. Colleen? No, that's crazy. Although to be honest, nothing is too crazy after this past weekend.

But someone is trying to replace me, the same way I replaced Colleen.

I saw her. I heard her. She was real.

When the door closes behind Byron, I sit at the kitchen counter, alone, for twenty-three minutes and thirty-one seconds, according to the clock. I glance at my phone, which is lying facedown on the counter within arm's reach.

Did you like drowning, Claire?

Reluctant, I pick it up. But there are no strange messages, no weird emails. And the incriminating one vanished overnight—it doesn't even surprise me this time.

Well, whoever this woman is, she will find out that Claire Westcott will not give up without a fight. I get up, head straight for Byron's office door, and tug on the door handle.

It's locked, which is something he started doing recently and thinks I haven't noticed because I never brought it up. Luckily for me, he hasn't figured out that I found the key. It's in the living room, in an ornate box stashed on one of the shelves. The box is a trophy from some fancy trip he took with Colleen a long time ago, and it contains a litany of small objects that didn't have their place elsewhere: lonely buttons, random coins, a sole earring, a stray cuff link. Also, a nondescript key that, after trying it all over the house, I figured out opens the office door.

Of course, ever since he started locking the door, he takes the key with him to work. But way back when I first found it, the first thing I did was make a copy, just in case. Despite what Byron might think of me, I always think of the future.

The lock is well-oiled, and the office door creaks quietly as I slip in. The term *man cave* comes to mind when I look at Byron's office: with walls densely covered with books, black-and-white photo prints framed on the desk, and his computer. Not the sleek little laptop he takes with him everywhere, but the desktop, a heavy and somewhat outdated beast that he won't replace with something more practical because he's just so used to it.

Usually, a man's private computer is his territory. Any woman knows better than to snoop in it because she won't like what she finds. But I'm not put off. I know that Byron, like any man, watches porn semiregularly. I know what kind, and frankly, it could be a lot worse. I never understood women who got their panties in a twist about porn. If anything, it's a harmless way to let off steam. As for my husband, he doesn't even have a favorite video— whatever random thing that's free and available seems to get the job done.

But that's not what I'm here for.

I turn on the monitor, and the welcome screen comes on. My first unpleasant surprise is that his password has been changed. It used to be our wedding date, which I found kind of sweet when I figured it out. But now I enter it only to be met with an error message.

I frown, my hands hovering over the keyboard, ready to enter something else. No. I need to think about it. I don't know how many attempts I have before the system locks me out. I try Colleen. Nothing.

I'm not sure whether to be relieved or alarmed. Drumming my fingertips on the desk, I think. Colleen plus her birthday doesn't work either.

Holding my breath, I enter COLLEEN04112010.

I hit Enter, and my breath escapes from me in a rush when the screen blinks and the desktop appears.

Her death date.

Facing the desktop with its image of a Bali beach and

its rows of icons, I chew my bottom lip. Finally, I decide to start at the beginning. His email is already open, one of the many open windows and even more numerous open tabs. Hello, westcott.byron@mansfieldcollege.edu! I don't even have to sign in.

Squinting at the too-bright screen, I scroll through generic messages from the college, emails from Emily and Andrew, and Amazon receipts for books he bought.

I'm ready to give up when a message catches my eye. It's one of those automatic emails. Your booking has been confirmed!

I glance at the date. Two months ago. An unpleasant tremor travels up my spine, and I click on the email. It opens, and I find myself looking at a familiar picture: an image of the cabin. It's a pretty, promotional photo taken on a bright autumn day, and it looks like a postcard, idyllic and welcoming. The cabin looks much nicer than it actually is.

Your booking for 09/21-09/23 is confirmed, I read. Below is the address of the property as well as the conditions. Please remember that, in case of cancellation, a percentage of the cost will be charged to—

I stop reading. There's no need to continue.

So the last-minute getaway idea wasn't exactly that. I remember his sheepish look as he apologized for the shabbiness of the surroundings. *It was hard to find anything better.* Right.

This was planned. Yet I feel no anger, no betrayal, not even hurt. I'm just numb. And just like that, it occurs to me: Maybe it *was* planned. Just not for him and me. For him and . . . someone else?

Then things went sideways, and he decided to take me instead.

Guided by an unknown intuition, I click on the icon at the top of the screen. A drop-down menu unfolds, containing only one item: widower@yourmail.com, reads the address, next to a blank user icon.

My heart begins to pound, fast and dull, as I click and open it in yet another tab.

I'm greeted with a nearly empty screen; widower @yourmail.com only has a single message in it—a single thread, it turns out on closer inspection. Without letting myself think or second-guess, I click.

The latest message in the thread unfolds.

I don't know what else to do. I can't take much more of this. Do you have any idea what it's like to live with her? To have to fall asleep next to her every night? I don't know if she suspects something—by now, she very well might. But to be honest, I don't care. Some days, like this week-end, I think, fuck it, I can just leave. Cut my losses, as awful as it must sound. Hell, she can have the house. She can have all my savings, I just don't want to be around her for another minute. But, as you know, M., it's not nearly that easy . . .

Yours,

B.

My body reacts before my mind can wrap itself around what I just read. My eyes film over with tears, and pain squeezes my throat, so sharp it takes my breath away.

Wiping my eyes with the back of my hand, I blink away the tears and scroll up.

> You have to be patient, B. I know it's going to take a lot of patience, and a lot of work, but we have to do this right or who knows what might happen? It's the only way. You know I'll be there to help you with everything I can. You can count on me.
>
> M.

M. My mind reels back to the Facebook discussion. What was the name of that girl? The grad student the others were gossiping about. Maya? Mila?

Mia.

I remember without having to look. It's Mia, the girl who gave me the dirty look over the edge of her heavy tome when I came to the college that day.

Scroll up.

> I can't even look at her anymore, M. Some days I used to watch her flit around the house and wonder if this is all a mistake and whether I can turn back, start over. You must forgive me for such weakness. I know there can be no starting over and no uncertainty. I have to get rid of her. I just don't know how.

And the reply:

> You have to tread extremely carefully here, B. With what happened to Colleen and the others, the situation is precarious. I won't lie, it looks bad. With that history—and that history will come floating up first thing should anything happen to her—the police will jump down your throat. You should have been more careful from the beginning.

The answer, time-stamped a couple of hours later:

> Don't you think I know that? I realize it fully; I'm in deep shit. But imagine yourself in my shoes. I have to come home to her every day, eat the dinner she makes me, sip the drink she pours for me. Playing the perfect woman, the perfect wife. How could I have been naïve enough to fall for that?

Reply, within minutes:

> It's not your fault. Any man would have. Be careful with yourself, B. Be careful what you do. Love you.

> M.

I can't read any more. I lick my dry lips and then click the window closed.

Mia. Mia Mia Mia.

I get up with a clatter of the chair. A familiar feeling pulses through my veins, bringing me back to the real world—back to life.

No way am I going to take this lying down.

# CHAPTER TWENTY-FOUR

I park the car in the small lot behind the literature building, where I know Byron won't see me because he parks in the bigger lot out front. But I can see the entrance just fine from where I'm sitting. I have time. And I have patience.

Mia Mia Mia Mia. He's replacing me. Replacing me with a grad student! She's probably not even younger than I. She's definitely not prettier. If she were, would it be less bad? I don't know. It would make more sense.

In the back of my mind, I'm still wondering, guiltily, what I did to cause this. Because surely, I must have done something. It's my fault—I taught him to always expect the best; I got him accustomed to having his every wish and whim and expectation met and exceeded. Making fancy meals, picking out good wine, maintaining charming conversation with his work friends, wearing beautiful dresses and looking good on his arm at college events. And now he got bored, and what he wants is something new.

No, no. It doesn't make sense. Why her? That awful hair, the hipster sweater she had on that time. The lip ring. He's not someone who goes for a girl with a lip ring. She's vulgar, mundane. She's so—

In that moment, I see Mia exit the building, her bag slung over her shoulder, and the realization hits me. Despair fills my lungs slowly, drowning me from the inside. Now I see all the other things she is, plain as day. She has a slight figure, her breasts nonetheless prominent enough even under the baggy sweater—propped up by a good bra, no doubt. Plain black leggings hug skinny legs topped with an inexplicably round ass. She only looks stumpy because she wears ballet flats that threaten to fall apart with every step—the sole of the right one is coming unglued. She squints in the sun. I can see now that the weird bob haircut emphasizes her long, fragile neck— I could wrap my hands around it and squeeze squeeze squeeze until there was no breath left inside her, those full lips bloodless and blue, those big brown eyes filmed over, shocked and still. The too-short bangs bring out her high cheekbones and highlight full brows. And that dull hair color I made a mental note of last time lights up in the sun. It's a natural dark blond, like ancient gold. As she hefts her bag into the trunk of her car, a battered Ford, her sweater rides up, and I get a flash of a pancake-flat stomach with a glinting ring in the navel.

I'd looked Mia up on Facebook. Just before leaving, I sent her a friend request from my dummy account, which she accepted immediately. Her profile is weirdly minimal. Her profile picture is that of a cat—I'm assuming hers. She only reposts stuff about politics and books, not a single original status in the whole feed. Instead of discouraging me, this lack of insight spurred me on. I didn't even put on makeup before I left the house, and I'm a fright, my hair tied back with a headband instead of a proper elastic tie.

But if I do everything right, she won't see me.

I know the thing to do is to follow at a respectable distance but I'm jittery, my hands tight on the steering wheel and my foot jumpy on the gas pedal. Driven by the panicked thoughts of her making a turn ahead of me and vanishing into the thin early afternoon traffic, I take risks. Dumb risks. I cut off another driver, switch lanes when I shouldn't. Someone rolls down their window just to throw a few choice words in my direction, words that, today, seem to burn into my skin like molten metal. My eyes fill with tears that I have to blink away.

Get hold of yourself, I mutter under my breath. I'm drawing attention. Not Mia's, not yet, but Mia isn't the only one I must worry about. Actually, Mia is at the bottom of the list. I should be worrying about anyone who might be motivated to remember my car, my license plate. I should worry about getting pulled over and slapped with a ticket—the kind of ironclad proof that always comes back to bite you.

I've never been like that. I've always had an eye for detail. Did the last two years make me this soft and stupid?

I fall back behind a line of cars waiting at a traffic light, three or four behind Mia's little Ford. Her hand is hanging out of the car window, casually holding a cigarette. A smoker. Did I ever smell smoke on Byron when he came home from work?

I can't remember.

The point is, I try to tell myself, she has no idea she's being followed.

Luckily, this doesn't go on for much longer. She lives in a duplex on the edge of the student ghetto—the place where "fully furnished off-campus suites" rent for fifteen hundred dollars a month. In reality, these "suites" are crammed into century-old buildings with oppressively low ceilings and small windows, where formerly working-class apartments have been further subdivided to create studios the size of a closet.

Engine idling, I watch Mia park and then grab her bag and saunter up the stairs to the double doors of her building. These doors were once ornate but the paint has peeled and one of the glass panels has been replaced with cardboard. She shoves the door unceremoniously with her foot and goes in, letting it swing closed behind her. It doesn't shut all the way, leaving a gap a few inches wide.

I stop the engine and get out of the car. Now what?

I could call and figure out a way to get her out of her apartment—if only I'd done my homework. But I don't have her number. I think of all the occasions I'd had, over the last two years, to snoop in Byron's office and get the info on everyone he comes into contact with, and groan at the missed opportunity. Maybe I did get soft and stupid.

But no sooner do I get back into my car than fate smiles

on me. Mia is leaving. She's had time to change into one of those baggy dresses and into a different pair of flats, this one not in quite such a state of disrepair. She's firing off texts as she hops down the stairs, never looking up from her phone, smiling at the screen. She's put on lipstick, I notice. The lipstick is garish orange, and for a moment, I think I must be insane. There has to be some mistake. She can't possibly be the other woman. Byron would never trade me for this.

But then I think about Colleen. If Colleen were alive today and a couple of decades younger, that's exactly how she would dress. Ugly on purpose, defiantly showing off how much she doesn't care about whether people find her attractive.

Mia looks up from her phone, her grin widening. I follow her gaze. There's a guy. She runs up to him and puts her arms around his neck. He dodges her lipsticked kiss, and it lands on his jaw instead. He puts his arm around her waist and off they go, unaware of my bemused gaze.

Unbelievable. Beneath the rage I'm already feeling, a new emotion briefly flashes: anger of sorts but on Byron's behalf. To have a man like Byron besotted with you, and to still need more. The nerve.

I make sure they're gone from sight before I start the car and park it a few streets down. My ragged attire serves me well. I blend in, unrecognizable. Not that there are many people to see me. Most of the neighborhood's inhabitants are in class right now.

Minutes later, I'm climbing the same stairs leading up to

the front door. The door doesn't lock so I go in and find myself in front of another staircase. It's all so small that I'm suffocating; my head all but brushes the ceiling above the stairs. From the mailboxes, I see that Mia Flynn lives in apartment 3. I climb the stairs and knock softly. Then I try the handle, keeping an eye on the other door across from it just in case.

Locked.

If I know anything about these buildings, they have balconies in the back. I go back outside and circle the building, going through a narrow alley. I need to maneuver around garbage bags and giant recycling bins but it turns out I was right. I can see the back window of apartment 3 from below. It's a French window, and right now it's open, nothing but a ratty sliding screen door to keep the world out. Metal stairs lead all the way up.

The sliding screen door is held in place by a latch but it's easy enough to make a neat hole in the net using the metal nail file I have in my purse. And I'm in.

I look around cautiously, a part of me still disbelieving. But then again, it makes sense. It's clearer to me now why she never noticed I was trailing her. It's for the same reason our generation—well, not me, but others my age— posts their location and shots of themselves dancing on the bar on public social networks. They haven't learned to be afraid. She has no reason to think someone might take enough interest in her to break into her apartment. Carelessness mixed with a hefty dose of delusions of one's own immortality.

The kitchen is an appalling mess. I almost gag as I take

in the sight: dirty frying pans on the stove, a mountain of dishes in the sink, a packet of instant rice on the counter, and the rice itself scattered on the stove top, practically fused to it with congealed fat. A cat enters, stretching. It yawns at me, unsurprised. I give it a look of loathing as it hops right onto the kitchen counter and, unfazed by my presence, begins to eat the bits of rice.

I never liked cats. My sister did but I always thought they were dirty, nasty creatures. They bury their shit in the litter box and then go on the kitchen table with those same paws. Byron suggested we get one once because he thought I was getting depressed, sitting at home alone all day. He thought it would do me good to care for something.

But I don't want a cat. It's a baby I want.

As I walk past the cat into the main (and only) room, the mess only becomes worse. There's dirty underwear on the floor, and I kick it squeamishly out of the way. Clothes are piled on every piece of furniture, stacks of books sitting here and there on the floor among the chaos. Empty cans of Diet Coke with cigarette butts crushed on top of them. The bed is unmade and half-buried in more clothes. And amid all this, the desk is curiously clear, only a neat stack of books and notebooks and a pen. I don't see a laptop or tablet anywhere. When I open the lone drawer, it's overflowing with stuff she had probably swept off the desktop: bits of paper, hair clips, miscellaneous junk.

One of the spines of the books jumps out at me. It's wrapped in brown paper, old-school. I remember seeing this book. She was reading it the day I came by Byron's office. A massive, heavy, old-looking hardcover.

I pry it out of the stack and open it.

The title page stares back at me.

THE MAGUS BY JOHN FOWLES, it reads in a small, retro font on yellowish paper.

This is Byron's favorite book, I think dully to myself. No, not just his favorite book. This is *his* book. The physical copy that used to sit on the bookshelves back at Colleen's house before migrating inexplicably to the office. Original first edition. Don't know how much it's actually worth but it's damn near priceless to him.

I slam the cover shut like something might leap out of the pages and bite me. My ears are ringing.

Mia Mia Mia.

I sweep everything off the desk onto the floor in one movement. I yank out the drawer and upend it onto the desktop and onto the floor; little papers scatter all over like scared butterflies.

I tear through the apartment like a tropical storm, an unconscious, unstoppable force. I shred clothes that get in my way. I smash dishes, tear pages out of books. A black veil of pure rage falls over my vision. It's only happened once or twice before. I don't think about what I'm doing anymore—I just coast along on the powerful pull of my id.

When the veil drops, I find myself standing in the middle of the destroyed room, panting. My hair has escaped from the hair tie and falls into my eyes, sticking to my sweaty forehead.

And someone is knocking on the door.

"Hey!" A muffled voice comes through the thin panel. "Keep it down in there. People are studying, you know!"

The understanding of what I've done crashes over my head. Oh shit. What was I thinking? How could I?

Panicked, I spin and spin around, as if I've forgotten which way is the exit. I stumble to the kitchen, tripping over the things I threw on the floor. The cat considers me with round-eyed indifference. God, I want to wring its stupid, skinny neck.

"Mia?" The pounding on the door resumes. "Is everything okay? Mia?"

I flee through the kitchen door, out onto the balcony, down into the alley, then to my car. When I turn the key in the ignition, I feel another stab of that disorienting, panicked feeling. It's past five in the afternoon. Where did four hours go? Oh God, Byron must already be on his way home. I hit the gas pedal and pull out of the parking spot. I do everything on autopilot, on the setting of Good Wifey Claire: drive back, stop at the grocery store, buy things for dinner—random things that don't go together that I just throw into the cart without thinking too much. Pay, load up the car. Drive back home. Pull into the driveway.

Except I realize at the last second that I can't—another car is blocking the way, parked illegally at the curb in front of our garage. I stop the engine and storm out, ready to smash the windows and key the paint and kick the doors until the damn thing is totaled, but I stumble and come to a halt.

There's a figure standing on the porch. A woman, in

too-tight black leggings tucked into those awful cheap boots. I can only see her back—boxy denim jacket, brittle hair pulled back in a ponytail—but then she turns around, and I stop cold. My mouth forms her name before my mind fully connects the face to it. "Chrissy."

# CHAPTER TWENTY-FIVE

"Hi," she says. Her smile is shaky and supplicating. She clasps her hands in front of her chest, and I can't stop staring at her nails: a tour de force of hideousness, acrylic pointy ends with some kind of plastic design glued to them. She always was the tacky one. "I couldn't get hold of you so here I am. You look nice."

"You ambushed me?" I ask in a low hiss. "How dare you."

"I didn't ambush you. We need to talk..."

"My husband is coming home soon. And when he gets here, you'll be gone."

"I'm afraid not. We're talking about this. You owe me, remember? Mom's life insurance? The money from the house?"

I spent the money a long time ago, and she knows it. On college tuition, on books, on piano lessons that never

came in handy, on the cooking and wine-tasting classes—
all the things she never would have considered in her
wildest dreams. Ways of self-improvement, something my
trailer-trash sister wasn't keen on.

"If that's what it's about, why did you show up here? In
front of my husband's house? When he's coming back any
minute? Cut the bullshit, Chrissy."

She gives a single hoarse laugh. "Oh, there she is. My
little sister. This life suits you."

I scoff.

"I have my own nail salon now," she says, her hooded
eyes boring into my face. "In Cincinnati. I put aside
enough money, finally, and I'm buying a condo. Not that
you care."

She's right. I don't care in the slightest.

"I have a boyfriend, too, you know."

I can't help but chuckle, imagining.

"Yeah, yeah, laugh. He may not be a literature professor
or anything but at least I didn't have to scrap who I was
to get him, am I right?"

And what you are isn't much, I think. My mouth twists.

Chrissy sees it and shakes her head. "Don't put on airs.
*Claire*." She shakes her head in disbelief. "Jesus. I never
thought you could pull it off—"

"Then maybe you underestimated me."

"Oh, I don't think I have. I think you've bitten off more
than you can chew, little sis. I think it's all closing in on
you now."

I draw a breath through flared nostrils. "Leave."

"Or what, you'll call the police? That won't happen."

"What do you want, Chrissy? You didn't drive up from Cincinnati to insult me. What, you didn't scrape together quite enough money for that one-bedroom with a garden view? You want cash?"

"For fuck's sake!" She takes a menacing step toward me, and I back away instinctively. "I wish I could shake some fucking sense into you. I don't even care about the money, you hear me? I don't care. I mean, you're a little shit for pocketing Mom's life insurance, selling the house—sole inheritor, my ass. No one ever notified me that Mom died. That's what it's all about. She died, and I learned it six months after the fact! I didn't even go to the funeral because I didn't know there *was* a funeral. How can you think you can possibly make it up to me?"

"If you'd ever called or visited, you would have known," I say dryly. I'm not going to put up with her shit, not going to let her stand there and spew venom. She's the traitor. She took off and never looked back and left me with that fucking alcoholic monster.

"How could I possibly have come back?" she shrieks. "With Mom in that state, out of her mind all day long, and you too, completely going off the rails? I was lucky to get away. Or I would have ended up like her." She glowers at me, her eyes shiny with tears. "Or you."

"Yeah, sure, it's better to glue rhinestones to strippers' acrylic talons all day long."

"Maybe," she says, sucking in a breath. "Maybe. Maybe you think it's a shitty life but at least it isn't all a lie."

She storms to her car. She's crying now, her tears tinged with cheap mascara.

"I'll come back," she says as she climbs into the driver's seat. "And we'll talk. We're not finished here."

"Yes we are."

But she's already slamming the door. The engine starts with a cough that grows to a hoarse roar, and for a moment, I'm dead certain she's about to slam her foot onto the gas and try to run me down. The hairs on my arms stand on end, and instinctively, I get out of the car's way, ducking behind my own. But she just screeches away from the curb and careens down the street.

Crash, I catch myself praying silently. But she doesn't crash, of course. She takes the turn at the last second and vanishes from sight.

Numb, I go into the house. It greets me with cool semi-darkness. I plunk my keys onto the counter and collapse onto one of the chairs, remembering that I forgot the groceries in my car.

I stare at my hands with a sense of loss, like they're not my own. I notice that two of my fingernails are broken, their edges ragged and crooked. On one, the cuticle is bleeding. Must have happened while I was trashing Mia's place. I think of the little bits of fingernail lost among the chaos. Loose hairs, bits of dead skin I left in my wake. How careless. How stupid. She'll know it was me, she'll call the cops, and then...

And then nothing. She doesn't know that I know about the affair. Neither does Byron. No one has any reason to be looking in my direction.

God, I have a headache. On heavy legs, I plod upstairs to the bathroom and dig out the plastic bottle of Advil. I twist the cap off and dump two pills into my palm. Yet moments before I toss them into the back of my throat, something makes me pause. Pause and look at them. Really look at them. They grow blurry as I bring them close to my eyes. Then focused again. They're oblong, they're reddish brown, but that's all they have in common with Advil. Something about them is wrong. The surface is rough. They look like little alien eggs.

I put the pills back into the Advil bottle and hide it in the back of the medicine cabinet. Next, I head back downstairs but remember there's no wine—everything ended up down the drain. The realization sends me scurrying to the recycling bin, digging for the empty bottles. I sniff the gullets with suspicion but they only reek of vinegary old wine.

I really must be going crazy. It can't be, right?

It can't be.

The sound of the key in the lock takes me by surprise, and I get to my feet so fast my head spins.

"Claire?" Byron's voice.

"Here."

"What are you doing?" He appears in the kitchen doorway, still in his light jacket with his bag over his shoulder. He looks genuinely puzzled and a little annoyed.

"Just . . . I don't know."

"Is there anything to eat?"

I shake my head.

"What did you do here all day?"

I open my mouth but don't answer.

"Don't tell me you wrote. You haven't written in

months." The offhanded way he makes the remark hurts the most. I clutch my hands to my belly, like I've been physically wounded. *So you knew, then.* Yet he never let on, allowing me to continue the whole charade. I don't know what I think about that.

I make a split-second decision and go on the offensive. "At least I'm not screwing an undergrad behind your back."

Color drains from his face, and I realize how I screwed up. I showed my hand. This is bad. I must backpedal. He doesn't yet know how much I know—

"Oh God. You think I'm having an affair?"

"Aren't you?"

"No." A small chuckle escapes from him, as if the very notion was ludicrous.

"What about Mia?"

"Who— Oh." His shoulders droop. He looks relieved, I realize with dismay. A terrible suspicion creeps into my mind. What if I have it wrong? If it's not Mia, it's got to be someone else. And now I'll never figure it out because he's on his guard.

"Mia? Are you nuts? She's nineteen. And I'm pretty sure, from that haircut of hers, that she's a lesbian."

I saw her kissing a guy but I don't tell him that.

"Claire," he says, and takes a tentative step forward, "I'm not having an affair. You can't seriously think that." He makes a motion to take my arm but I move out of the way.

"Claire." A note of tension in his voice, not yet a threat. "I'm not a cheater by nature, Claire. I've told you this a million times. I'm a one-woman person."

He has. And I realize now that, sure, it could very well be true but I have always assumed that the one woman was me. But now it occurs to me that I might not be.

"I'm not having an affair," he repeats. He reaches out, and I let him brush the side of my face. The gesture, a reminder of how much he once loved me—how much I still love him, even right this minute, in spite of everything between us—almost hurts.

I step toward him and grab him, pull him close, and cradle his face in my hands.

"Claire—" he starts to say. Then, "Stop," but I don't want to be stopped. I kiss him hard on the mouth and start to unbutton his shirt. He shivers but he doesn't pull away. Once upon a time, I could make him rock hard in seconds with just the lightest touch of my fingertips, and I still can, and I'll show him; I'll show him no matter what it takes.

"I love you," I exhale in his ear. "I love you more than anything, and more than anyone else ever has or will love you. Do you understand that?"

His gaze meets mine. I look up close into those pale blue-gray eyes I once admired so much it hurt, and I don't see the man I love. I only see a glassy surface.

"Yes," he says, never blinking, and for a moment, I think I glimpse something beneath the glass, something mysterious and primal. It's there and gone again, like the splash of a fish on the surface of a still lake. "I understand."

He leads me over to the couch, untucking my shirt from my jeans as he does. He pulls it over my head, violently. My hair tumbles out of my loose ponytail and falls around my face, crackling with static.

"Byron," I murmur, but he's already moved on to my jeans. He yanks the button, then grabs the waistband and pulls it apart until the zipper pops. "Byron!" I say louder, my voice hoarse. "What are you—"

He pushes me—shoves me in the chest so I lose my balance and fall on my back on the couch. He pulls the jeans down my legs, rough, careless, leaving burning skin in his wake.

"This is what you wanted, isn't it?"

He stops, panting, glowering at me as he straddles me, and I realize he's expecting an answer. I give a tiny, terse nod.

"The love. The marriage. Sex. A baby. Is that what you want, Claire? A baby? *Then* will you be satisfied?"

A smile spreads over my lips. "Yes."

"Will you do anything you have to do to make it happen?"

"Yes." No hesitation.

He lowers on top of me, unbuttoning his pants with one hand. His weight pins me to the couch, and I put my arms around him and then my legs as he finds the right spot and begins to thrust, his muscles rippling in my embrace.

My husband. My Byron. My love.

I'm not letting go of what we have so easily.

# CHAPTER TWENTY-SIX

*I screwed up. I screwed up so bad.*

*If you knew, you'd never want to even look at me. I'm so ashamed. I feel like I failed us both, failed our future—failed fate itself. I only needed to do what had to be done, and I screwed up. Now the plan is all messed up, and I don't know how it's going to play out.*

*She saw me. I made a mistake, I was sloppy, and she saw me. Now she knows my face, what my car looks like. She must have followed me, somehow, without me noticing. I got overconfident, sensing the end was close. I forgot to pay attention, and now I'm going to pay the price.*

*She knows I exist, when she never should have known. No one else does. Not even you, my love. That's disastrous enough on its own. But she also knows my license plate number; she knows where I live.*

*She knows about me; she followed me. And now she's coming to my home.*

*I don't know what to do.*

*I have to think fast.*

# CHAPTER TWENTY-SEVEN

I wake up the next morning with renewed hope. I swear to God, for the first time in months I feel hopeful, happy, and full of energy.

Byron wakes me up with a kiss. Just like old times. While he's splashing in the shower, I get out of bed and put on the pink satin robe he gave me for Christmas last year. In front of the mirror, I quickly fix my bed hair and pinch my cheeks so there's color in my face. I'm still a little gaunt, worn-out-looking from all these months of unhappiness, but I'll recover. I just need to take care of myself. To start paying attention to the little things again. And everything will be back under my control in no time.

While I'm making breakfast, I hear the shower stop and then his footsteps upstairs as he gets dressed. Coffee is already hissing out of the spout of the coffee machine. Eggs

sizzle on the stove. I make three for him, two for myself.
And I'll eat every bite, and the toast. I set the plates and
cups on the table so that everything is ready and served
when he comes down.

I greet him with another kiss. I catch him watching
me with astonishment as I shovel scrambled eggs into my
mouth.

"Storing up for winter?"

I give a laugh and try not to choke on my mouthful.
Then I notice that his plate is barely touched. He follows
my gaze. He must notice how my smile fades because he
hurriedly picks up his fork.

"I want us to do something special this evening," he
says.

"Special? Should I make reservations?"

"No need. Let's have dinner at home. But afterward, I
have a surprise for you."

"Okay. Any special requests? Should I wear something,
or—"

"Whatever you want. You always look great in whatever
you pick. You have an innate sense of style, have I told
you that?"

Yes. He has. I remember everything he ever told me.
But I don't say so; I just nod and laugh.

Tonight, he finishes work at six. This leaves me just
enough time to do everything I have planned.

I have a busy day ahead of me.

\*　　\*　　\*

The first thing I do is call Derek Hollis. I get his voicemail and leave a message, doing my best to sound casual and vague enough to intrigue him. Sure enough, fifteen minutes later he calls back, and we agree to meet.

There's nothing new in my email this morning. Still, my faith in my novel is somewhat renewed, and I email a couple of literary agents on my list.

Ideal love is possible. Perfect happiness is not naïve. And I'll show them—Colleen, my sister, Mia, the world. I'll show them all.

After much deliberation, I decide to dress businesslike for my meeting with Derek. After all, that's exactly what this meeting is about: business. I don't want him to think it's about anything else. So I put on the pencil skirt and blouse I bought when I thought I was going to be looking for a job. I've lost a little weight since then but I still look my best, the fitted skirt highlighting the slender curve of my hips, the cream silk blouse complementing my skin.

Sadly, as soon as I open the door of my car, I'm assaulted by the stench of something rotten and remember the groceries I forgot in the trunk. Trying not to breathe, I extract them, tie the plastic bag, and throw it in the trash can. Then I saturate the inside of the car with air freshener spray that instead reeks of synthetic lemons. It's not much of an improvement.

Anyway, none of it is important now.

Nothing can stop me.

I arrive at the same café where we met the first time, early and nervous. Since I'm already jittery, I get a chamomile tea to calm my nerves while I wait and check my phone every two seconds.

Where is he? We said we'd meet at noon. It's 12:02. My foot does a nervous dance, bouncing in its low-heeled pump. Maybe I should text him; 12:03 now.

*Ding.*

I jump at the message alert on my phone. God, don't tell me he's canceling. What am I going to do? I can only keep stalling for so long before the doctor gets suspicious and starts asking questions. I need his help.

I glance at the phone screen and frown. It's not a text, it's an email, and it's not from Derek. It's from a vaguely familiar address.

I tap on it to open it. My gaze strays along the rows of words, snatching out one or another out of order, unable to make sense of them.

Bafflingly unprofessional . . . disgraceful. Small industry . . .
word of mouth . . . total lack of self-control . . . seek help.

Seek help?

What?

I feel myself sinking into unreality again, like I did back at the rented cabin. Like I did too many times recently. The world around me recedes into the distance, becoming distorted. A fog fills my head. The tiny screen of my phone blurs, and I have to squint to make it come back into focus. I zero in on the beginning of this missive, whatever it is. Dear Claire . . .

"Hey! Claire!"

My head snaps up, and I see Derek, looming over me. I didn't see him come in. Or hear him call my name. Which, judging by his mildly impatient tone, he did at least a couple of times.

I don't have time to wipe the look of confused devastation off my face, and he mirrors it.

"Is something wrong?"

Considering our last conversation, it wouldn't be a far reach to assume that. I make myself smile.

"Oh, no. Not at all. Just got a...weird email. Doesn't matter." Remembering my manners, I turn off the phone and turn it over, screen-down. I get up and give him the customary loose hug and peck on the cheek. But he's keeping his distance, I notice. Like I have a cold he's afraid to catch.

I need to distance myself from this slipup before I can broach the subject. "Did you want to get a coffee or something?"

He shakes his head. "I'm good. I'm actually kind of in a hurry..." His glance strays, fleeing mine in shame, and I understand that he's not in any hurry at all. *This is bad, Claire, very bad. You fucked up.* The smart thing would be to abandon mission, try on another day. Or better yet, get someone else.

But who?

"Oh, please, have something. It's my treat."

"I really shouldn't—"

But I'm already getting up, fumbling for my wallet. He's clearly uncomfortable but he asks for a coffee, black. I take my time getting it and bringing it back. Noticing that he doesn't touch the cup I've set down in front of him, I fidget in my seat.

"You look good today," he points out.

Yeah, last time we spoke, I was a complete mess. Thinking about it momentarily fills me with shame. But I accept the compliment as you're supposed to, with grace.

"Things have been going better," I say offhandedly, and take a sip of my chamomile, remembering how much I hate chamomile and tisane in general. It's as bad as last time. "With Byron. I just wanted to tell you how much I appreciate your help last time. And that you came down to meet me today too."

"Always happy to help," he says. If not for his orientation, I'd assume he's flirting with me. And by this point, men usually become compliant. But I must tread carefully. "I'm glad to hear things are improving. So anyway, how *is* Byron?"

Just as I open my mouth to tell him Byron is great, as great as can be, something occurs to me. "What do you mean, how is Byron? Don't you guys see each other, like, every day?" I barely notice that I let a *like* slip into the sentence, a verbal tic I eradicated years ago. Byron hates girls who say *like* every two words.

He shrugs. "It's a big campus. And besides, he's been out a lot—home sick, he says. Bad back? Something like that?"

I'm caught unawares, staring back at him with round eyes like a cat. "Yeah," I say, smiling. A touch too late. "He has back problems."

Absent from work a lot? He's been doing overtime. Or

so he told me. I think of the surprise he was telling me about this morning and try to tell myself that maybe it has something to do with that.

Yeah, right, says a sarcastic little voice in the back of my mind. I momentarily screw my eyes shut. I won't think of it right now. I must focus.

I ask Derek how he's doing, how his boyfriend's art exhibit went—I think it was an art exhibit he went on and on about at that party when last I met him. I could be completely off the mark and would never know it because I can barely bring myself to listen to the answers. Maybe his boyfriend is a writer like me, or maybe he makes avant-garde sculptures with animal bones and computer parts. Who knows? Who cares?

Then, when Derek's body language relaxes again, once he leans closer like he trusts me, I lean in too and tell him I need a big favor.

He listens to me, perfectly still. A couple of seconds tick by. Maybe more. The coffee shop buzzes like a beehive, the noise setting my teeth on edge.

"You're completely out of your mind," Derek finally says. I spring back instinctively. The look on his face isn't neutral anymore. It's a look of shock. I completely missed the moment it made the transition. "You're crazy."

"Listen," I implore. But he pulls away. It's too late—I know it. I fucked up. Again. "It's just— It's the only thing that will mend our relationship. Don't you see? Byron and I will never end up like his marriage to Colleen. The reason it fell apart is because she couldn't give him a baby, right? Isn't that what you said?"

"I never said any such thing." He gives a vehement shake of his head. "And right now, to be honest, I'm starting to regret I told you anything at all."

"So I have to give him one. A child. He'll come around once I give him the news. I just know it. The thing with Colleen left him cynical and bitter and disillusioned but I can fix it! I can fix everything."

I stop when Derek shakes his head with a look of disbelief, and jump right back in, breathless. "But there's one problem. It has to be the real thing. I don't want him to know I did in vitro. I want it to be a miracle baby, made with love, not in a tube. It's the only thing that can make a difference at this point. And he'll never find out you helped!"

"Helped? You think that's helping? You just asked me to go to a fertility clinic and pretend to be your husband."

"So?"

"Should I also jerk off into a cup while I'm at it? Byron won't find out, after all."

"No!" I laugh nervously because the suggestion is so ludicrous. He has no idea or else how could he even have thought it for a second? Me, having another man's baby. "I'll get him to do it. I thought of a way—"

"Do you hear yourself, Claire? This is completely insane. You are insane. You should see somebody."

He gets up, nearly tipping over the chair.

"Derek," I plead. I must stop him—I must at least stop him from telling Byron. "Wait. I can pay—"

"You have problems, Claire," he spits. "I feel very sorry for you." His face twists with disgust. No one ever looked at me like that. Not for a really long time. Claire doesn't provoke disgust or pity; Claire is admired and envied and wanted.

Rage makes my throat clench.

"Then fuck you," I snarl. "Fuck you!"

He turns to go, and when I pick up my cup and throw it at him, it misses his head by inches. The cup crashes to the floor, breaking into a hundred pieces. Someone shrieks. Everyone turns around to look. Tears fill my eyes.

Derek doesn't turn around. He walks out without another glance at me.

I wait until the door closes behind him, flee to the bathroom, and then make my escape through the back door. Once I'm behind the coffee shop, in the stinky alley next to trash bags and recycling bins, I let myself sob.

*     *     *

Fine. Whatever.

I'll pay off Hassan. Ten thousand dollars in cash—that has to be good money even to a doctor. It's only a matter of finishing what I started.

I always finish what I start.

The house is empty and drenched with sunlight, in sharp contrast to my mood. As if even the weather is laughing at me. Stupid girl. What did you think you were getting? A little suburban dream? True love eternal?

I slam the front door behind me and catch my breath. The living room reels before my eyes, lilac walls, Colleen's murky painting above the couch—everything as I left it, familiar. Yet different. Like someone came in while I was gone and moved the furniture, the knickknacks, the photos and paintings, the TV, just a couple of inches in the wrong direction. Everything the same but also wrong. Unwelcoming. A house but not a home.

I slide to the floor and bury my face in my knees. In my back pocket, my phone buzzes.

I take it out and look at the screen. I can't focus at first but then my husband's name swims out of the blurriness. Hi honey. Don't forget about the surprise tonight!

A sharp exhale leaves my lungs, like a sob. I thumb the screen, unlocking the phone, only to find myself staring at the mystery email from earlier.

Bafflingly unprofessional behavior. The phrase leaps out, searing my eyes. I read the message over and over, trying to put the words together.

I jump to my feet so fast I get vertigo. The moment everything steadies again, I race upstairs and get my laptop. Then I plop down into a kitchen chair, flip it open, and click on my email.

The same message splays out across the screen. I reread it again, just to be sure. Now I recognize the sender's name and address.

I have to shut my eyes for a minute. Gold sparks dance under my eyelids, and I dare hope that, when I open them again, everything will be different. The message will be gone, and the incident earlier will be just a bad dream, and everything will be fine again, as it should be.

But when I look at the screen again, it's all still there. The house has sunk into silence, punctuated only by the muffled chirping of birds outside the window and the distant ticking of the clock in the living room. The air here, in the kitchen, is hot and stifling. I'm starting to sweat.

I click on the Sent folder. There they are, in a neat row: messages without a subject line, to each and every agent I'd emailed about my book. I open the first one, and my gaze races up and down the lines of obscenities. Uncomprehending. I didn't write this.

I'm reasonably sure I didn't.

This can't be happening, I think, confused. A stupid thought. Of course it's happening—it's right in front of me.

Letting go of the breath I was holding, I close the laptop lid. Where to now? I circle the first floor, as though the living room couch and bay window and decorative vases might hold answers. Then I go to the garage.

The place is dusty and neglected, Byron not being the most hands-on type. There's an old bicycle there and plastic boxes filled with old junk—mostly my stuff from my old apartment, from before Byron. If there ever was such a time *before Byron*. It feels like there never was a time I didn't know him. A time when he wasn't constantly on my mind, even when I was doing something else. Cooking, writing, getting my hair done, cleaning the house, shopping for winter boots—and him, always him, on my mind every second of every day. He wasn't always the focus of my thoughts but he never left them, always there in the background. He never even knew it. Was I on his mind the same way? I don't even need to think about it.

Was Colleen?

Good God, I'm thinking of my husband like he's some apocalyptic event. A world war or tsunami.

I spin around. There are a few tools hanging on the wall, and I grab the biggest hammer I see. It's ice-cold in my hand and heavy as lead. Good.

I take it back into the house. To the door of the basement. I try the handle first, and only once I've made sure it was locked, I swing the hammer and smash it into the lock. The impact travels through my bones and makes my teeth clack but I clench my jaw and ignore it. I swing the hammer again, and again, and again.

The door splinters, and the lock comes loose. I pry it out with my hands. A splinter sinks into the pad of my thumb. I pull it out with my teeth, barely aware of the pain. I faintly realize I'm leaving behind a small smear of blood as I reach along the wall to flip the light switch.

It smells like dust in here, dust and old things. I make my way down the stairs. The lone light bulb swings on its cord, illuminating stacks of boxes. Colleen's easel stands in the corner, covered with a piece of plastic. It casts an enormous shadow on the wall behind it, crouching there like a monster.

*Why couldn't you just forget her? Why couldn't you leave her in the past?*

I pull the plastic off the easel and then topple the easel itself onto the boxes next to it. The boxes topple in turn, and their contents spill all over the floor. The cloud of dust that rises makes my eyes and throat itch. But there it is, rolled up, just like the last time I saw it, the painting from the bedroom. I unroll only the edge to make sure. I don't want to see it right now, don't want to lay my eyes on that obscenely embracing couple. The thought alone makes me feel dirty.

I tuck it under my armpit, and that's when my gaze falls on the array of small objects scattered at my feet. I crouch, then kneel right on the dirty floor and pick through the objects, one after another. Just miscellanea: half-empty, calcified tubes of paint, sponges, brushes, a bottle of nail polish, a pen. I follow the trail to the box lying on its side and turn it upright. There are more things in it, at the bottom. I plunge my hand in, and my fingertips find something soft.

I pull out a small plush toy, a pink teddy bear. It has that eerie aura of a thing never used. It's dusty and smells faintly of damp but the fur is still new and glossy, the colors unfaded. There's even a little tag still attached to its paw.

What?

I grab the box and upend it, unable to hold in a little shriek when I see the things that tumble onto my lap. Clothes. Tiny clothes, pink and white and lilac. I hold up a tiny sweater with the tag still on—just like the teddy bear.

It's impossible. Impossible.

I unfold it. On the front, a pattern of sewn-on flowers.

This can't be. It's not possible. She—

I pick through the rest of it in a panic: baby clothes, baby shoes, a rattle, a doll.

There can't be any doubt.

I pick up the sweater again, bring it close to my face, and breathe in its smell of dust and synthetic fibers.

It can't— I don't believe it. I don't even notice when I start to cry until I break out in full-on sobs, my body shaking.

\* \* \*

The ringing of my phone pulls me mercilessly back to reality. I sit up, disoriented. What is this dark, dusty, ugly place?

Then I see the sweater and the toys, sitting in a pile next to me. I swing at them blindly and send the teddy bear flying across the room.

The phone keeps trilling stubbornly. I paw around for it and look at the screen: an unfamiliar number.

"What?" I snarl into the speaker, shocked at the hoarseness of my voice. "What do you want?"

There's no pause or hesitation on the other end. The voice is male, young sounding, devoid of emotion but polite. "Ms. Connie Wilson?"

I shut my eyes, trying to control my dizziness. Something is very wrong here, but what? It's like one of those puzzle pictures, and I can't make any sense of it. "Yes," I say, snapping back to my well-mannered self on autopilot. Thank God.

"This is the Mansfield Police Department, ma'am. I was given your contact information by Dr. Hassan at the Ova Clinic."

"Yes," I repeat dumbly. "It's me."

"I just have some routine questions. As you might know, the receptionist at the clinic, Ms. Burke, was the victim of a serious cybercrime—"

I tune him out. Cybercrime. What, are they joking? How can they call me at a time like this?

"Ma'am?"

"This isn't a good time," I say flatly and hang up. I half expect the phone to ring again but it doesn't. Blessed quiet surrounds me. That's all I want. Quiet.

Lucinda Burke, that awful, impertinent girl with her smacking gum deserved what I did to her, and if anyone asks me, I don't know a thing. They can't prove it. They don't even know who I am because I gave them a fake name and they never bothered to check my ID, as long as I kept forking over their exorbitant fees.

I scoop up the sweater, the one thing that's still within reach. I press it to my cheek and then curl up in a ball and close my eyes.

*     *     *

"Wake up. Hello."

Byron's voice above me, soft and gentle. Oh God, what have I done? Where am I?

I'm passed out on the floor, on the pile of unworn baby clothes.

Colleen's baby's clothes.

The baby she never had, because she went to the clinic and had an abortion. She did—I know she did. Otherwise... What if I had it wrong, and she didn't go through with it? Changed her mind at the last second? Decided to keep it? But...

This can only mean that she was pregnant when she died.

Byron is going to kill me, I think. But I can't bring my-self to panic. Everything is dull, my emotional responses blunted.

"Claire, get up." He leans over me, his broad back blocking the only source of light.

"No," I moan.

"Yes. Come on. Up you go. Let's take you upstairs."

"I don't want to go."

"You have to. I have a surprise for you, remember?"

I don't want a surprise. I don't want anything. Just leave me alone, please.

But he's already threading his arm around my waist, grabbing me under the armpits, and hauling me to my feet. My knees buckle, and I refuse to stand, slumping against his shoulder.

"Stop it," he chides in my ear. "Walk."

I won't walk. When he realizes it, he groans but lifts me up into his arms and carries me upstairs.

There's too much light in the living room. The window is dark but it feels like every light in the house has been switched on. God, just dim it all a little, please. I can't take it.

I turn my head and bury my face in Byron's neck. He smells like soap and cologne and shampoo, a familiar scent. A scent I used to love so much I'd keep one of his shirts next to me all day just so I could take breaks from whatever I was doing to press it to my face and bask in that scent again, even for a second.

"Claire," he says. "Wake up. Be an adult."

They were going to have a baby after all—a girl. It's all

so close to coming together in my head. But the jagged
pieces float around and never connect fully. The answers
slip away. I never stood a chance, from the very beginning.

Everything I've ever done was fucked from the beginning. It was all for nothing.

It's the only thing I know for sure.

"Claire," Byron says again. He sits me down on the
couch, like a doll. He folds my hands in my lap, and I
don't move. I look straight ahead and blink.

"There," he says, taking a seat on the armchair across
from me. "Good. We can talk now."

"There isn't anything to talk about."

"Yes. There is."

"I don't know what's happening," I say, shocked with
how broken and plaintive my voice sounds. "I do things
I don't remember doing. I sent emails that I didn't send.
Everything is such a mess. What's going on, Byron? Can
you tell me what's going on?"

"I think you know pretty well what's going on . . .
*Claire.*"

"Was my sister here?" I crease my forehead. "What did
she tell you? She's a liar, Byron. She's an evil, malignant—
You can't believe a word she says. She's poison. It's all her
fault. She set me up—I'm sure of it. It can't have been anybody, anybody . . ."

I trail off. My face goes numb when he slowly puts a
little square box on the coffee table.

"Do you know what's in there?"

I look up into his face. Seeking . . . answers. Seeking

anger, love, pity—something. But there's nothing. No emotion at all. Like there never was.

"I found it. I found the ring."

My breath, weak as it is, catches. He opens the box, and there it is. Emeralds—real emeralds, more than a hundred years old—glimmer the color of envy from the rich setting of platinum and tiny diamonds that sparkle like tears.

The ring. The real ring.

"You need to tell the truth now. It's all over, Tracy."

# PART TWO

# TRACY

# CHAPTER TWENTY-EIGHT

*You need to understand. Everything I did, I did because I love you. I love you like mad, they say, but that's a lie—it's not like madness, it is madness, pure and absolute madness. No one else has ever loved you like that, I assure you. Not Sarah Sterns, not that Melissa girl, not Isabelle, who left you behind as soon as the going got tough, at the first sign of trouble.*

*Not Colleen.*

*One day you might understand that.*

*The day I first saw you is still clear in my mind. The end of junior year of high school was looming, but to me, those couple of months might as well have been a hundred years. I was not motivated in class; I didn't like school. I didn't see what it could possibly bring me—me, who didn't seem to be good at anything, who was chubby and average looking, and who was, worst of all, hopelessly devoid of that cool gene that made you stand out, that drew people to you. The same way they flocked to my older sister, for instance.*

*Chrissy was hardly prettier than me. We looked alike, at least as far as physical features went. We took after our mom: same round face, a slightly bulbous nose, dishwater-colored hair. Chrissy didn't have stellar grades but she had friends and even a boyfriend whose sole purpose in her life seemed to be creating drama. Most of the time, she pretended we weren't related. Nobody had any particular reason to look at me, and so I learned to be invisible.*

*It all changed the day I met you.*

*You didn't see me either but I sure saw you. It was the first time I felt tempted to leave my shell of a world. The first time I thought there might be something out there for me, in the murky world after high school.*

*We had guest lecturers come in from universities all month. It was optional. During lunch hour and right after school, you could go to the gymnasium and hear some professor from this or that college try to sell you on social science or psychology or biochemistry. I wasn't going to go. After all, there was no chance of me ever getting a scholarship, and my family had no money to pay for college.*

*But that day, Chrissy was bringing the useless boyfriend home to study—meaning sloppily make out in the room we shared while I camped out in the living room with Mom, pretending it wasn't happening. I needed to kill an hour or two. The lecture wasn't crowded so there was no chance of running into any nasty characters. So I went. I sat in the back and listened to you lecture about literature.*

*You know you're good at it. I think you're selling your-*

*self short at that horrible liberal arts college, where they've never appreciated what you have to offer. I know you only went to work there because of Colleen—another way her self-absorption ruined your life. But you could do so much better.*

*And that day, you were on fire. You talked about F. Scott Fitzgerald and Faulkner and other names I hadn't heard. You told funny anecdotes, and even the most hardened cynics of a small-town high school giggled. And I looked at you—you were enjoying the attention, I could tell. You were having a good time. You were glorious. To me, you were something akin to a god.*

*After the lecture, you took questions but I didn't dare raise my hand. Even later, you stayed near the gymnasium doors to chat with anyone who still had something to ask. You were a natural. The god was down here on earth, walking among us.*

*I watched from afar, concealed behind a large group of girls. Then they started to leave, and one of them said, "God. This guy. So up his own ass, right?"*

*The others laughed. Another girl said, "Yeah. I thought he was cute; that's why I went..."*

*"Ew. No. He's gotta be, like, forty."*

*"Still hot. Hot older man, right?"*

*I felt dirty on your behalf. Sullied. Profaned. I remembered who they were and put glue in their lockers. Childish, maybe, but I risked a lot. If the teachers found out, or worse, if the girls themselves found out, it could have been disastrous.*

*But you never even knew about my sacrifice.*

*That was okay by me. Glue in lockers was only the beginning.*

*I had found my purpose now. I went home a different person, and nothing mattered: not Chrissy's bullshit; not her asshole boyfriend, who'd laugh at her put-downs of me but leer when she wasn't looking; not our mom, who was passed out drunk half the time. For the first time, I felt like I was somebody.*

*Or like I might become somebody, in the future. But that would take a lot of work.*

*I was ready.*

# CHAPTER TWENTY-NINE

To: M1970@yourmail.com
From: widower@yourmail.com

Dear sister,

I think this email is secure. She doesn't know anything. I don't think she suspects. Maybe she's not
as vigilant anymore, now that she has what she
thinks she wanted.

I checked her laptop again today. The bad news is
there's still nothing that could help us bring her to
justice. The only thing I could determine from it is
that she's not working on her new "novel" like she

said she does. Who knows what she does all day. But the good news is I have her passwords now. I can log on to her email accounts from another location.

I admit that it took a lot to convince me. Believe me, Em, no one wanted to find a sensible explanation more than I did. Maybe it was all a coincidence. Maybe she got hold of Colleen's ring some other way. Maybe she simply found it in the bathroom of that restaurant, and she has nothing at all to do with the whole mess.

But rest assured, we aren't tormenting an innocent young woman. She's deranged, and I don't say this lightly. I know you're a psychologist, and you're opposed to the use of that word. When I got the report from the background check firm I hired, I knew. All the lies, the name change, the sister I never heard of.

She told me stories about her past, Em. Fabrications. Pure fiction. She told me her parents died in a car crash when she was nineteen—that never happened. Her father left when she was little, and he still lives somewhere in Oklahoma. Her mother died only five years ago. She's not from where she said she's from.

Everything is fake. There never was a Claire Greene. Her name is Tracy Belfour, and she's from a town called Peake Falls, Ohio. It's a short drive from where I live, not even an hour. A blip on the map, population 4,000. I saw pictures of the house she grew up in. An absolute dump. She told me her parents were environmental lawyers.

I'm telling you, the moment I found that ring (in a tampon box, of all places, if you can believe it! I can't decide if it's charmingly naïve or utterly horrifying), I knew. It's our grandmother's ring, it's one of a kind. The emeralds and diamonds, the setting. There can be no mistake.

Of course, I'm well aware that none of it will hold up in court. Forget court—none of it is enough to even get her arrested. The ring means nothing, and changing her name and lying about her past is sketchy but hardly a criminal offense. Our only hope is to get her to slip up and confess. I need your help, as a psychologist and as my sister. I need to know you're behind me on this.

Best,
B.

Byron,

I am behind you 100%. But if you're right, this is going to be difficult. And what's more, it's going to be dangerous. This girl—Claire, Tracy, whatever—has a mania, and that mania is you. She's fixated on you. Or, at least, her idea of you.

The fact is people like her don't really understand what love is. What she feels is more akin to a compulsion. Underneath, she's a tormented and miserable person who thinks you're the only key to happiness and a fulfilling existence. She doesn't really have a solid sense of self, only a persona that's based around her obsession, and that's what makes her so volatile. If she convinces herself that it's necessary in order to preserve the narrative she's built in her head, she can seriously hurt you.

I will help you, but I beg you to be careful. You can't bring back Colleen, and I don't want to lose you as well.

Love,
M.

# CHAPTER THIRTY

I look at the ring. It sits on the table in front of me, undeniably real. The exact replica of the one on my finger.

Then I look up at my husband. Tears blanket my eyes.

I remember how he proposed to me. I think I remember every second of every minute of that day. The day that I knew it wasn't all for nothing. That I fulfilled my destiny.

It was a whirlwind courtship—just the way it should be, as I always thought. When you've met your true love and you know it, you don't drag your feet and wallow in doubts for months and months, maybe even years. And when you haven't met the one, you should be out there looking for him, not hopping in and out of undergrads' beds.

I did know better, and I steered him to this step with meticulous care. Just like it was clear to me we belonged together, it had to be as clear to him. I did everything I was supposed to do. I made meals, showed up on weekends with pizza and rented Blu-rays. And if I sensed he was getting overwhelmed, I pulled back. Even though it was hard. God, he'll never know how hard it was! I kept track of him during those times, of course. It was so much easier now that I had legitimate access to the house. A man must never be left to his own devices for too long.

The point is I made it easy for him. Every step of our courtship, he never once had to agonize over what to do with me next. That was my job, to make his life easy, and I did.

I knew he was going to propose because I kept track of his computer, looking in while he was in the shower or in another room. I checked his credit card statements and the receipts in his desk drawer—luckily for me, he's way more organized than Colleen used to be. Sure, it ruined the surprise a little but that's okay.

But when he finally got on one knee, I opened the little velvet box and saw it there.

The awed smile on my face didn't waver, but inside, I felt myself wilt. It wasn't an exact replica—there were subtle differences. The work on the real ring, the ancestral one, had been too fine to reproduce accurately. Or maybe he didn't have enough money. But it was definitely a replica, emerald and diamonds set in platinum. I confirmed it later—took the ring to a jeweler to appraise, where I was told that the platinum was real but the emerald was lab grown, and the diamonds were cubic zirconia.

Why did he choose to do that? To recreate that other ring, instead of getting something new? *It matches your eyes*—that's what he said. I still remember it. But that's a lie. Is that what he wanted from the start? I found myself wondering. To recreate that ring and to recreate that marriage? That horrible failure of a marriage he had with the starter wife, where he had been so miserable?

I said yes, of course. I decided not to be petty. I put the ring on and agreed to marry Byron—the love of my life. But I never could bring myself to love that ring. Every time I looked at it, it was nothing more than a reminder. The ring should have been my first warning bell.

He wasn't over her and never would be.

And now he found the real ring. How many times have I thought of just flushing it down the toilet or throwing it out of my car window? Why didn't I ever do that?

He sits calmly across from me. He doesn't look angry or sad. He waits.

I want to say something he probably expects to hear. Like, *You have to hear me out.* Or that eternal chestnut, *I can explain!* But I know it's the last thing I should say.

"The baby clothes," I say hoarsely. "Did she really—"

"It's not the point." He runs his hands through his hair. "Don't you see?"

"I just want to know about the baby clothes."

A long silence. The clock ticks. I find myself wanting to smash it to tiny pieces.

"Tell me what you did," he says. "And then I'll tell you about the baby clothes."

I look him in the eye for what feels like a long time. Neither of us looks away. "I didn't do anything, Byron."

"Tell me what you did."

"I only did . . ." The plan unfurls in my mind as I speak. Saving me. "I only did what you told me to do."

"What the hell are you talking about?" He gets up. He's towering over me. I have to look up to keep my gaze on his.

"If you call the police," I say, "that's what I'll tell them."

A shaky laugh escapes from him. "You have to be kidding. You psycho, crazy, stalker *bitch*."

I can't help it. I flinch. "I love you, Byron."

"Like hell you do."

"I want you to think about it," I say. "Really think about it. Before you do anything you might regret, like calling the authorities."

"If anyone should be worried about police, it's you," he spits.

"Why is that?"

His reaction is so immediate and intense that it scares me. He lunges forward. I think he's going to hit me but his fist stops just inches from my eye. I don't have time to shriek. I just sit there, trembling.

"You murdered my wife, you bitch!" He's yelling but his voice breaks midsentence, trailing off to something close to a howl. It makes my hair stand on end. "You drove her to suicide. I don't even have a grave to visit because of you."

Inwardly, I catch myself smiling. I feel relieved.

There's still a chance. He doesn't know. He doesn't know anything.

"You're wrong," I say, and it's the truth, in a way. "Byron, you need to think about this. Carefully. No one will believe you. You know I'm right."

He storms past me. I don't follow him. I sit on the couch, listening to him rummage around upstairs. He throws things. *Crash, boom.* It all takes only minutes, although it feels much longer. Then he's thundering down the stairs. There's an old duffel bag thrown over his shoulder. It looks like it's about to burst at the seams.

"I'm going away," he snaps. "To Emily's."

"There's no need for that," I say. I sound like I'm pleading. "Stay. We can talk about this. Work it out."

"I won't stay for another second in the same house with you. You have two days to tell the truth," he says. "Then I'm going to get the authorities involved."

"And what, they're going to torture the confession out of me?" I give a little laugh. "Listen to yourself. You're being absurd. Put the bag down."

Without another word, he grabs the ring off the table and heads for the door. In the doorway, he stops. He looks like he's thinking. Then he turns around.

"About the baby clothes," he says. His voice is dripping with venom. "She wasn't pregnant. She never wanted kids. I planted the clothes. I knew you'd go looking for the painting you keep trying to sell, and I wanted you to come across them. I knew you'd lose your shit."

That's it. Enough is enough. Breathless, I leap off the couch but he's already slamming the door behind him. Tears burst from my eyes. "Come back here!" I scream, my voice shrill and ugly. I've never used that voice with him. "Come back! You bastard!"

I grab the closest object—an empty glass—and hurl it blindly. But he's already gone, and it shatters against the door.

# CHAPTER THIRTY-ONE

To: m1970@yourmail.com
From: widower@yourmail.com

Em,

I know the psychologist in you wouldn't approve but I keep thinking about Colleen. How she was in that last year. All the little things that I didn't notice at the time. I can't believe I was such an idiot. I was so self-absorbed that it never occurred to me she might genuinely not have known what was happening to her. She kept denying it, saying she wasn't high, and I could see it on her face— I thought it was a look of guilt. I thought she was lying. But now I realize she was telling the truth, and that look was fear.

I should have understood what was going on after that party at our place. It's messed up—there are so many happier times with her I could be remembering but they're all foggy, and that horrible evening is clear, after all these years. Maybe it's because that was the night everything really started to fall apart. Or maybe it's because all the people from work were there, and I'm not stupid—I know *someone* must have overheard. She was so disoriented, and she was screaming at me in a rage. She thought it was all about the stupid ring she lost, that I was still mad. She kept repeating it wasn't her fault she lost it. And looking back, I realize that of course it wasn't her fault. But what's worse is that I also realize that I did blame her.

I have to wonder if a part of what happened was my fault. She was wild, and creative, and strange from the day we first met. She was so far beyond me that it thrilled and scared me a little, and I couldn't believe a woman like that wanted to be with me.

But time went by, and I began to realize the very things I loved about her had sharp edges, and those sharp edges refused to fit into the life I envisioned for myself. They kept poking through and cutting and bristling. So I started trying to shoehorn her into being something she wasn't. I had my own ideas, you see, of what our ideal life should be. I loved her for what she was, yet at the same time, I kept trying to change her.

I still ask myself: did she ever think I was the one trying to drive her insane? She must have. I was a bad husband. I had failed her.

Because of this trailer-trash bitch, my wife killed herself, thinking I wanted her dead.

Yours,
B.

Byron,

I won't lie—it's going to be extremely difficult to prove that it was Claire—sorry, Tracy—who drove Colleen to suicide. Our best option is to get her to confess. For that, we must break her spirit. As the object of her obsession, you're also in a singular position of power. She lives for your love, or whatever she perceives to be your love. That need was her motivation for everything she did, and it can also be her undoing.

I have to remind you, once again, to be extremely careful.

This Friday I'll come over for dinner. I'll try to get a picture of her mental state.

Hang in there.

Your sister.

# CHAPTER THIRTY-TWO

*After Colleen was gone, I spent the next week or two in a kind of limbo. Every time someone looked at me, I was sure they could see it. An indelible mark, like Lady Macbeth: Out, damned spot, out, I say! I was convinced everyone could magically know I was a murderer. But of course, if that were true, people wouldn't get away with crimes every minute of every day, all over the world.*

*Those were a tough two weeks. I will never forget them. I promised that, should I ever reach my goal, I wouldn't take a single minute I spent in your company for granted. I missed you dreadfully in those two weeks. But of course, I had to stay away.*

*It was the price to pay, and then the coast would be clear, at last. Except it wasn't.*

*I wasn't ready for you, you see. And I realized it. I'm not completely delusional. Trailer-Trash Tracy—that's what some people at school called me behind my back, even though it was unfair because we didn't live in a trailer. It was a real house. Not much of a house, but a house nonetheless. As I was, I would never in a million years be good enough for someone like Byron Westcott, literature professor.*

*So over the next few years, I set about killing Tracy Belfour. Little by little.*

*I'd already improved my grades somewhat, and by the end of the year, I was squarely on the "average" end of mediocre. My English grades stood out: I paid special attention in that class because the materials reminded me of you. That, and I'd need to be well-read so I could keep up a conversation with you, when the time came. I ended up with an A-minus in English for the year and did well enough on my tests to get into college. Definitely not an Ivy, and definitely not on any scholarship, but it was worth a try.*

*So I tried, and I failed. All my applications came back with rejections. And anyway, I had no way to pay for it, and my mom could certainly not be counted on to help. Her medical bills ate up all the welfare money.*

*I spent a year waiting tables at the same restaurant. I still remember that one night, when I came home from work past midnight. My legs burned in agony after a twelve-hour shift, and my hair smelled like grease. I almost forgot to look in the mailbox, like I did every night. All I wanted was to take a shower and collapse onto my narrow bed. You could never understand these struggles, Byron. It's not how you grew up. And I would never, ever dream of telling you. I don't want you seeing me that way.*

*But I took the time to look anyway. The mailbox was empty. I went inside to find Mom passed out on the couch with the TV still on, like she did more and more often lately. The bottle of cheap wine on the floor by the couch was empty. A syringe sat on the side table. At least she remembered her insulin, I thought.*

*I threw down my bag and kicked off my shoes and then went to shower and wash my hair, like I did every night. I wasn't blond yet but I already decided that I would be. I always pictured you with a blond. I'd lost weight—I didn't even have to cut back on food; the endless waiting tables did the job. That, and I quit my soda habit. I pictured you with someone who drinks only Evian.*

*When I got out of the shower, I saw that my mom was awake, sitting up on the couch, blinking at the TV with bleary eyes.*

*I called out to her. She didn't seem to hear. I called again.*

*"What?" she grumbled. She barely turned her head.*

*"Did we get any mail today?"*

*"If we got mail, it would be in the mailbox, wouldn't it?"*

*I didn't want to argue. I went to bed. It took forever to fall asleep because she didn't feel the need to lower the volume of the TV. There was some kind of reality-show marathon. It seeped into my ears and into my dreams. I woke up with the alarm the next morning, puffy faced and barely rested.*

*The house was silent. When I ventured out of the room I used to share with Chrissy, I saw my mother passed out in front of the TV, which was, mercifully, turned off.*

*I went into the kitchen to make a cup of instant coffee but realized we were out. I threw the coffee jar into the trash, and that's when I saw it.*

*A small pile of ads and brochures: takeout, grocery store discounts of the week, the usual junk mail. I don't know what made me reach in and lift it up. There, underneath a flyer for Premium Quality Doors and Windows, sat a thick white envelope.*

*My heart stopped beating. I snatched it out of the trash with trembling hands and tore it open.*

Dear Ms. Belfour, *I read*. On behalf of the Creative Writing Department at Ohio State University, we are pleased to welcome you—

*I couldn't keep reading. The letter slipped from my hands, and I barely caught it before it hit the dirty floor.*

*I did it. It was happening. Another sign from above that I was on the right track.*

*And my mother threw it in the trash. She didn't even look. Told me there was no mail. She was so out of it, the fucking alkie. She couldn't even be bothered to remember that I was waiting for this letter, waiting for months and months and months.*

*Unless she did remember. Unless she told me there was no mail because...*

*"Mom?" I bellowed. No answer came. She must have been passed out cold. I set the letter carefully down on the kitchen counter and stormed into the living room.*

*Sure enough, she slept peacefully on the couch. Hadn't even stirred.*

*Standing there, by her head lolling on the armrest, I*

*remembered the tantrum she threw when Chrissy left. A frightful alcoholic rage.* You're abandoning your mother, you ungrateful little slut. How dare you. I gave my health to have you. *And so on and so forth, spittle flying from her lips in a haze of boozy breath.*

*Chrissy packed her bags and walked right out the door, leaving me to bear the brunt of most of it.*

*She doesn't want me to leave, I realized. Doesn't want me to move on, go to college, have a better life. She wants me to stay here forever and take care of her, make liquor store runs and pick up her insulin at the pharmacy until finally, one day, her kidneys or heart or brain gives out.*

*She found the letter and threw it away on purpose.*

*I felt an intense rush of hatred.*

*Enough. I'd had enough of her, of this house, of Trailer-Trash Tracy. The ticket to my new life—the ticket to being one step closer to you, Byron, the meaning of my existence, the reason for everything I've ever done—sat on the kitchen counter, ready to spirit me away and out of here.*

*She wasn't going to tie me down.*

*I picked up the syringe from the end table, went to the bathroom, and then found the insulin in the cabinet. I filled the syringe. I felt no anxiety. My hands were steady and calm. I'd done this before, a number of times. She wasn't that good at managing her illness.*

*Looks like she finally made the last, fatal slipup.*

*And now my good-for-nothing mother would free me— and finance my future in the same stroke.*

*You—and our beautiful life together—waited for me.*

# CHAPTER THIRTY-THREE

What matters is that I'm in control of the situation again. I sweep up the shards of glass like I would have done any other time, diligently, leaving nothing behind.

Byron will come around. We are stronger than that; we are meant to be. Surely, he will see that.

In the meantime, I can nudge him in the right direction.

I record the video with my phone. I prop it up against a coffee mug and turn on the video function. With a tap of my fingertip on the big red button, the seconds begin to tick away.

I wipe the tears from my lower lashes with my fingertips and then press the heels of my hands over my eyes and take a deep, shuddering sigh of resolve. Making sure it's all recorded. This isn't easy for me, Byron. You'll never know.

"My name is Claire Greene Westcott. I'm married to Byron Westcott, literature professor at Mansfield Liberal Arts College in Mansfield, Ohio. Claire Greene wasn't always my name."

I take a short breathing break. I'd put on some mascara, and now it's artfully smudged under my lower lashes. I look like a woman crushed by guilt, worn thin with remorse.

"I first met Byron Westcott more than ten years ago, when I was a junior at Peake Falls High School in Ohio. He came to give a lecture at my school. Afterward, I stayed behind to ask him questions. That's when our relationship began."

With another artful sigh, I lower my eyes, the very picture of shame.

"Over the next year, I met Byron Westcott in secret. He was in his late thirties; I was sixteen. We met..." I let my voice tremble just the right amount. "We met at his house when his wife was away. Several times we met at my mother's house, when no one was home. I lost my virginity to Byron Westcott a week before my seventeenth birthday."

I take another pause, letting the words sink in.

"He told me he wasn't happy in his marriage anymore. That his wife was distant, that they were going to get a divorce soon. I listened to him. I wanted us to have a future together, and he told me we could. Just as soon as he got Colleen to give him a divorce. But it was hard, he said, because she would take the house, and his savings, and make his life a living hell. He didn't use those exact words, but it was the meaning. That's why we had to keep our relationship secret. If Colleen suspected anything, she could use it against Byron in the divorce.

"Shortly after my eighteenth birthday, when I was in my senior year of high school, he broke up with me. Briefly. I was devastated but he contacted me again a week later. We met at an empty house that he later told me was his sister's. She and her family were away for the weekend. There, he told me he couldn't live without me, and I'm ashamed to say, I felt the same way. And I told him so. He asked me if I was ready to do anything to have a future with him. I said yes."

The lies come so easily that I hardly need the brief outline I jotted on a napkin to help me keep track of stuff. As far as I'm concerned, it might as well all be true.

"We devised a plan to get rid of Colleen. He never said the word *murder*; we were getting rid of her, getting her out of the way. He would need an alibi so I had to do the work. No one would ever suspect me, he said. *No one knows we're seeing each other, do they?* he asked me. I told him no one knew. I was proud of myself"—I heave a tiny sob—"proud of never letting him down. He kissed me and said I was the only person in the entire world he could count on. He could put his life in my hands.

"He devised the plan and told me he needed me to pull it off, so no one would suspect anything. Not just Colleen. He said no one would believe it was a suicide if it came out of nowhere. So we set it up, over several months. He drugged her food, made her look unstable in front of their friends. Whenever I told him about my reservations, he changed, became violent. Then he told me he loved me over and over, until I stopped objecting.

"He told Colleen to come to the pier in Cleveland that night. Said it was a surprise. Instead, I was waiting for her there. I pushed Colleen May into the water.

"Byron Westcott composed the suicide note and made it sound real enough to convince everyone she did write it.

"We continued seeing each other for more than five years afterward. All in secret. He told me it was necessary, to avoid arousing suspicion. He would act normal, he said. He would date here and there, after enough time had passed since Colleen's death. But it was all a front, he told me. He only ever loved me, and one day, we'd be together."

I make another shuddering sigh and look straight into the camera. My lips tremble.

"But a few weeks ago, he hit me. And I threatened to tell the truth. Then he said he'd kill me if I ever tried. He said, *Do you think I'll hesitate when I killed my wife—the only woman I ever loved—for the pathetic, whiny mess that you are?* He is insane, and he wants me dead. And I am so, so sorry for everything I've done. I was just a teenager, and I was naïve, and Byron . . . Byron took advantage. In case anything happens to me, consider this my confession."

I'm full-on sobbing now. Real, genuine tears run down my face, tinged with mascara—a beautifully grotesque display. Maybe I should have gone into acting instead of writing. "I'm so sorry," I repeat, my voice breaking, "and I wish to God I could undo what I did—may God have mercy on my—"

I raise my hand and deliberately knock the phone over, screen-down, before pressing the button to stop recording. Then I wipe the tears and the mascara.

This is the last time I cry because of Byron Westcott. My faithless husband. My beloved traitor.

I pick up the phone and send the video to Emily's email. It's a risky step but I feel safe enough. She, of all people, will never send it to the police. She loves her brother far too much to implicate him.

For the time being, let it be a warning.

# CHAPTER THIRTY-FOUR

*It wasn't easy, all that time between. Again, I found myself in a limbo, and the end seemed so far away that it might as well never have come. So many variables, so many obstacles, and the whole time I had to keep track of you so I wouldn't lose you again. But I endured it—endured it all without a word of complaint—all out of love for you. I wish you could understand.*

*In the meantime, I received my mother's life insurance payout, just in time to pay for my first semester in college. I put the house on the market. Sure, it was little more than a hut but any amount of money was better than nothing. I had to think about it, hard, to wonder if it was worth the risk. On one hand, unloading that house severed my last ties with the past, with Tracy Belfour, with what happened inside these walls. On the other, who knows what the new owners might accidentally discover?*

*People are so nosy. In the end, I decided to chance it. I
needed the money.*

*Before the term started, I officially changed my name
to Claire Greene. Trailer-Trash Tracy was now gone for
good. For the next four years, I got into my new role: Claire
Greene, the creative writing student. New name, new haircut, new look—I was a different person, even though I
didn't quite feel like one yet.*

*And in the meantime, I had to keep up with you. And,
Byron, you didn't make it easy.*

*Isabelle Herrera cleared out on her own. After the
whole debacle, after having to alibi you for the police, after the rumors about the two of you started circulating,
she couldn't just go on flirting with you like nothing happened. She may have wanted to, no doubt. But she's one
of those people who feels an overwhelming need to be the
good guy—or girl—and hitting on the man whose wife
just died in a suspicious suicide is the opposite of a good
girl.*

*There was also Sarah Sterns. It wasn't hard to get rid
of her. I found out about her late, but not too late, and
could excise the cancer before it sunk in its tendrils. Without too much bloodshed. I even felt a little bad for her. It
wasn't her fault she didn't know you were taken. And I
no longer judge you for having sex with her that night. I
understand that it had been a while and a man has needs.
Why shouldn't she fulfil them, as long as she leaves the picture afterward?*

*But at the time, I was furious. Don't be angry—I was
overworked at school and exhausted, and I couldn't wait*

*much longer. I wanted to be with you. I thought it should be me, in your house, in your bed.*

*I sent you the message in the morning, calling you to the college. But soon enough you'd discover there was no emergency and come back, and she was in no hurry to leave. She sat around, drinking your coffee and going through your cabinets like she belonged there! But one phone call and she was out. And then I made sure she didn't contact you again.*

*I realize that extraordinary luck played a part in all of it. But I took it as my due. As more signs from above that what I was doing was good and right, and we belonged together.*

*I would make you so happy. Happier than any other woman ever could. Colleen or Sarah. Or that Melissa character.*

*I feel a little bad about what happened to her. But she left me no choice.*

*And I always do what needs to be done. Especially when it comes to you, my love.*

# CHAPTER THIRTY-FIVE

I end up falling asleep on the couch. In fact, I only realize I'd managed to nod off when I open my eyes and the room is filled with thin morning light. Sitting up, I blink my dry eyes, disoriented, and then it all comes back, like a crushing weight settling onto my shoulders. *He knows. He knows the truth, and everything I've done has been for nothing.*

No. I have to keep myself under control. This isn't the time to do something rash and stupid. Like slash every single painting in the house to ribbons and wreck the furniture, no matter how much I want to.

I pace the room and then start cleaning up to get my thoughts in order. It feels weirdly normal and soothing: I pick up the stray coffee mugs, start the dishwasher, sweep the floor, clean the kitchen counter.

I open the sliding door and go out onto the deck. It's

morning, and the sun has come out, but there's that autumn chill in the air. The plants in the boxes are looking out of shape. Time to cut them to the root so they can grow back next spring. And leaves litter the deck and the yard. It needs cleaning. So I go get the pruning shears and the broom and get to work.

"Everything must be perfect," I say out loud. "For when he comes back. Right, Melissa?"

Melissa doesn't answer, of course. She hasn't answered anyone since that email I sent from her phone about moving away. I think the revenge is fitting, really. She got to watch us being happy all these years, having our morning coffee all summer long right above her.

She pretty much asked for it. I tried to resolve this peacefully but she was having none of it. I remember her tacky acrylic nails and shudder. I missed three days of school because she'd clawed my face with them, the witch.

Everything about her was so tacky. I don't know why men go for these appalling women. Especially Byron. They met on a dating site—the only way their paths could ever cross. She was a hairdresser. Reminded me of my sister, but worse.

From the start, I'm sure he saw nothing in her besides sex—a fun, little fling without a future. But she—she got ideas. Sank those acrylic talons in and wouldn't let go. I went to have my hair trimmed by her and then got her fired from the salon, but still, she wouldn't leave.

I did what had to be done, like always.

Once the deck is swept, I go back indoors. Upstairs, I collect all the clothes lying around, put them into the hamper, and take it to the laundry room. I sort everything, fill up the washer, and start the cycle.

When I go back to the living room, a cold breeze ripples through the house, and I freeze in my tracks. The little hairs on my arms stand on end as gooseflesh races across my skin.

The front door is open a crack. My sister is standing there, her hands on her hips.

"Hi, Tracy," she says.

\* \* \*

Understanding dawns. "Byron sent you," I say.

She flinches. "He didn't send me. But we spoke."

I should have remembered to lock the door.

"We spoke about you at length. I told him—"

"About Tracy Belfour," I say, and my mouth twists.

"I told him the truth," she says levelly. "Tracy, you really need to hear me out."

"If you want me to listen, maybe use my real name."

"That is your real name. Claire Westcott doesn't exist. You'll have to face the facts sooner or later. It's all fake."

"I don't have to listen to you. Get out of my house."

"It's not your house. It's Colleen May's house."

I swallow hard. It won't be easy to get rid of her but lashing out will only make it worse. I have to make her think she's getting somewhere. That I'm listening.

"Is that what you came here to say?"

"Tracy, you need to admit that something's wrong and get help. It's not too late."

It is definitely too late. She must know that. And I realize that I can't get her on my side. She won't listen to reason. There's only one thing left to do.

"Chrissy, please." I let my voice tremble, blinking like I'm about to start crying. "You don't know the half of it. You don't understand what's going on here. He called you and told you things but he's lying! My husband is trying to get rid of me. He's trying to kill me like he killed Colleen!"

"Tracy," she murmurs. She covers her eyes with her hand.

"Please. He just wants me to sound like the crazy one. But he has a mistress, a young mistress—a student from the college named Mia—and they're trying to get rid of me."

"You're unwell."

"Because he drugged my food," I sob. When I look up and meet her gaze, she's unmoved. Her eyes are hard and dark.

"You really thought I didn't know anything?" she snaps.

I stop sobbing. Even the tears stop like I turned off a faucet.

"What?"

"You really thought I was blind," she says with a shaky, disbelieving laugh. "Why do you think I left? Because of Mom? No. I left because I couldn't watch you anymore, mired in your weird fucked-up little obsession. It was fucking scary, Tracy! I thought you were going to drag us all down with you into your madness. I wanted no part of it. So I left."

"Chrissy—"

"I just didn't realize how far you'd go," she says, shaking her head. "Remember when you sent me the invitation to your wedding?"

Do I ever. I sent it out of spite more than anything else. And because I knew she would never accept.

"That was the first I'd heard from you in years. And suddenly there's this kitschy-as-hell wedding invite in my mail, with a name I never heard before in my life, but the picture is of you and that professor of yours. If you meant to shock me, to show off—congratulations, you succeeded. But then I looked you up. Claire Westcott. And I found the story of Colleen."

I close my eyes.

"I didn't want to believe you had anything to do with it. I did my best to put it out of my mind, and for a while, I succeeded. I didn't even contact you for my part of the inheritance, the life insurance, my half of the house. I said to hell with it. I just didn't want to be anywhere near you. Then one day a background check company contacted me on behalf of Byron Westcott."

"No." I open my eyes, my fists clenched at my sides. *He can't have done it; he can't have betrayed me to this extent, gone behind my back like that. He—*

But he did. Of course he did.

*It's all fake, Tracy, every last little bit of it.*

"At first, I refused to talk to him. But he emailed me saying he found his late wife's missing ring in your stuff. The ring she lost months before she died. So we talked on the phone, and then we met. I told him the truth, and he did the same."

I'm this close to losing it. And when I lose it, bad things happen. She must realize it, if she knows as much as she pretends she does.

"So what are you going to do?" I ask, my voice toneless.

"I'm going to ask you to get help."

Silence lingers between us, and again that fucking clock ticks in the background.

"Look, Byron wanted me to talk you into confessing to killing Colleen but you know what, Tracy? You're my sister. I still care about you, in spite of everything. We can just leave." She's pleading. I can't tell how honest she is. "Just get your things. We're going to my place. You can stay there for as long as you need. But you have to get help. I'll find you someone to talk to, to get over this...obsession. Then you can get a divorce and move on with your life."

I have to wonder if I'm hearing correctly. I shut my eyes. When I open them again, she's still there, same hopeful look on her face, forehead scrunched up, eyebrows forming a little dome over her eyes. Are her eyebrows tattooed on or something? They must be. It's so Chrissy.

"Move on...with my life?"

"Yes. You can get any man you want. One without a wife. You're beautiful, you're young, you're smart. You have a college degree. You can start over. Leave Byron Westcott be."

I breathe deep. Leave him be. Like nothing happened.

"But he loves me."

"He doesn't love you. Not anymore."

Bitterness teems in my chest. I can taste it. I need to make all this go away. I gulp and then give a curt nod.

"You'll do it?" Chrissy asks, hopeful.

"We leave and never come back, right? And no police."

"Absolutely no police. You just made one teenage mistake—that's all. No need to get the police involved."

So she doesn't know. She doesn't know about the rest of it. I think of Melissa, buried under the deck. It was just being built back then. Byron left her alone in the house while he went to pick up some papers he forgot at work. I rang the doorbell, and she opened the door like she owned the place. She stood there, at this same front door—my front door—in this hideous negligee thing, and she was smacking gum, her headphones in her ears. I came in and told her Byron had a girlfriend and was playing her. She was supposed to leave—any woman with any self-respect would have. But she didn't want to. Even her name was tacky. Why are the ones with the bad hair extensions always called Melissa?

I strangled her with those stupid pink headphones, the cord wrapped around her throat. It's harder than it sounds. My hands were bloody. But then it was done, and she was in the hole in the earth, and the next day they poured concrete on top of her, and that was that.

I look at Chrissy, who seems relieved. And what would happen if I were to refuse? I think. You'll go to the police and tell them everything? Turn me in?

But all she has are her crazy theories. A ring and an almost decade-old death, not even a body.

Except she knows. She knows I've pursued Byron since

I was sixteen. She knows I followed Colleen, that I spied on her and Byron. She can fill the gaps in Byron's case.

It cannot happen.

"Chrissy," I finally choke out, "I'm coming with you."

"I knew it." She smiles. "I knew you'd come to your senses. Pack your things, and—"

"I'll be quick. You can wait for me in the car. I'll be right out."

She turns around to go.

Mistake.

My gaze darts to the side, to one of the decorative tables, where I notice it. No, I lie—I had noticed it some time ago, the moment I found her standing in the door of my house.

Our house, because Byron and I are one, and nothing she can say or do can change that, nothing—

I pick up the hammer, the one I used to break the lock of the basement door. With two leaps I'm behind her, and I swing it, and it lands with a sharp crack on the back of Chrissy's skull.

# CHAPTER THIRTY-SIX

A gurgle escapes from her lips, and Chrissy drops at once, without another sound. I step over her. The front door is still open a crack, and a breeze works its way in, chilling the room. I can't have that; it's bad for the baby—

Stop. No. There is no baby. First, I have to solve this. Make it go away.

I shut the door and turn the lock this time. Then I crouch next to my sister. There's blood on the back of her head, and she's immobile. Is she breathing?

Who am I kidding? She's gone. I cracked her skull.

I get up and grab hold of her ankles. Her boots are cheap, fake leather trimmed with fake fur. I drag her across the floor without resistance. Once or twice I think I see her move or hear a faint moan. But maybe it's my mind playing tricks on me.

Damn Byron. All I ever did was love him. Why punish me like this?

I drag Chrissy down the stairs to the basement—all she needs is a little push, and she topples to the floor at the foot of the staircase, next to the boxes of Colleen's things. Dead things belong together.

I will deal with her later. I pat her down and find her phone in the pocket of her jacket. She sure loves pleather. She has one of those old Android phones that unlock with a pattern you have to trace instead of a code, and when I tilt the screen, I can see the greasy tracks of her finger clear as day. I try the pattern twice before I get it right.

She's been texting Byron. He's Mr. Westcott in her phone. It's hard not to cringe. First, it's Dr., and second, how dare she. They've been talking for some time now. I don't have the patience to scroll up to the beginning of the texts. *He's* been diligent about deleting their conversations from his phone, but then again, my sister never was particularly bright.

As I read the last exchange of texts, anger boils within me. It was an act from the start. The whole "let's just go away together" thing. Totally fake. A ploy.

That fucking bitch—she belongs with Melissa. But Byron's betrayal hurts more than I anticipated. The pain is sharp, almost more than I can handle. I need to sit down on the living room couch for a minute or two and catch my breath. I'm still sweaty from the altercation and from dragging Chrissy's body to the basement.

Then I pick up the phone again. Mr. Westcott, I type. She's crazy. She's going to kill me! Please come!

Then I send the message, and I wait.

\*　　\*　　\*

*It was a wine bottle, in the end.*

*I still don't know how she spotted me. Or how she knew where I lived. I must have gotten reckless. I sensed that victory was within my reach. Colleen was being driven closer and closer to the precipice every day. It was only a matter of time.*

*You think I'm some kind of evil genius, a mastermind. You think I planned everything meticulously from start to finish but I'm ashamed to say I had to improvise. This was one of those instances but my luck—my extraordinary, magical luck—was on my side again. It was fate. It was God bringing us closer together.*

*Maybe it was after I'd followed her to and from the abortion clinic downtown, watched her go in and out, all pale and sweaty. I was so caught up in my own rage and excitement that I might have followed her too closely. She must not have been as out of it as I thought. She must have noticed the nondescript old car trailing her. Or it could have been any of the other times.*

*And then she must have followed me home. The tables turned, the watcher being watched. She acted stupid though. What happened is her own fault in a way. She should have called you or called the police or something. But instead, she went to ring the doorbell.*

*My mom was out. She had a doctor's appointment that afternoon, and as I knew well, she'd stop at the pub afterward for a drink that always turned into ten drinks, and for all I knew, she wouldn't come home until the next morning. This was only the beginning of my luck.*

*When I saw Colleen there, I could have freaked out. Instead, I calmly went to open the door. She invited herself in.*

*I remember it all very clearly. How could I ever forget?*

*She looked around, incredulous. I read it all on her face. It was surreal to her. Incomprehensible.*

*She stuck out incongruously in our shabby living room, with its disintegrating seventies couch, the old TV, the beer cans. She was showing wear and tear on her face, traces of the last several months. The hollows under her eyes were deep and blue, the lines around her mouth etched dark and sharp. But she was wearing bright lipstick, and her glossy brown hair had recently been dyed and cut, nicely and expensively. Her coat alone cost more than every item of clothing I owned. I remember looking at it, wondering whether it was made of real leather. Seething with envy. And something else. Shame. I was ashamed of the place I came from, the house where I grew up: How could someone like me ever compete with her? And she saw all that and doubtlessly thought the same thing. For that, I hated her even more.*

*She looked around, moving as if in slow motion. She looked me up and down. Her eyes were wide. "How old are you?" she asked. I was a little surprised that it was the first thing she wanted to know.*

*"Nineteen," I said.*

*"What do you want from me?" Her voice was different.*

*I'd overheard her countless times by now but always from a distance, and when she addressed me directly, it didn't sound the same. It was soft and soothing but it cracked a little when she said the last words.*

*And when it cracked, I understood everything with stunning clarity. I was the one who had the upper hand. Yes, Trailer-Trash Tracy with her alcoholic mother and runaway sister and bad grades and a roll of fat on her belly, with her cheap clothes and mousy hair, had triumphed over this statuesque, successful, well-dressed woman. She thought she was here to confront me, but really, she was here begging me to put her out of her misery.*

*I could not deny her that.*

*"I want Byron," I said simply.*

*Instead of lunging for me and trying to claw my eyes out—as I surely would have done in her place—she nodded, absentminded. I see.*

*"You're a teenager," she said, staring off into space as if hypnotized. "And you want my husband. Why?"*

*Because he's Byron. Because he's wonderful, and you don't deserve him. You're a bad wife, Colleen Alexandra May.*

*But it didn't look like she wanted, or expected, an answer.*

*"You think a man will make you happy but that's a lie. You think this man, the man I'm married to"—I kept noticing that she avoided saying his name—"is what you need to complete you. You're young, and you're stupid. It's all fake, a sham—don't you see?"*

*She sounded like she was close to tears. I took a step away from her. Clearly, she was mad.*

*"They've only changed on the surface. The last sixty, one hundred years of feminism, equality, emancipation—all horseshit. Deep down, they just want a housemaid, someone comfortably inferior that they can boss around. But you're not listening to me, are you? Of course you're not. Or you wouldn't have jeopardized your whole life just to get this one man."*

*I didn't jeopardize anything, I thought furiously. And who was she to lecture me anyhow?*

*"All this," she said, shaking her head. "All this for my husband? You can have my fucking husband."*

*I stood there, stunned. She circled the room with the same look of awe on her face.*

*"Is this it? Tracy? Is that your name? Will you leave me alone now?"*

*It was too good to be true. After all this hard work, she was just giving him away, giving him to me. It was like those Victorian comedies of manners that you hate. The wicked woman goes away, and the virtuous couple are united in their love. And I knew that it would never happen in a million years.*

*I had done too much. Gone too far. I knew that she would go to the police if I let her leave this house. She would tell them I stalked her, that I infiltrated her house and sabotaged her life. She would tell them I admitted that I wanted her husband.*

*And then everything would be over. She would get to keep you, or leave, and something terrible would happen to me. I would never be with you.*

*I could not allow that to happen.*

*I always do what needs to be done.*

*One of my mother's empty wine bottles was left on the floor by the couch. I picked it up by the neck. Colleen didn't have time to react. I hit her across the face as hard as I could. It connected with her cheekbone and temple.*

*She fell—she spun around and landed on her stomach and didn't move again.*

*Just like that, Colleen was gone.*

# CHAPTER THIRTY-SEVEN

I see Byron's car through the crack in the curtains. He got here fast. Everything can still be saved, I think. All I need to do is make him understand.

He finds me sitting on the couch. The curtains are still drawn, and the room has that slightly surreal look, sunlight breaking through every crack.

He closes the door and looks around him. "Where's Chrissy?" he snaps.

"Hi, Byron."

"Where's your sister?"

"She left." I look up to meet his eye. "She wanted me to come with her but I refused."

"Why?"

I blink, taken aback by the question. "What do you mean?"

He groans. "Why do you act like nothing is happening?"

"Because nothing *is* happening," I start to explain but he cuts in.

"What could there possibly be here for you anymore?"

I answer without hesitating. "Why, Byron, you, of course. My love."

"I don't love you anymore. I thought you were evil but you're just dense, aren't you? You don't understand that I could never, ever love you now."

I must be patient. It's hard for him to understand. It can take a while. I'm okay with that—I waited eight years, and I can wait longer than that, if I have to. Love is worth it. It's worth all the sacrifices.

"And that fucking joke of a video you made? Do you think it'll save you?"

I smile with just the corners of my mouth. "Byron, darling, I still don't see the police kicking down the door."

"You think anyone will believe that?"

I don't answer. I must tread carefully with him now.

To my surprise, he heaves a sigh and then comes to sit down on the other end of the couch.

"Why me, Claire?" He winces. "Tracy. What's so special about me? I'm a college professor without tenure who could barely make ends meet if it weren't for my famous artist wife. Why not a rock star or an actor?"

*Because you're you*, I want to say. "Because I looked at you that day, at school, and you were the most beautiful thing I'd ever seen." My voice sounds broken but it's genuine this time. I'm aching to reach out and touch his face. His chin is rough with stubble, salt and pepper with a lot more salt lately. Wrinkles surround his eyes and mouth.

He's getting old. I never noticed over the last eight or nine years. I never thought of him as someone who could get old.

"But I'm not a thing, Tracy," he says softly. "People aren't things. You can't just move them around like pieces on a chessboard."

"Unless you can. And I could! And I did, all for you."

"It wasn't even me you loved, just your idea of me. And I fell short of that idea, didn't I? You could never have been happy with me anyway. Do you see?"

Do I? What he said couldn't be more wrong, and it makes me angry with him. How can he still not understand that my love is deeper than anything?

He was always my ideal. Except for one thing.

He still loved Colleen. It was the one failing I could never live with and would never forgive him for. And I couldn't excise her from his mind the way I excised her from life.

My gaze wanders, looking for the hammer. But I left it on one of the decorative tables on the other end of the room.

"You need to move on, Tracy. Move on and get help. Not everything is lost. You could still find someone, someday, whom you can love for real. And someone who will love you back."

I sit still like a doll. Those last words out of his mouth ignite something inside me—something that won't be so easy to extinguish. The fire catches; it leaps from synapse to synapse, engulfing my entire being.

"Never," I say, and my voice is hard like glass, filled with resolve. "I will never leave here."

"Then you leave me no choice. Emily will testify, and so will Chrissy. You'll be leaving here in a police car."

Finally, I grin, but it feels like my mouth is full of needles. "Chrissy is dead."

A shadow flits over Byron's face. He doesn't know what to think, whether to believe me, and he's trying to hide it.

"You tried to turn my own sister against me," I say. "But I forgive you. She had to go anyway. She's the last of Tracy Belfour, and it's better that she's gone."

He slowly shakes his head. "You are completely out of your mind. I'm calling the cops."

With increasing panic, I watch as his phone appears out of his pocket. He thumbs the screen.

"No!" I blurt. He doesn't look up.

"If you call the police, I will never talk. You will never know what really happened to Colleen."

It works. Just like I thought it would. He lowers the phone slowly.

"Put it on the table."

He obeys, every movement careful, like I'm some dangerous criminal.

"Tell me," he says.

I smile and close my eyes. I'm in control again. Everything is going to be okay.

I open my eyes again to see him literally on the edge of his seat, his eyes intense on my face. Waiting. That's all he cares about anyway, what happened to his precious Colleen.

I lunge forward, knocking the phone off the table with

a swipe of my hand. It skitters across the floor and under one of the bookshelves.

And I wrap my hands around my husband's throat.

\*       \*       \*

*Colleen lay dead on my living room floor. There wasn't even that much blood. It was that simple, in the end.*

*I can't leave her here, I thought. My mom will come back. People will look for her. I have to do something.*

*Before the plan had time to fully form in my head, I was kneeling next to her, lifting her up. She was so much heavier than she looked, even though she was so thin I could feel her ribs through the layers of clothes. I stripped off that beautiful coat and held it to my face. It smelled like expensive perfume with that musky tang of real leather. It smelled like money. Like the life that should be mine.*

*And then I knew what to do.*

*I went to the kitchen to get a pair of rubber gloves and put on my hairnet from work. Then I put on the coat. She was tall and slender, and I was short and still a bit chubby, but the coat fit like it was my own. In her purse, I found a scarf and a hat made of soft cashmere. I put them on, wrapping myself in the scarf up to my chin, the hat pulled low. I also found her car keys. Her car, a silver SUV, sat by the sidewalk in front of our house.*

*I knew I had to hurry. I grabbed Colleen's body and dragged it across the floor, into the kitchen and into the garage we never used. It could hardly be called a real garage, just a ramshackle structure with a dirt floor, but our mom used it to store whatever random things she was hoarding. I put a bunch of old tarps on top of her. It wouldn't last but it would have to do for now.*

*Then I got into Colleen's car. It was like driving a truck—a fancy truck with beautiful tan leather seats. I drove it all the way to Cleveland.*

*Do you realize how much luck and skill I needed to pull it off? At any moment, I expected to screw up. I could have accidentally mishandled the car, gotten pulled over, and everything would have fallen apart right there. I could have been seen, spotted, caught on a surveillance camera. But I parked near the waterfront and used Colleen's credit card to pay for the parking spot. Then I put her wallet in the glove compartment.*

*The waterfront was deserted. In the early spring, it was cold. Rain drizzled in tiny, icy droplets, and the wind whipped my face, penetrating Colleen's little coat like it was made of tissue paper. But I didn't stop there. I walked to a secluded spot in the less developed part of the port. There were barely any streetlights, and I couldn't see any cameras in the vicinity. I stood there for a few moments, looking over the dark water. My heart was beating too fast, frenzied. It wasn't just the exertion or the adrenaline. It was the anticipation of the life that now lay at my feet. All I had to do was reach out and take it.*

*There was one thing to do first. I took out her phone. She had a fancy-model smartphone even then, when they were only starting to become ubiquitous. By today's standards, they were so easy to unlock. So I wrote an email with my clumsy gloved hands.*

Dear Byron,

I can't take it anymore. I don't recognize myself.
I'm sorry I couldn't be the person you wanted me
to be.

Love,
Colleen

*I reread it several times. And...this is going to sound
crazy but my eyes filled with tears. It felt so real. Like I
didn't write it myself just a few seconds ago but was really
reading someone's final words. The whole story—there was
something romantic about it. I hated her for having you
and taking you for granted, but at the same time, I envied
her. Does that make sense to you? She would get to be the
perfect dead wife. Not just an ex or some bitter divorcee—
but the woman gone tragically before her time. Her death
would erase all her sins and failings, make her perfect in
your mind. I envied and respected her for it.*

*You see, your life together is not what you remember. It's
only perfect because I made it that way, by killing her. Even
those bright, precious memories you owe to me.*

*I put the phone in the coat pocket, where I'd already
stashed some rocks, and threw the coat into the water.
Watched it sink and disappear in the depths.*

*Then I walked back to the well-lit streets and took a bus
home.*

*No one ever knew I was there.*

# CHAPTER THIRTY-EIGHT

When you love somebody, there is no sacrifice you won't make. And I love Byron—I think I've already proven that, time and time again. Colleen, Melissa, Sarah. Chrissy. Let's not forget Tracy Belfour, Trailer-Trash Tracy, whose entire existence I annihilated without pity.

And now it's my turn. Claire Westcott will disappear.

Sometimes, love means pretending to attack him so that he turns on me and kills me, in self-defense.

Go on, Byron. Free your hatred. End all this.

But to my shock and surprise, I meet no resistance. My hands wrap around Byron's neck. My thumbs sink into the thin flesh over his windpipe. All I have to do is keep squeezing.

Why isn't he fighting back? I need him to fight back. He can throw me off with ease. He's older but he's a man, bigger and stronger.

*I can't do it.*

His eyes meet mine, and it's enough to make me stagger back. The look in them doesn't look like him at all. We are both panting, like after a bout of vigorous fucking.

"Do whatever you want," he rasps. "Just tell me what happened to her."

"No. You're not going to make it about her again."

"It was always about her."

"You're not going to die with her name on your lips."

He cracks a pained smile. "Colleen."

"Liar!"

"Colleen, Colleen, Colleen. You lost. Don't you get it?"

I stand up, gobsmacked. My legs are unsteady, and I sway a little. Byron stands up in turn. We face each other.

"I want you to stop lying!" I lose it and yell out the last word, surprising us both. "You love me. You know you do. Just say you love me."

"I don't love you."

"Say you love me."

"I hate your guts."

A shudder courses through me.

"It's over," he says evenly. "It's time for you to die."

"You'll—"

If he kills me, Byron will go to prison. As far as the police are concerned, he killed one wife and then another. If anyone ever discovers Melissa, it will only be the cherry on the sundae. Emily's testimony will count for nothing. There's Chrissy's body in the house, the confession video on my phone.

He nods. "I know. I don't really care. At least I will
know justice was done."

He steps toward me. And the look on his face is...
maniacal, resolve and relief all in one. I did this to him, I
think, incredulous.

And in the same moment, I realize, as fear fills me, that
I don't want to die.

I turn around and start to run.

*     *     *

Byron makes it to the front door before I do, blocking
my escape. I spin around, my bare feet skidding on the
floor, and dart in the opposite direction but he makes no
attempt to follow me, to stop me.

The hammer.

I see it on the edge of a table and grab for it. My hands
shake wildly, and a vase comes crashing down and shatters on the floor. One of Colleen's.

My hands grip the hammer's handle. It's slippery.
Blood? Colleen's blood. No, Chrissy's. Colleen was buried
deep in the dirt floor of my mother's garage many years
ago, concrete poured over her a short while before I sold
the house, a grave forever without a name. It will pass into
oblivion along with me.

I didn't kill her with a hammer either; it was a wine bottle. Why is everything so confused?

I can't do this. Not like this. I put the hammer back
down and take one, two, three tiny steps toward Byron,
who stands still in front of the door. He waits.

But he doesn't look like Byron anymore. His face is an anonymous ripple, blurred out like on one of those true-crime shows. I squint. Sweat drips into my eyes—that must be what's messing with my vision. I blink it away furiously, and Byron's face refocuses. But it's still the wrong face. It's not Byron, it's Brandon—that boyfriend of my mother's, the one who always told me to watch TV with the two of them. He'd sit right next to me and grope my leg.

Then he cornered me one day, a week before my sixteenth birthday. Mom was in her bedroom, passed out, and Chrissy was out with her popular friends—Chrissy never seemed to be around when Brandon came over, I remember with a rush of confusion. I remember finally understanding why too late as he pulled my jeans down my legs, pinning me facedown on the living room couch, his elbow in my back, its sharp point right between my shoulder blades. I didn't really struggle, and it was over quickly. He didn't stick around too long after that.

Something seemed to flicker out inside me after. Like someone flipped a switch. All my emotions, everything I felt, became gray and flat: joy, sorrow, shame, anger—everything seemed to skim the surface.

Until I saw Byron in the school gym that day. Then everything became real once more.

I blink, and my husband's face becomes his face again. Indescribable relief fills me. My heart is lighter than a balloon. It wasn't a mistake after all. I did everything I was supposed to do. I did everything right. Fate guided me, and I followed—I followed it through to the very end.

Byron is my husband, and I love him, even if he doesn't

love me. That's what true love is. True love only gives and asks for nothing in return. True love is magnanimous. True love is self-sufficient.

Everything around me disappears. It's just the two of us in my tunnel vision, and everything else goes dark. My lips start to form his name—*Byron, Byron, Byron*—but don't have time to complete the first syllable.

Something crashes over me from behind. A vicious pain flares in the back of my skull. My vision bursts with white sparks and then white begins to encroach at the edges, flooding everything. I feel myself begin to topple, my knees giving way. The floor rushes toward me but there's no shock or pain of impact. It's like falling into a cloud.

I want to laugh but I can't feel my lips anymore. What a burden true love is. No one will ever understand. They will all think I'm crazy, insane, psychotic, but what else is love but madness? Isn't that what all the great novels are about?

My husband should know. He teaches them to naïve teenage girls every day, year in and year out. And those girls in college who have always been so contemptuous of me, who whispered behind my back and called me a pathetic throwback and prude—they will never know one-tenth of the pain I went through, all in the name of the great love they only read about in Byron's class. They think they know hardship and suffering but they know nothing. They kiss their boyfriends, whose names they won't remember by senior year, they make out with each other in bars, but they know nothing of true love. The love that kills.

Faintly, before my sight flickers out, I see a figure standing over me. A woman. Brandishing something. I think it's a hammer—it's all so out of focus that I can't tell. Maybe it's a lamp or a vase. Or a wine bottle. The only thing I can see clearly is her boots. Shiny fake leather trimmed with fur, also fake.

No. It can't be. A synapse fires deep within my damaged brain but fizzles and flickers out to nothing. I know who she is but can't make the connection. Only one name rises out of my murky memory and floats to my lips.

*Colleen.*

The last thing I see is her dropping the hammer. It clatters to the floor, inches from my face. And then I fall away, tumbling into the white nothingness.

# EPILOGUE

The Mansfield College Canvas Official Blog

OPINION:

MURDERER OR VICTIM? LET'S NOT JUMP TO CONCLUSIONS

by Mia Flynn

Controversies continue to surround the case of Mansfield professor Byron Westcott and the death of his wife, Claire Westcott. The bizarre case has captivated nationwide media attention, but no one is more affected than us—students and faculty who have worked and studied with Prof. Westcott for more than a decade.

Westcott, beloved professor of literature, was previously married to painter and former Mansfield professor Colleen May, whose death under suspicious circumstances in 2010 was ruled a suicide following a short investigation. And three months ago, police responded to a frantic 911 call from Byron Westcott. They found him next to the body of his second wife, Claire, with Claire's sister, Christine Belfour, seriously injured on the floor next to her. It appeared that Ms. Belfour had delivered the fatal blow to Claire Westcott after a violent struggle. Christine Belfour, a manicurist from Cincinnati with a history of alcohol abuse, is still in the hospital following injuries to her head and spine. Byron Westcott remains in custody.

However, so much about the case is still shrouded in mystery. What happened between Byron and Claire Westcott? Troublesome testimonies about Claire Westcott's character have surfaced— namely, from other faculty members at Mansfield as well as a doctor and staff of a local fertility clinic.

How did Christine "Chrissy" Belfour, who's been reportedly estranged from her sister for years, find herself in her home that fateful day? Is it all connected to Colleen May? How did Dr. May really die, and where is her body?

And the big one: Is Byron Westcott the victim or a cold-blooded and manipulative murderer?

The police investigation is underway. But it looks like we won't know the truth for a while, if ever.

Which leaves us with more questions that may never have an answer. How well do we know those closest to us? So many of us have taken Dr. Westcott's classes and loved his lectures. I have been his TA for the last year, and it's hard for me to imagine this kind, generous man guilty of any kind of wrongdoing. Right now, it looks like he might never come back to Mansfield or to teaching ever again.

In this strange and complicated case, it's easy to designate a scapegoat or jump to conclusions. But I, for one, choose to believe in Byron Westcott's innocence.

COMMENTS:

**ValerieJ:** yeeeeeah. *sarcasm* believe the guy about the dead woman. How convenient!

**Ramonathepest:** the victim blaming in this piece is SICKENING imho. What are mods thinking??!?? Take it down!!!

*WokieMcWokeface:* uhuhhhh. Dead women tell no tales, especially when a Straight White Male is telling the TRUTH, everybody!!!

*Ramonathepest:* See Wokie we were right about him all along.

*Jake015:* You're all crazy. CW basically brained her sister w/a hammer. I saw it on the news the other day. It was self-defense. Poor guy.

*Ramonathepest:* STFU Jake015 before I report you

*Notyourmothersfeminist:* Ugh, everyone knows Mia is

*Notyourmothersfeminist:* [comment removed by moderator]

# ACKNOWLEDGMENTS

As always, thank you to my agent, Rachel Ekstrom Courage, and everyone at Folio Literary. Also thanks to Miranda Graeme, one of the earliest readers of this book, for her feedback and notes.

Thank you to Alex Logan (without whose editorial guidance I'd be a meandering mess), Kristin Roth Nappier, Mari Okuda, and the team at Grand Central Publishing for helping me unleash Claire Westcott upon the unsuspecting world. Huge thank-you to Kamrun Nesa and Tiffany Sanchez, publicity and marketing team extraordinaire!

As usual, thanks go out to Maude Michaud and The Ladies, in whose encouraging presence I wrote parts of the manuscript that would become *The Starter Wife*.

No real people were exploited as inspiration for this book but I'd like to thank the authors whose fiction fuels my crazy ideas. Thanks to David Bell, Heather Gudenkauf, Meg Gardiner, Wendy Walker, and others who have said kind words about my writing.

Thank you to Patrick and to my family for your unwavering support.

And finally, thank you to all the readers who pick up my books! You are truly what it's all about.

I look up at the TV screen, and my twin brother's face is splashed across it, life-size. It's a shock that makes my breath catch. This is my brother as an adult, my brother whom I last saw fifteen years ago after the fire that killed our parents, covered in soot, clutching a lighter in his hand, his knuckles stark white against the dirt and ash.

What did you do this time, Eli?
What the hell did you do?

Please turn the page for an excerpt from *What My Sister Knew* by Nina Laurin.

Available now.

# CHAPTER ONE

APRIL 10, 3:44 A.M.

A sticky thread of saliva runs from the corner of my mouth down to my earlobe, cool across my cheek. My vertebrae feel like a bunch of disconnected Lego pieces but I manage to hold up my head.

Humid April wind howls through the car. That's not right. Then I realize there's no windshield and the gleaming uncut diamonds scattered all over the passenger seat are glass shards.

My temple throbs with hot, clean pain, and I realize I need to call someone: Milton, or better yet, an ambulance. Why didn't the airbag work? The light from the car—the one surviving headlight, like a beam of a lost lighthouse in the night—shines into emptiness filled with stray raindrops, catching the side of the tree that I wrapped my car around.

When I raise my hand to my forehead, my fingers

come away coated with slick, shiny blood. More of it is already running down my neck under my collar— foreheads bleed a lot. An ambulance sounds better and better, but I don't know where to even begin looking for my phone. Was I texting when I crashed? Checking my email? They're going to ask that, and I have to say no. I sometimes use my phone as a GPS, but not tonight. I've taken this route a million times. When there's no traffic, and there's never any traffic, it takes me forty-five minutes to get home.

The door is stuck, and for a few moments, I tug and push and pull on the handle, consumed by ever-growing panic. But then, once I give it a kick, it comes unstuck and swings open. Getting out is a feat. I unfold my aching body and have to hold on to the car door to keep from falling over. After stumbling through the usual debris on the side of the highway, I breathe a sigh of relief when there's finally flat, solid asphalt beneath my feet, the yellow stripe in its center curving into the dark distance. I follow it. Down the road, there's a gas station. If I were driving, it would be right there around that curve. I don't know how far it is on foot but, hopefully, not that far.

I take one step after another until the road steadies itself beneath my feet and stops swaying. Next thing I know, when I turn around, I can no longer see my car. The one headlight went out, and now it's just me and the sky and the road.

My heart starts to thunder, which makes my forehead bleed more—or at least it feels like it, that little throbbing pulse intensifying. Maybe I should have stayed and looked for my phone in the wilted grass of the ditch. Anything could be out here on this road. The darkness is alive.

I wrap my arms around myself and do my best to walk faster, but a rush of dizziness stops me in my tracks. When I close my eyes, an image flashes in front of them, a shadow. A figure. Except this isn't imagination—it's memory. It's vivid, fresh. I'm driving, twin beams of my car's headlights intact, my hands firmly on the steering wheel, my mind calm in that dull way it is after a long, late shift. I'm thinking about a bath and a bowl of ramen noodles in front of the TV I will only half watch because nothing good is on that late.

The shadow flickers out of nowhere, my headlights snatching it out of the darkness. It's the silhouette of a man, standing stock-still in the middle of the road, right over that yellow line.

I open my eyes, and there's nothing—no car, no lights, no figure. A glow in the distance suggests that I'm getting closer to the gas station and, hopefully, a phone and an ambulance. At the same time, the dizziness settles in, and I fight the temptation to sit down, just for a moment. Or better yet, lie down, right here on the side of the road. This means I have a concussion, which means I need to do precisely the opposite, as I learned in my mandatory first aid courses.

A spike of headache drives itself into my temple, and when I flinch, the image springs back up, like a movie I paused in the middle of the action. I'm careening toward the figure at eighty miles per hour. When I react, it's already too late to slow down, to give him a wide berth. The car's headlights bathe him in bluish light, erasing facial features, bleaching out everything except a strange harlequin pattern of splotches and spots that look black against his ghostly skin. Just as I swerve the steering wheel and hit the brakes, I have time to see that I was wrong—it's not black. It's red, red like ripe cherries and rust.

Then the world spins, the road is gone, and so is the figure. My eyes snap open just as everything explodes. *Bang*.

I'm panting and need to stop to catch my breath, hands on my knees. The gas station is finally in view, deserted but all aglow like a church on Christmas Eve.

Only a few more steps and I've reached salvation.

\*     \*     \*

What follows is a blur but somehow I find myself on a gurney with a blanket around my shoulders, and an ambulance tech is shining a flashlight into my eyes. Whether I have a concussion or not, the cut on my temple keeps oozing blood so they tape a gauze pad over it. I expect someone to ask me what happened but no one does. Through the open doors, I watch the ambulance lights bounce off the rain-slicked road. Is that what happened? Did my car skid? Maybe I fell asleep at the wheel.

"Ms. Boudreaux?" the ambulance tech is saying. They already know my name, which means they ran my car's plates. Then I see my open purse just sitting there in the middle of the wet road, my wallet splayed open next to it. Oh. How did it get here? I don't remember grabbing it as

I got out. "We're taking you to Saint Joseph Hospital, all right? For observation."

I hate that soothing tone, maybe because I've oftentimes used it myself, on frightened teenage runaways who show up at the shelter where I work. But whether I like it or not, it has the intended effect: He could be saying literally anything in that calm, measured voice. It's the intonation and timbre that have the effect.

"We'll notify your family," the tech says. It's that word that wakes me up, overriding whatever he just shot into the crook of my elbow. I make a clumsy move to grasp his forearm.

"Wait. There's someone else there." I must have hit my head harder than I thought—I can barely get the words out, slurring and misshapen.

He frowns. "Someone else?"

"I saw someone. Maybe they're hurt."

"You mean you hit someone?"

I give a vigorous shake of my head. I'm disoriented as hell, but this I'm sure of. Certain. Although when I think about it, I have no reason to be so certain, considering I still go to AA meetings once a week. "No. I saw someone." I didn't drink, I didn't take anything, I haven't even smoked a joint in months. That part of my memory is crystal clear. I wasn't wasted, and I didn't run anyone over.

But there was a man, covered in blood. And by the time I came to, a few minutes later—or maybe hours later, for all I know—he was gone.

# CHAPTER TWO

This is what they tell Milton when he gets there: I was driving home from work, crashed my car, and hit my head. They think I have a concussion. They don't hook me up to any machines, only an IV and a heart rate monitor. I'm in a room with four or five other people. I can't tell exactly how many because the space is separated by white plastic curtains that smell faintly of cleanser. When all of them are closed, the space I have to myself is just big enough to accommodate the bed itself and the plastic chair next to it.

My health insurance through work only covers the most basic stuff. In retrospect, I should have swallowed my pride and let my adoptive mother put me on the family plan. The family plan includes separate rooms. And probably a monogrammed bathrobe as a souvenir. That same plan once gave me braces for my teeth and laser treatments for the burn scars on my chest, neck, and upper arms. The braces did their job; the laser treatment...not so much.

Far over my head, positioned at an angle above the curtains so that everyone in the room can see it, is a TV screen. It's hard to watch without painfully craning my neck, and anyway, the channel is fuzzy with static.

The curtain crinkles, and its metal rings clink against the curtain rod, alerting me that Milt is back. I lower my head onto the flat hospital pillow and try to look appropriately injured.

He's brought me sour candies and a can of the exact no-name orange soda I like, presumably from the vending machine downstairs. There's nothing like favorite childhood junk foods to make you feel better but right now I can barely bring myself to look at the treats.

"Quick," he says, tossing me the bag of sour candies. I catch it in midair. "Before the nurse comes in and sees you." He winks, and I do my best not to cringe.

Few people wear their name quite as badly as Milt does. My gorgeous, six-foot-two, blond, blue-eyed, college soccer champion fiancé—pardon, ex-fiancé. It's easy to forget. Even when I still had the ring he gave me, I hardly ever wore it, not because I didn't appreciate it but because I'd never think of wearing a two-carat diamond to work at the homeless youth shelter. When the ring disappeared, my first logical thought was to tell him that someone stole it.

Milton wasn't my type until I met him. In fact, he was the opposite of my type. I always liked the dangerous boys, dark eyes and hair in need of clippers, a tattoo peeking out from under a collar or sleeve. When we met, I was at a party where I barely knew anyone, pursuing one or another such boy—I don't even remember which anymore. I remember getting stupid-drunk on those canned, premixed, malty-tasting sex on the beach drinks because the boy failed to show.

It wasn't a love-at-first-sight thing; Milt was there with somebody else. I never really knew who that girl was or what happened to her, because the next time Milton and I met, I pretended not to remember that party. It was more than a year later. I'd had time to grow out my ugly haircut and realize that black lipstick wasn't for me. I hoped he wouldn't recognize me, but I underestimated his ability to notice details. Because he recognized me, all right.

And within another two years, I somehow had not just Milt but also the diamond, the town house, all those things so normal and conventional it made them magical somehow. Everyone sort of expected me to die in a ditch, and here I was, with a mortgage and a reluctant subscription to a bridal magazine.

Of course, it couldn't have lasted. Just as we were already deciding on venues and caterers, I went and fucked it all up. Milt doesn't have the heart to leave me, so we're not broken up—we're taking a break. Same word, different formulation, but he doesn't see it's essentially the same meaning. He let me have the town house while he lives in his parents' summer residence.

I tear open the packet, and sour candies go flying all over the pale-blue hospital sheet. I snatch them up and pop two or three into my mouth at once. My taste buds writhe in acidic agony, and my eyes start to water, but I figure, with a mouthful of chewy high-fructose corn syrup, I can't be expected to talk.

"So you're going to tell me what happened?" Milt asks. He's not angry with me. It's not really in his nature to get angry. He's anxious, although he tries hard to hide it—it's not so easy to hide things from a psych major, even one who only made it to the end of senior year on a prayer.

"I'm fine. It's just a concussion." I have a feeling like I just said the same words less than five minutes ago. I gulp down the half-chewed sour candy that sears the back of my throat. "Where's my phone?"

His gaze darts back and forth. "I don't know. I checked at Reception. They gave me your coat and purse, but I don't think your phone is in there." He clears his throat, which is one of his tells. "Maybe, er, the police—"

"I wasn't texting," I say. I feel like I already said this too. "And I wasn't drunk."

Have they taken my blood to test for alcohol and drugs? My upper lip breaks out in beads of anxious sweat. They have no reason to do that, do they? No one else got hurt. Even I didn't get hurt...too badly. Besides, even if they did the test, I have nothing to worry about.

"So what happened?"

"Milton," I say. I catch his wrist and feel the muscles in his forearm, sinewy and ropey through the sleeve of his jacket. They tense and pop as he instinctively pulls away. This is bad. I hold on but my grip is weak. "Milton, you do believe me, right?"

"Of course I believe you." Milton sounds sad. Milton knows more about me than almost anyone—because I told him things I've told very few people who weren't shrinks. And also because his parents hired a PI to look into my background when we started dating, and he accidentally blabbed about it months after the fact. "It's just, you're a good driver."

For just a moment, I consider telling him the truth. Blink, and it's gone. "The road was slippery. Or maybe...maybe I fell asleep. I don't know, okay? I was exhausted. I don't remember exactly. I hit my head."

"Yeah." He finds it in him to grin and ruffles my hair. "You're going to look like a football for a while. Completing your gangsta cred?"

I chuckle. I want him to keep touching me.

His look turns serious. "I believe you, Addie." He knows I hate the nickname, but the more I protested the more he made it sort of a playful tug-of-war until it stuck, whether I liked it or not. "But I have the right to be worried. And your airbag—it didn't deploy."

"My bad for buying a crappy used car." Last year, he did offer to buy me a brand-new sedan, one with the top safety rating in its category. But I always had an issue with accepting his money—by extension, his parents' money—ever since I found out about the PI.

I can handle the fact that they hate me, but investigating me is another thing.

"Have they told you when they're letting me go home?"

He shrugs. "I tried to ask at Reception but they barely acknowledged I was there, so..." He gives me a guilty smile. "Can I at least get you something to pass the time? A magazine from the lobby? A book?"

Yes. As a matter of fact, you can get me a phone, hopefully one with a signal and a full battery and an internet connection. But I just return his smile in a properly pained way and shake my head.

"I'll see if I can find a nurse. Or someone who knows what's going on." He makes a motion to leave but slowly, reluctantly, as if he's hoping I'll ask him to stay.

"Milton," I blurt, like it's my last chance. For all I know, it is. "Wait. There's a . . . thing I think I remember. Or maybe I imagined it. Or dreamed it, if I really did fall asleep."

Alarm crosses his features. He doesn't have time to hide it, and I nearly change my mind but realize it's too late to go back. "I saw something," I say, swallowing. My mouth immediately goes sandpaper dry. "On the road, someone jumped out in front of my car. I didn't have time to see. A figure."

Milton's brows, a few shades darker than his sandy-blond hair, knit as he frowns. "Addie," he says, "have you told anyone? Have you told the police?"

"Police?" I stammer. "Why would I—"

But in that moment, I'm miraculously saved from the mess I got myself into. I hear rapidly approaching clacking steps that don't sound like a nurse's orthopedic sneakers, and a moment later, someone yanks the plastic curtain out of the way. No *hello*, no *are you decent*.

"Jesus Christ, Andrea. Not this bullshit again. What on earth were you thinking?"

With maroon lipstick at seven a.m. and fury blazing forth off her gold-rimmed bifocals, the formidable Cynthia Boudreaux has arrived.

"I wasn't drunk," I say through gritted teeth. "I fell asleep at the wheel." I don't glance at Milt, and he keeps mum, thank God. The mysterious-figure-in-the-middle-of-the-road version of events has been forgotten for now.

The woman who raised me from age twelve dismisses me with a wave of her hand. She probably already knows I wasn't in a DUI-related accident—the nurses or the police would have told her, because no such nonsense as patient confidentiality ever got in the way of Cynthia Boudreaux. I don't understand why she's here. Certainly not out of concern for me. Even if she had any, once upon a time, I sure did everything in my power to make sure this was no longer the case.

"They'll be releasing her soon," she says over my head at Milt. "I'm going to take her *home*."

The ominous way she says the last word, with a subtle but present emphasis, tells me she doesn't mean the town house.

"No way," I protest.

"Did you get her stuff from Reception?" Cynthia's icy gaze doesn't waver from Milt, like I don't even exist.

"Here," he says, complying, handing her the plastic bag with all my belongings. I'm stricken speechless by the betrayal unfolding right before my eyes, and Milt studiously avoids looking at me. She snatches the bag out of his hand and peers in.

"Is her phone in there?"

"No."

She fishes unceremoniously through my things, unzips my purse, and plunges her veiny hand with its gold rings into its depths, retrieving my wallet that she flips open and fleetingly inspects. "Anything else missing?"

"Why would anything be missing? Mom?"

For once, the *m* word fails to get her attention.

"Go check at Reception again," she says to Milt. "Make sure we have everything. Her car keys. Where are her car keys?"

Milt looks uncertain. He opens his mouth to say something but cuts himself off, silenced by my adoptive mother's sharp glare. The second he vanishes on the other side of the white curtain, Cynthia drops the act—it's an instant, head-to-toe flip, a shape-shifter changing form. She takes her glasses off and rubs the bridge of her nose where the little plastic pads have left two kidney-shaped red marks in her foundation. Her shoulders drop, relaxing from the perfect politician's wife posture; even her face itself seems to fall an inch or two, a mask with loosened strings.

"Do you think I don't know what you're up to?" she says in a hoarse, loud whisper. "Do you think you're the only smart person around here? And if I can figure it out, so can the police." She heaves a noisy sigh that smells like her herbal supplements and mouthwash. "I knew it would come back to bite you. I knew it."

I lift myself up on my elbows. "Mom, what are you going on about?"

"Don't *mom* me," she snaps. "We're well past that, Andrea, and you really should have thought about it when—"

"I wasn't driving drunk, and I wasn't texting. I swear." I make a move to catch her hand, which she eludes. "Why did they take my phone? Was it the police?"

"And they have your thermal cup too," she says dryly. "They're analyzing the contents."

A thought flits through my head: *Good, let them think I spiked my coffee with some dregs of cheap whiskey I confiscated from one of my shelter kids; let them think I swallowed pills, whatever.* I don't let the thought show on my face.

"But that's not the point," Cynthia adds. "Anyway, we're going home now; I already called our lawyer, and if they want to talk to you, not a word without him present, understand?"

"I'm not going to your house," I say, struggling to contain the anger that fills my chest. "I'm going home. I'll ask Milt to drive me."

"Milton is coming too," she says, not missing a single beat. "Just keep in mind, your sister is there, so at least have the decency to behave."

At the news that my adopted sister is home, an electric tingle of alarm shoots down my spine, and I know that whatever it is might not have anything to do with the crash after all.

And it must be really, really bad.

"Mom—"

A nurse comes in, her bulky presence overfilling the small space, all canned hospital cheer and smell of disinfectant. Cynthia puts her glasses back on and reluctantly steps aside, letting the nurse yank the catheter needle out of my arm and disconnect me from the heart rate monitor. For better or for worse, I'm being let go.

The nurse is professional and efficient, and before I

know it, I'm seated in a wheelchair, a piece of folded-up gauze stuck to the crook of my elbow with clear tape. The whole time, she manages not to look me in the eye once, and whenever she speaks, I feel like she's talking at me, not to me. Like Cynthia's been giving her lessons.

Just as she hands me over to another nurse, a short Filipino woman, I turn and glimpse at her over my shoulder—in time to catch her looking. An expression races across her face but vanishes before I can make anything of it, facial muscles relaxing and eyebrow creases smoothing back to a waxy neutrality.

I recognize this look, or one like it, from many years ago.

From after the fire. When I forever became That Boy's Sister.

# CHAPTER THREE

*The woman whose friends knew her as Cassie hid a difficult start behind her cheerful, optimistic demeanor. Photos from her youth show a beautiful, smiling girl with piercing green eyes and long, glossy brunette tresses, teased up per the dictates of late eighties fashion. But by the time her children, Andrea and Eli, were born in 1990, that smile had faded.*

*The children's father had an extensive arrest record for felonies ranging from petty theft to battery and assault. Cassandra had lost touch with her only remaining family, an elderly aunt, and dropped most of her friends. Her coworkers reported that she showed up with bruises poorly concealed by makeup.*

*When the twins were only two years old, she finally snapped. After a particularly violent episode, she pressed charges against her first husband and spent several months at a women's shelter. She could have easily gone down a familiar path: more dysfunctional relationships, alcohol, drugs, and eventual tragedy. But instead, things took a good turn. She found a job, which allowed her to leave the shelter and move into an apartment with the twins. For several years, Cassie worked long hours on minimum wage, still managing to support herself and her children. Eventually, she got a cashier job at a furniture store, and shortly after that, she married the store's owner, Sergio Bianchi.*

*Now a housewife living in a spacious suburban home, Cassie's future looked as bright as ever. But everything was shattered when tragedy found its way back into Cassie's life, from the place she least expected it.*

—*Into Ashes: The Shocking Double Murder in the Suburbs* by Jonathan Lamb, Eclipse Paperbacks, 2004, 1st ed.

*FIFTEEN YEARS EARLIER: BEFORE THE FIRE*

Crouched on the brick border of a flowerbed across from the school playground, Andrea stares at the face of the hot-pink watch around her wrist. She wiggles its translucent strap with bits of glitter trapped in the plastic. It's uncomfortable, even on the loosest setting, too small for a twelve-year-old, and the buckle leaves a sweaty red welt in the plump, pale flesh of her wrist. That's why she keeps the watch hidden under her sleeve at all times.

Other girls don't wear watches with cartoon characters anymore. Other girls paint their lips in front of the bathroom mirror during breaks and smoke during lunch, perched on the windowsill next to the window that only opens a smidgen. Andrea thought she might like smoking: The smell of it, whenever she dashes in and out of the bathroom unnoticed, tickles her nostrils in a way that's not unpleasant, and it makes her ponder other exciting possibilities like stealing sips of Miller beer at a high schoolers' party, or even making out with boys. She's not entirely sure what making out consists of and how it's different from just kissing. But she knows these are the things she's supposed to want, even though she can never quite get a clear mental image.

And besides, the cigarette smoke makes her think of Sergio, her mom's husband. Sergio is supposed to have quit, but she knows he still sneaks cigarettes on the balcony when her mom isn't home. She caught him once, when she came home from school fifteen minutes early. She felt strange watching him, leaning on his elbow on the balcony railing as he exhaled smoke through flared nostrils. He looked different alone, lost in his thoughts as he tapped the ashes over the railing. A tiny spark detached itself from the glowing tip of the cigarette, drew a luminous orange arc in the air, and winked out gracelessly to a black point. She felt like she was seeing something she wasn't supposed to. Like watching scary movies through a crack in the door.

He caught her looking after only a few seconds, but he must have thought she'd been standing there for a while. He didn't look alarmed. He waved her over, and she trudged through the backyard, right through the snow Sergio was supposed to shovel from the pathway but didn't. Now it had developed a grayish crust that crunched under her boots. Sinking to midcalf, she stumbled over.

"Let's keep this a secret, hmm, kid?" he said. "I'll get you something you want, and you don't tell Mom, all right?"

This was when she could have asked for one of those charm bracelets, or a new set of gel pens, or a Discman, or bedazzled jeans with the butterflies above the hems like the other girls had. She would have gotten it—she was fairly sure—because if she told her mom about the cigarette, there would be yelling, and there was a chance Sergio wouldn't get to be her dad anymore, which was not what she wanted. She still isn't sure why she didn't ask for something nicer.

Now she glances at the watch, and the long, thin hand with the jumping pink heart on it seems to twitch and jerk in one place without ever moving. Only ten minutes are left until the lunch hour is over, and Andrea considers going back, slinking along the wall to wait in front of the classroom even though you're not supposed to before the first bell. Bathrooms have been her respite until this year, but now the lip gloss and cigarette girls have claimed them as their fiefdom, and she'd sooner throw herself off the roof.

A noise, and her head snaps up. It's a wrong noise. It's coming from the fire exit by the gym where she snuck out. The door wails and groans as someone swings it wide open, and then it crashes shut. She hears giggling and excited shrieks. She knows who she'll see before they come into her range of sight.

Andrea is twelve, and the girls are thirteen. Her December birthday not only shortchanges her on birthday gifts, which double as Christmas presents, but it also makes her one of the youngest in her grade. And in those few months that feel like a chasm she'll never be able to get across, all the others seem to have picked up on things intuitively, things Andrea still has no clue about. Andrea isn't a pretty girl. She's not rich enough to compensate, and she's never been smart. She's just a strange, lonely girl, in an age before smartphones, before the internet was ubiquitous, before strange, lonely girls had online friends to confide in and blogs to fill with bad poems.

She is, however, smart enough to know what they're here for. Under the sleeves of her sweater, yesterday's bruises make themselves known, and her right ribs throb with every inhale. The girls are coming. There's one especially, Leeanne, who is the worst of them all. Whenever Andrea thinks of her, even when she's not at school, even on Saturday mornings when Sergio is making pancakes for all of them, her stomach twists with dread. Her heart starts to race like when the teacher makes them run laps in gym.

The laughter and voices grow closer and closer, and Andrea knows she must hide. A panicked glance around confirms that she has nowhere to go, only open space everywhere; the playground won't hide her. So she does the only thing she can: She ducks behind the brick border and flattens herself against the earth. She lets herself think that maybe, just maybe, the border is tall enough to hide her. Maybe if Leeanne doesn't see her right away, she'll think Andrea is hiding somewhere else, and Leeanne and her posse will leave.

The ground is mind-bogglingly cold, and damp seeps through Andrea's gray sweater, the one Leeanne called a dishrag last week. Andrea stuck it in the trash once she got home, but her mom fished it out and made her wear it again. Her jeans are black, and the mud won't show as much, but the sweater will be ruined. Andrea presses her cheek into the earth and flexes her fingers in the dirt. It's so cold that her hands go numb at once.

The steps grow closer, and Leeanne's peals of laughter ring out right over her head. She squeezes her eyes shut.

"Oh my God. Look at her. What is she doing?" The voice belongs to another girl, and every word drips with disdain.

Andrea barely has time to draw a breath. A hand grabs the back of her collar and pulls her up as if she were a kitten.

"Eww! Let her go, Leelee. So gross," says the first voice.

"You disgusting little pig," Leeanne's voice sneers, so close to Andrea's face that she can smell her strawberry gum. "Look at yourself. You're repulsive."

The other two girls start to make oinking noises. Andrea's collar cuts deep into her neck. She tries to steady herself on the brick border but her hands slip off it. Tears are stubbornly sneaking from under her shut eyelids.

"What a shame. You got mud all over that nice sweater. What will Mommy think?"

Andrea opens her eyes to see Leeanne's rapturous grin just inches from her face. She has a little bit of glittery pink gloss on one of her front teeth. The light of day brings out the pimple on her forehead that she coated with concealer. She wears that cropped puffy coat with the white fur trim that all the girls envy. Leeanne's parents are rich, and she has everything. Lip gloss, platform shoes, bedazzled jeans, rabbit fur collars.

Suddenly Andrea knows what to do. Leeanne is leering while her two cronies keep on oinking, pressing their fingertips with pink-polished nails into their noses to turn them up. Andrea raises her hand, unclenches her fingers, and plants the handful of mud into the dead center of Leeanne's white coat.

For a moment, everyone is stunned into silence. Then Leeanne's shriek nearly splits her eardrums. The girls yelp *oh my God* and *look what she did* and *what a little bitch*. Leeanne's grip loosens on Andrea's collar, and just as Andrea draws in a lungful of air, Leeanne's palm connects with her right cheek.

The slap goes off like an explosion and sends her flying right back onto the muddy lawn. The world tilts as she lands on her side, the impact knocking the wind out of her.

"You bitch! You'll pay for this," shrieks Leeanne. Andrea realizes her mistake, but all she has time to do is curl up on her side, pulling her knees up to her chin. Leeanne's pointy-toed boot digs into her side, right into yesterday's bruise, drawing a gasp from her. Her mouth fills with mud as more kicks rain down from all directions. Suddenly, they stop, and she realizes the ringing isn't inside her skull—it's the bell far overhead.

When she opens her eyes again, the girls are gone. But she can't go to class—she knows that. She barely finds the strength to sit up. Tears are running down her face freely now, and she smears them along with the mud all over her cheeks.

"Hey! Addie."

She spins around and sees a lone, lanky silhouette sauntering toward her. She wants to call out to him, but if she opens her mouth, she knows she'll start to sob.

"What happened?" He crouches to be at her face level, and she turns her head away. "Shit. Leeanne again?"

"Mom will kill me," Andrea murmurs, surprised that it's the first thing that comes to mind.

"Why? It wasn't your fault."

"For the sweater."

Her brother's face blurs with the tears in her eyes. Eli is everything Andrea is not, like he'd leeched all the bright colors out of her when they were still in the womb, and some of the girls are already starting to look at him in *that* way, giggling behind their hands.

"Don't worry about the sweater. I'll switch with you." Their mom buys their clothes at Walmart, and he's wearing the same gray sweater with fitted cuffs, except scrupulously clean. "Come on, Addie. Let's go get you cleaned up."

She lets go of a tiny sob. Eli grins and picks up some of the mud at his feet.

"Hey. Look." Under her puzzled gaze, he smears the dirt along his hairline and down his cheek. She can't help but giggle. "Feel better? Come on. We'll be late for class."

"You're not going to go to class like this," she says.

"Sure I am. Boys will be boys, right?"

# CHAPTER FOUR

They smuggle me out the back like some celebrity after a stint in rehab. So it really must be that bad, I think, trying not to let myself panic.

Milt takes the back seat on the passenger's side, next to me, in Cynthia's black, shiny Cadillac SUV. The morning is obscenely bright and sunny, and the car is stuffy like a toaster oven from soaking up the sunshine in the parking lot. I watch my adoptive mother jab the buttons irritably with her manicured finger until the fans start their quiet hum in the four corners of the car. My sweat cools on my upper lip. Here, in the gauzy aroma of Cynthia's lilac air freshener, I notice the sour, stale smell wafting from me. It can't be coming from the clean clothes Milt brought me from home, my favorite old jeans and a sweatshirt I'd left thrown over the back of a chair in the bedroom, in another life. It seems to seep from my very pores, and I detect my own fetid breath, which means it's even worse than I can tell. I smell not too unlike my charges when they show up at the shelter, hoping for a place to turn in for the night, or at least for a cup of coffee and five minutes in a tepid shower.

As soon as I'm home, I'm going to run a bath, I think automatically, my mind on the oversize oval tub in our town house. Except I'm not going home and there will be no bath, not for a little bit.

"Can I have my phone now?" I pipe up.

"You don't have a phone anymore," Cynthia says flatly. My snappish retort dies when I see her eyes in the rearview mirror. Her regular Botox appointments maintain her face in a pleasing, smooth expression, but in spite of all that paralyzing toxin, her glare manages to convey murder. So I decide to keep quiet.

When we turn the corner onto the quiet street where the house sits at the very end, I sit up straight and look around. My adoptive parents used to live in an honest-to-God gated community, right up until the out-of-nowhere divorce that came as a surprise even to me. The ensuing move from the McMansion to the neat Victorian-style cottage in an upper-middle-class area was a comedown Cynthia never got over. That was when Cynthia's own biological daughter began to hate her. I, for one, was glad to be out of that mansion. Maybe it's all the memories of life right after the fire that I was glad to leave behind. Maybe I just liked the cottage that smelled like home—not my home, maybe, but a home.

Right now, there are cars—not our neighbors' quaint Toyota SUVs and dated Jeeps, but other cars, vans splashed with logos. One or two have that telltale tower sticking out of them, like something from a cartoon.

"Milton," Cynthia says in that reserved voice that nonetheless manages to be commanding. He nods, shrugs out of his jacket, and throws it over me. It's big enough to cover me entirely, like a large, warm tent that smells like him. Except right now it's anything but comforting.

"What the hell is going on?" I ask, peering out from under the collar.

He gives me a look so apologetic it borders on pity. "Come along, Addie."

We make our way through the swarm of reporters, and all I can see are legs and feet: my own once-white work shoes, Milt's brown leather boots, Cynthia's maroon stocky heels and massive nylon-clad calves in front of me. And other shoes, crowding in from all sides: loafers, sneakers, pumps. Voices descend on us, overwhelming despite the coat that covers me from head to midthigh.

"Do you have any comment, Andrea? What can you tell us about what happened?"

Milton yells at them to get the fuck away from me, or something like that—I don't make out the actual words. Cynthia's shrill voice chimes in: *Please disperse; she will not be talking to anyone right now.* Finally, the front door opens, swallows us up, and shuts behind us. I throw the coat off me with all the violence my painkiller-weakened muscles can muster, just in time to see Cynthia turn the two locks and slide the latch into place too.

"I was afraid it would be worse," Milt is saying.

"Worse?" Cynthia hisses. "How can it possibly be worse?"

That's when I realize I've had enough. "One of you is going to tell me what the fuck is going on," I snap. "Right fucking now."

They turn to me as if on command, and their faces soften, expressions shifting.

"Addie," Milt says in that pacifying tone, the same one he used when we had The Talk months ago about taking a break.

"You should go to your room and rest," Cynthia cuts in. "You have a concussion, for goodness' sake. You're not thinking clearly."

"I think I'm the only one here right now who's thinking clearly."

Cynthia looks at Milt, half-pleading, half-exasperated. He steps forward, tiny steps like he's about to tame a wild horse, and tries to take my arm. I throw him off. He grabs it again, more insistent this time, and I'm reminded that he's an athlete who still works out five days a week, and the heaviest thing I've lifted in years is a beer can. He leads me along to the staircase up to where my old room used to be, next to my sister's.

"I hate to say this, Addie, but this time, you should listen to her," he mutters into my ear.

"What happened? Don't lie to me, Milt. Not you too. Please. What happened?"

"Nothing you need to worry about. Nothing that has anything to do with you."

"Did I do something?"

"No."

"Did I . . . did I run someone over? Did I kill someone?"

# ABOUT THE AUTHOR

Nina Laurin studied creative writing at Concordia University, in Montreal, where she currently lives. She arrived in Montreal when she was just twelve years old, and she speaks and reads in Russian, French, and English but writes her novels in English. She wrote her first novel while getting her writing degree, and *Girl Last Seen* was a bestseller a year later in 2017. The follow-up, *What My Sister Knew*, came out in summer 2018 to critical acclaim. Nina is fascinated by the darker side of mundane things, and she's always on the lookout for her next twisted book idea. She blogs about books and writing on her own site, thrillerina.wordpress.com.